SEX AND DRUGS AND SAUSAGE ROLLS

ROBERT RANKIN

Sex and Drugs and
Sausage Rolls

Doubleday

LONDON • NEW YORK • TORONTO • SYDNEY • AUCKLAND

TRANSWORLD PUBLISHERS
61–63 Uxbridge Road, London W5 5SA
a division of The Random House Group Ltd

RANDOM HOUSE AUSTRALIA (PTY) LTD
20 Alfred Street, Milsons Point, Sydney, NSW 2061, Australia

RANDOM HOUSE NEW ZEALAND
18 Poland Road, Glenfield, Auckland 10, New Zealand

RANDOM HOUSE SOUTH AFRICA (PTY) LTD
Endulini, 5a Jubilee Road, Parktown 2193, South Africa

Published 1999 by Doubleday
a division of Transworld Publishers

ISBN 0385 600569

Typeset in 11½/13pt Bembo by Falcon Oast Graphic Art

Printed in Great Britain
by Mackays of Chatham Plc, Chatham, Kent.

1 3 5 7 9 10 8 6 4 2

*For my very good friend Jonathan Crawford,
whose postcards are always from
The Edge and sometimes even beyond.*

In the Future There Will Be Nothing
But the Past

There's a Chef and His Name Is Dave

There's a frog in the Kenwood blender.
There's a cat in the microwave.
There's a mouse in the waste disposal.
There's a chef and his name is Dave.

There's a cockroach that lives in the pâté,
And the salt is an earwig's grave.
There are droppings all over the butter.
There's a chef and his name is Dave.

There's a nasty fungus under the stove,
Where the creepy crawlies wave.
And squeezing his spot in the beef hot-pot
There's a chef and his name is Dave.

There's a man from the Health Department
And he's just been sick in the sink,
And the Watermans Arts Centre kitchen
Will be closed for a while, I think.

1

'She does what?' John Omally looked up from his pint and down at Small Dave.

'Reads your knob,' said the wee man. 'It's a bit like Palmistry, where they read the lines on your hand. Except this is called Penistry and they can tell your fortune by looking at your knob.'

It was spring and it was Tuesday. It was lunchtime. They were in the Flying Swan.

'I don't believe it,' said John. 'Someone's been winding you up, Dave.'

'They have not. I overheard two policemen talking about it while I was locked in the suitcase.'

'Excuse me, Dave,' said Soap Distant, newly returned from a journey to the centre of the Earth. 'But why were you locked in a suitcase?'

'There was some unpleasantness. I don't wish to discuss it.'

'Small Dave was sacked from his job as chef at the Arts Centre,' said Omally.

'What Arts Centre?'

'The one they built on the site of the old gasworks.'

'Oh,' said Soap. 'So why did they sack you, Dave?'

'I was unfairly dismissed.'

'The manager gave Dave his cards and Dave bit the end off the manager's knob.'

'It was an accident. I slipped on some mouse poo, and anyway he hit me with a frying pan.'

'I thought that was in self-defence, because you came at him with the meat cleaver.'

'I just happened to be holding the cleaver at the time.'

'You bit off the end of his knob,' said Soap. 'That is disgusting.'

'It was an accident. I slipped, he hit me on the back of the head, I fell forward and my teeth kind of clenched.'

Soap's teeth kind of clenched and so did Omally's.

'So what happened to the manager?' Soap asked.

'He's recovering in Brentford Cottage Hospital. The surgeon sewed the end back on. It's no big deal. Mind you' – Small Dave smirked wickedly – 'from what I heard he's going to sue the surgeon.'

'I know I'm going to hate myself for asking,' said Soap, 'but why is he going to sue the surgeon?'

'Well,' said Dave. 'What with all the blood and it being an emergency operation and everything, it was the kind of mistake any-one could make. Especially if you're Mr Fowler.'

'What, fumble-fingers Fowler? He's not still in practice, is he? I thought he was struck off years ago.'

'He probably will be this time. He sewed the manager's knob end on upside down.'

'I think I'll go for a walk,' said Soap. 'I feel a little queasy.'

'I'll come with you,' said Dave.

'I'll stay here,' said Soap.

'Just one thing, Dave,' said Omally. 'Why exactly were you locked in a suitcase?'

'Because I escaped from the police cell. I squeezed through the bars. They caught me again and locked me in a suitcase and that's when I overheard them talking about the Penistry. The policemen were having a good old laugh about the manager's future prospects being cut short.'

'I still think it's a wind-up,' said John, applying himself to his pint.

'You should sue the police, Dave,' said Soap. 'Locking you in a suitcase must be against the Geneva Convention, or something.'

'I think I'll pass on that. There was some further unpleasantness after I made my escape from the suitcase. I put a bit more work Fowler's way. But the Penist said that I'd have happy times ahead.'

'Hold on,' said Omally. 'You mean to say that you actually went to see this woman?'

'I had a consultation, yes.'

'And she gave you a—'

'Reading. She gave me a reading. She was a very nice woman. Warm hands, she had. She said she saw a long and happy future stretching out in front of me.'

'It *is* a wind-up,' said Soap. 'It's just an excuse for a lot of cheap knob gags.'

'It is *not* a wind-up.' Small Dave gnashed his teeth.

Soap and John took a step back apiece.

'It is *not* a wind-up. She said she saw me galloping to glory and I'm sure she would have told me a lot more if she'd been able to make herself heard above all the noise.'

'You ask him, John,' said Soap. 'I don't like to.'

Omally shrugged. 'What noise, Dave?' he asked.

'The noise the policemen were making, shouting through the loudhailers. All that "Come out with your hands up" stuff. And the helicopter circling overhead.'

'The helicopter,' said Soap.

'The helicopter. I had to take my leave at the hurry-up and it's hard to run with your trousers round your ankles.'

'So you ended up back in the suitcase?'

'I did not. I shinned over her back wall and holed up on the allotments. I've spent the last week in John's hut.'

'*My* hut?'

'Living on nothing but John's spuds.'

'*My* spuds?'

'And his spud gin.'

'*My* spud gin?'

'And his nudie books.'

'I don't have any nudie books.'

'You don't now. I used them for kindling. It gets bloody cold on that allotment at night.'

3

'My hut, my spuds, my gin—'

'And your nudie books.'

'I do *not* read nudie books!'

'Nobody *reads* nudie books,' said Small Dave.

'I've had enough,' said Soap. 'I'm off.'

'I'll come with you,' said Dave.

'You bloody won't. No offence, Dave, but I find all this kind of talk most upsetting. Penistry and nudie books and knob ends getting bitten off. It leaves a very bad taste in the mouth.'

Small Dave looked at John.

And John looked at Small Dave.

Soap looked at the two of them looking, so to speak.

'What?' said Soap.

'Nothing,' said Small Dave. 'But if you're leaving do you mind if I use you for cover? You could smuggle me out under that big black coat of yours.'

'Use me for cover? I don't understand.'

'I think the police probably followed me here. They'll have the place surrounded. Probably.'

Soap let out a plaintive groan. Omally slipped over to the front window and took a peep out. 'He's right,' he said, 'there's police cars everywhere and a couple of marksmen on top of the nearest flatblock. I think it might be better if you just went out with your hands up, Dave.'

'No way,' said Small Dave. 'They're not taking me alive. Top of the world, ma.' And with that he drew from his trouser pocket—

—a pistol.

Now, it had been a quiet Tuesday lunchtime in the Swan. Very quiet. There had just been the three of them. And Neville, of course. Neville the part-time barman. But Neville hadn't been listening to the conversation. He had been quietly polishing glasses up at the public bar end of the counter.

Quiet, that's how it had been.

But with the arrival of that pistol . . .

It got *very* quiet indeed.

Dead hushed. Like.

'Dave,' said John, when he had done with quietness. 'Dave, where did you get that gun?'

'I dug it up,' said Small Dave. 'From under your hut. It's your gun.'

'Dave, it's not my gun.'

'Like they weren't your nudie books?'

'All right. They might have been my nudie books. But that isn't *my* gun.'

'So whose gun is it?'

'It was my grand-daddy's gun. Michael Collins gave him that gun.'

'It's mine now,' said Small Dave. 'And I'm not afraid to use it.'

'Be afraid,' said John. 'Be very afraid.'

'Oh yes, and why?'

'Because it doesn't have a firing pin.'

'Yeah, well they won't know that, will they?'

'No,' said John. 'Which is why they will shoot you dead.'

'He has a point there,' said Soap. 'One that might be worth considering.'

'I'll hold you hostage, then,' said the small fellow. 'I'll demand a helicopter and one hundred thousand pounds in cash and a takeaway Chinese with all the trimmings and a cat named Lofty and a pair of pink pyjamas and some chocolate cake and—'

'Have to stop you there,' said Omally.

'Why?' asked Small Dave. 'I was just getting into my stride.'

'Out of your tree, more like,' said Soap.

'What did you say?' Small Dave brandished the gun.

'Nothing,' said Soap. 'I just sneezed. Out-a-ya-tree. Like that, see?'

'Yeah, well you be careful. Or I'll shoot you.'

'Eh?' said Soap.

'*We know you're in there,*' came that old loudhailer voice. '*Come out with your hands held high.*'

Neville looked up from his polishing. 'Did someone order a mini-cab?' he asked.

'It's the police,' said John. 'They've come for Dave.'

'Oh, that's all right, then.' Neville buffed a pint pot on his apron. 'Does he want another drink before they cart him off?'

'Same again?' asked Omally.

'Yeah, thanks,' said Small Dave. 'Let me get these, though. Here, hold the gun while I find my purse.'

Omally took the gun. 'If this could only speak,' he said, turning it upon his palm.

'What do you think it would say?' asked Soap.

'I think it would say, "I'm sorry I had to do that. But you'll thank me for it later."'

'Why would it say that?'

Omally raised the gun and brought it down upon the head of Small Dave. The midget collapsed unconscious on the floor.

'Ah, right,' said Soap. 'I got you now.'

Neville gave Omally a hand. Together they managed to stuff Small Dave up the back of Soap's big black coat. Soap wasn't keen and he put up a lot of protest. But he did agree with Omally that Dave was a very bad man to cross. What with him being such a vindictive, grudge-bearing wee bastard and everything and how it would probably be in everyone's best interests simply to smuggle him out of the Swan and set him free on the allotments.

Because he would thank them for it later.

And everything.

Which he didn't. Of course.

Small Dave seemed anything *but* grateful. He awoke all spluttering and demanded to be told why he was being ducked in a water butt. He fussed and he bothered and he cursed and he swore and then he asked about the trowels.

'Trowels?' said Omally. 'What trowels?'

'Those trowels.' Small Dave pointed. 'Those trowels you're both wearing, strung round your waists and hanging down your fronts like sporrans.'

'Oh, *these* trowels, they're just—'

'A wise precaution,' said Soap. 'In case—'

'A fashion thing,' said Omally. 'They're all the rage up West. The Kensington Set are rarely to be seen nowadays without a trowel about their persons.'

'Especially at the Chelsea Flower Show,' said Soap.

'Especially there,' said Omally.

'You're bloody mad, the pair of you,' said Small Dave. 'And what happened to my gun?'

'Got lost,' said Omally.

'The fairies took it,' said Soap.

'The fairies?'

'No, not the fairies. Did I say fairies? What I must have meant was—'

'I'm leaving now,' said Small Dave.

'Oh, must you?' said Soap.

'Yes, I must.'

The sound of police car sirens swelled in the distance.

'Yes, I definitely must.'

And with that said, he definitely did. Without a by-your-leave, or kiss-my-elbow. No thank yous, no fond farewells.

Just off.

As fast as his little legs could carry him.

The two men watched him until he was gone. Then Soap raised a cup of Omally's spud gin.

'Do you think he's galloping to glory?' Soap asked.

'No,' said Omally. 'I don't.'

'Do you know what I like about Brentford?' Soap asked.

'No,' said Omally. 'I don't.'

'What I like about Brentford,' said Soap. 'Is that nothing ever changes here. I've been away on my travels beneath for nearly ten years and now I'm back and it's just as if I'd never been away.'

'Cheers to that,' said Omally.

'Cheers to that,' said Soap.

The Lord of the Old Button Hole

It was plain he'd come out for a stroll,
The Lord of the Old Button Hole.
The fêted celebrity dead in the wreck.
The keys to the boathouse at rest in his neck.
The vandals who did it are far off by now,
And I'm blessed I'll be had for a bumpkin.

Some kind of a chump in the goal,
Said the Lord of the Old Button Hole.
Hunting the hedgerows for samples and stuff.
The house is deserted, the ball's in the rough.
The vandals are rattling locks at the back,
And I'm blessed I'll be had for a bumpkin.

A little more cheese in the roll,
Cried the Lord of the Old Button Hole.
Since I came back from Burma, I'll frankly admit,
I've had scorpions crawling all over my kit,
And if that's in the contract, then I'm bowing out,
Cos I'm blessed I'll be had for a bumpkin.

2

Soap Distant strode up Brentford High Street.

There was the vaguest hint of stagger to his stride, but this was the inevitable consequence of two hours spent in Omally's company. Not that Soap was unacquainted with the grape and grain. Like most of Brentford's manly men he took his sup, but rarely to excess.

However, on this particular occasion Soap had felt the need for a drop of that courage which hails from the Low Countries. And why not? For hadn't Soap lately returned from some very low countries himself? Had he not planted the nation's flag at the Earth's core and claimed the realm for England? And was he not, even now, on his way to keep a three o'clock appointment with the editor of the *Brentford Mercury* to negotiate the serialization rights for the account of his epic adventure?

In short, he had, and he had, and he was.

Soap paused before the window of Mr Beefheart the butcher to peruse his reflection. He wanted to look his very bestest. Create a favourable and lasting impression. Exude a certain air. Make a presence. Be the business. And things of that nature, generally.

Soap adjusted the filters on his solar goggles. His eyes, still sensitive to sunlight, would sort themselves out in time. But what about the rest of him? He removed his broad-brimmed black hat and reviewed his facial featurings.

A gaunt and deathly face peered back at him. It was a white'n and that was a fact. Turning his head a little to the right, Soap noticed that the sunlight shone clear through his hooter. His hair had become similarly transparent, lending the crown of his head the appearance of a fibre-optic lamp.

Soap nodded in approval. He looked mighty fine.

Within Mr Beefheart's, a lady in a straw hat caught sight of the ghostly visage staring in at the window, took it to be the shade of the husband she had done to death and buried in the sprout patch and fainted dead away.

The way you would.

Soap replaced his hat and continued up the High Street.

The offices of the *Brentford Mercury* were just as Soap remembered them. Worn at heel and down upon the uppers. At ground level the Electric Alhambra, Brentford's only cinema, its doors long closed to an indifferent public, slept in the sunlight. Peely paint and crumbling brickwork, rubbish strewn upon its mosaic entrance. And above, behind the unwashed windowpanes, the borough's organ.

Soap squared his shoulders and made up the cast-iron fire escape. The door at the top lacked a sign, but Soap gave it a knock.

The door swung in and so did Soap.

The place was a bit of a mess. Packing crates and cardboard boxes filled the outer office. Soap did the old 'Cooee' and 'Shop?'

'Hang about, hang about,' called a voice. 'I'm all in a tangle here.'

Soap steered his sturdy boots between the towers of boxes, bits and bobs and came upon a woman who was worrying at wires. She had many wires to worry at and wires they were of many different colours.

'Why are you worrying at those wires?' asked Mr Distant.

'We're going on the Web,' said the woman, and there was pride in her voice as she uttered these words. 'We'll soon have our own Homepage.'

'Your words are strange to me, dear lady,' said Soap in a suave and silken tone. 'But I have every reason to believe that you know what you're on about.'

'Yeah, but I don't know what goes where,' she said, and she looked up at Soap. 'Oh my Gawd!'

'Soap Distant's the name.' Soap removed his hat and goggles.

'Oooh, your 'air,' went the woman.

'My apologies for my appearance. I have been many years below.' Soap got some serious timbre into that final word: *below*. It was a belter of a word, *below*. One of his all-time favourites.

'Below?' said the woman.

'Beloooooooooh,' repeated Soap. 'I would present you with my card, but at present I do not possess one. I thought I would wait until after my knighthood before I had any printed.'

'Knighthood?' said the woman. Loony, she thought.

Soap smiled and nodded and bowed a little too. She's a fine-looking woman, he thought, and it's clear that she's taken with me.

'The door's that way,' said the fine-looking woman, pointing with a fine-looking hand. 'Don't forget to close it on your way out.'

'I am expected,' said Soap. 'I have a three o'clock appointment with the editor.'

'Ah, you've come about the job.'

'Job?' said Soap. 'No, I am Soap Distant. *The* Soap Distant. Would you be so kind as to inform your employer of my arrival?'

'Are you from outer space?' asked the woman of fine looks.

'Eh?' said Soap. 'Do what?'

'Are you one of those Men in Black? Because we had one of your bunch in last week giving it all that.' She mimed mouth movements with her fingers. 'I said to him, "On your bike, sunshine, or off in your saucer." That told him, I can tell you.'

'I'm mighty sure it did,' said Soap. 'Would you please tell the editor that I've arrived?'

The woman, whose wires were now all over the place, made a face, flung down her wires and flounced away between the box-piles bound for God knows where.

Soap scuffed his boot heels and wondered at the wires.

Presently the woman returned and told him that he could go in now.

'Thank you,' said Soap. 'And good luck with your wires.'

★

11

The editor's office was a big old room, but it was also given over to boxes. Soap stepped between and through and over them and made his way to a large desk at the window.

Behind this sat the editor. He did not rise at Soap's approach.

Soap stretched his paw across the desk in the hope of a hearty handclasp. The editor viewed Soap's paw with distaste and folded his arms.

Soap viewed the editor. The editor viewed Soap.

Soap saw a man in his mid to late twenties. Smartly clad with long brown hair swept back behind his ears. An intelligent face, good cheekbones, calm grey eyes and a look about him that said, 'I'm going places.'

The editor, in his turn, saw a loony. 'What do you want?' he asked.

'Mr Bacon?' asked Soap.

'Mr who?'

'Bacon. The editor.'

'I've never heard of any Bacon,' said the editor. 'My name is Justice. Leo Justice. Known by many monikers. The Magnificent Leo. The Lord of the Old Button Hole.' He gestured to the red rose he wore in his lapel. 'Leo baby to the ladies, and Mr Justice to yourself.'

'I am Distant,' said Soap. 'Soap Distant. You were expecting me.'

'Ah, you've come about the job.'

'No,' said Soap. 'Do you mind if I sit down?'

'If you can find a chair. But you can't stay long. I'm busy.'

'Moving out,' said Soap, who, finding no chair, pulled up a box.

'Moving in,' said the editor.

'In?' said Soap. 'But the *Mercury*'s offices have always been here. Ever since the paper was founded in Victorian times.'

'Are you one of those Men in Black?' asked the editor, 'because if you are—'

'I'm not,' said Soap, comfying himself upon the box to the sound of cracking glassware from within. 'I am Soap Distant. Traveller through the hollow Earth. The man who has claimed the planet's heart for England and her Queen.'

'Queen?' said the editor. 'Are you taking the piss?'

'I'm sorry,' said Soap. 'I'm becoming confused. Before I embarked upon my journey I communicated with your predecessor, Mr

Bacon. Only by telephone, as he never seemed to have the time to see me. I told him that I intended to journey to the centre of the Earth and he agreed that when and indeed *if* I returned from doing so he would print my story. I offered him an exclusive. He was all for it. Said he'd hold the front page and everything.'

'I suppose he would have,' said the editor.

'And when I returned, successful, just two days ago, I telephoned this office and spoke once more with Mr Bacon and made an appointment and now I'm here.'

'I suppose you are,' said the editor.

'But you're not Mr Bacon,' said Soap.

'No,' said the editor, shaking his head.

'I'm now extremely confused.'

'Why don't you just go home and sleep it off? Would you like me to phone for a minicab?'

'What?' said Soap.

'You are clearly delusional,' said the editor. 'Does your condition manifest itself in bouts of uncontrollable violence? Because I must warn you that I am an exponent of *Dimac*, the deadliest martial art in the world, and can brutally maim and disfigure you with little more than a fingertip's touch, should I so wish. And I will not hesitate to do so should the need arise.'

'Come again?' said Soap.

'It's just that it's my duty to warn you. *The Dimac Code of Honour.* I have a badge and a certificate and a little plastic card with my photo on it and everything. Would you care to see any of these?'

'No,' said Soap. 'And I am not delusional, nor am I violent. I am Soap Distant, traveller beneath, and I demand to see Mr Bacon.'

The editor sighed. 'Mr Distant,' he said. 'If you really wish to pull off this scam you are going to have to work a lot harder, get your facts straight, make your story more convincing.'

'Scam?' said Soap. 'Story?'

'I see what you're up to,' said the editor, 'and it doesn't lack imagination. In fact it has a whole lot going for it. The centre of the Earth. The last frontier. Planting the flag for England. Admirable stuff.'

'But it's all true!' Soap's pale face took on a pinkish hue.

'No,' said the editor. 'It's not. You should have done your

13

research. Found a newspaper where a former editor had died or something. Forged his signature onto some kind of contract.'

'I . . . I . . .' Soap began to colour up most brightly.

'You see,' the editor continued, 'for one thing there never was a Mr Bacon on the staff. For another, this paper was only founded eight years ago, and for another yet we only moved in here today. Look, *I* founded this newspaper. *I* should know.'

'No,' said Soap. 'Oh no no no.' And his head began to swim and he began to rock both to and fro. And then he toppled off his box and fell upon the floor.

There is a deep dark pit of whirling blackness that detectives who work only in the 'first person' always fall into in chapter two. After a dame has done them wrong and a wise guy has bopped them over the head. Soap did not fall into one of these. Soap fell headlong into full and sober consciousness and leapt to his feet with a fearsome yell.

'Kreegah Bundolo!' cried Soap, which all lovers of Tarzan will recognize to be none other than the cry of the bull ape.

'Have a care,' cried the editor in ready response. 'Beware the poison hand that mutilates your flesh.'

'Pictures!' shouted Soap. 'I have the pictures!'

'Pictures?' went the editor. 'Look, I was young and I needed the money.'

'Eh?' went Soap. 'Whatever do you mean?'

'Oh, nothing, nothing. Do you want me to duff you up a bit? I'm feeling quite in the mood.'

'No,' said Soap, swaying on his toes. 'I am a Buddhist, I abhor all forms of violence. But I do have the pictures. To prove my story.'

'Whip 'em out, then. Let's have a look at the buggers.'

'Ah,' said Soap. 'Well, I don't have them on me.'

'Ah,' said the editor. 'Isn't it always the way?'

'They're at Boots the Chemist, being developed. I'll have them back by Thursday. I've got the receipt, here, I'll show you if you want.'

'Don't put yourself to the trouble. Why don't you just come back on Thursday, *with* the photographs, and we'll talk about it then. I think we might be able to come up with something moderately convincing, if we put our heads together on this one.'

'Moderately convincing?' Soap was now clearly appalled. 'But it's the truth. Everything I've told you is the truth.'

The editor settled back in his chair and sniffed at his bright red rose. 'Mr Distant,' he said. 'I am a professional journalist. The truth rarely plays a part in my work. I sell papers. The more papers I sell, the more money I make. If papers told nothing but the truth they wouldn't be in business very long, would they? Most news is terribly dull. You have to put a bit of a spin on it.'

'What's a "spin"?' Soap asked.

'It's a slant, if you like. An interpretation.'

'A lie,' said Soap.

'Just because it isn't the truth doesn't mean it's a lie.'

Soap Distant picked up his hat from the floor and stuck it once more on his head. 'I will get to the bottom of this,' he told the editor. 'Getting to the bottom of things is what I do best.'

'Do whatever you like, Mr Distant. But if you wish to pursue this, and you *do* have some pictures, and the pictures look moderately convincing—'

'Grrrr,' went Soap.

'If the pictures come out OK, then I'll see what I can do.'

'Right,' said Soap. 'Right. Well, we shall see what we shall see. But when I get my knighthood from the Queen—'

'Ah yes,' said the editor. 'The Queen. This would be Queen Elizabeth, I suppose.'

'Of course it would be, yes.'

The editor set free another sigh. 'You really must have been underground for a lot longer than ten years,' he said. 'Queen Elizabeth was assassinated twenty years ago.'

'Twenty . . . twenty . . . ass . . . sas . . . sass . . .' Soap's jaw flapped like a candle in the wind.

'Fair pulled the old shagpile rug from under us all, dontcha know,' said Mr Justice, shifting suddenly and seamlessly into his Lord of the Old Button Hole persona*. 'But listen, me old pease pudding, can't spare you any more time for the mo'. Got me personal Penist popping over in five little ticks of the clock to give me me Tuesday

---

*It was a case of either Multiple Personality Disorder or Demonic Possession, depending on your particular belief system. However, given events which are soon to occur, it is safe to assume the latter.

15

reading. So why don't you cut along like a nice gentleman and call back Thursday with the old snip-a-snaps. And here' – the Lord fished out his wallet and extracted from this a one-pound note – 'you seem a decent enough cove. Take this as a down payment on the exclusive. Can't say fairer than that, can I?'

Soap took the oncer in a pale and trembling hand.

'And no naughties like going to another paper, eh? I'm blessed I'll be had for a bumpkin, you know.'

'No,' said Soap, 'no,' and he shook his head numbly and dumbly.

He gazed down at the oncer in his hand and then he screamed very very loudly.

For the face that grinned up from that one-pound note was not the face of Her Majesty. It was instead a big and beaming face. A bearded face. A toothy face.

It was the face of Richard Branson.

Rain of Frogs

Down it came in great big buckets,
Emptied from the sky.
Watch the batsmen run for cover,
Cursing you and I.
Cursing rain and speedy bowlers,
Ill-timed runs and garden rollers.
Saying 'This is not my day, I wish that I would die.'

Down came frogs and fancy footwear.
Down came trees and tyres.
Raindance wizards on the hillsides
Dowsed their pots and fires.
Saying 'This is not too clever.
Will this rain go on for ever?'
Saying 'Blame the rich land barons. Blame the country squires.'

Down came dogs and armadillos.
Down came latex goods.
Turnips ripe and avocados.
Full sized Yorkshire puds.
Packets of nice Bourbon bikkies.
Ancient Bobby Charlton pickies.
Ivy Benson tea dispensers, small Red Riding Hoods.

My mum has left the washing out.
She was well peeved.

3

The blue sky clouded over and the rain came pissing down.

In his present state of mind it was pretty much all Soap needed. He trudged back down the High Street, striking out at the rain with a rolled-up copy of the *Brentford Mercury*.

The Lord had given it to him. Free, gratis and for nothing.

As a sign of good faith. Or something.

The three-inch banner headline had done nothing to raise Soap's spirits. It read 'LECTER' ON THE LOOSE. Followed by the tasteful subhead '*Knob-gobbling cannibal psycho-chef evades police dragnet.*'

Soap splashed his feet through puddles and as knife-blades of water rained down on his hat, confusion reigned in his head.

What was going on here? This wasn't April Fool's Day, was it? He unrolled the sodden paper, lifted his goggles and studied the date. April the first it was not! He scrunched up the press and consigned it to the gutter.

'That's where you belong,' he told it. And then a little thought entered his head. There was one easy way to find out the truth of all this. Well, of some of it anyway. Soap rootled in his pocket and dragged out the one-pound note. Go into the nearest shop and try to spend it. Simple, easy, bish bash bosh.

He stopped dead in his trudging tracks and looked up at the

18

nearest shop. The nearest shop wasn't a shop as such, though it was a shop of sorts. It was a cop shop. It was the Brentford nick.

'All right,' said Soap. 'If you want to know the time, ask a policeman. So . . .' And then he paused and he stared and he went, 'No no no.'

Soap knew the Brentford nick of old and, like most of Brentford's manly men, had seen the inside more than once (though never, of course, through any fault of his own). But this was not the Brentford nick he knew. This was a smart, updated nick. A nick dollied up in red and white. A nick that no longer had the words METROPOLITAN POLICE above its ever-open door. A nick that now bore a big brash logo instead.

And what was printed on that logo?

What was it that made poor Soap go, 'No no no' in such a dismal way?

The words *VIRGIN* POLICE SERVICES.

That's what!

Soap took a step back, tripped on the kerb, fell into the road and was promptly run down by a red and white police car.

He awoke an hour later to find himself inside the nick. Happily, not in one of the cells, but all laid out on a comfy settee. His hat and his goggles had been removed. Soap rubbed his eyes and squinted all around. The room was large and well appointed and had the look of a gentleman's club. The walls were bricked, with leatherbound books upon shelves of mellow mahogany. Parian busts of classical chaps stood on columns of pale travertine. There were elegant chairs of the Queen Anne persuasion. Tables that answered to every occasion. Rather nice whatnots. Lancashire hot-pots. Rabbits of yellow and purple and green.

All very poetic. All very nice.

Soap blinked and refocused his eyes. 'No,' said he, 'not all very nice. Well, nice enough, but for the hot-pots and the rabbits.'

'I tend to agree with you there.' Soap now found himself staring into a face that loomed in his direction. It was an elegant face. It had cropped white hair at its top end, a pince-nez perched upon its nose at the middle, and a long chin sticking out at the bottom. 'I am Inspectre Sherringford Hovis,' said the mouth of this face, exposing a gold tooth or two. 'And I trust that you are all hunky-dory.'

'Hot-pots,' said Soap.

'Hot-pots and rabbits,' said Hovis. 'Part of my grandmother's collection. Bequeathed to me by my late mother. She was mad, you see. Quite mad.'

'Quite,' said Soap.

'And you are?'

'I'm *not*,' said Soap.

'No,' said Hovis. 'I mean, your name. You are?'

'Soap Distant,' said Soap Distant.

'That name rings a little bell. Didn't I once run you in for an unsavoury incident involving a handbag, some chopped liver and a little boy's bottom?'

'No, you did not!' Soap struggled up to a sitting position.

'Must have been another Soap Distant, then.'

'Yes, it must.' Soap steadied himself. The room with its hot-pots and rabbits was doing a bit of a waltz.

'You just take it easy. I'll have someone fetch you a cup of tea.'

'Thank you,' said Soap.

'And then, when you're feeling up to it, we'll discuss the damage you did to the squad car and how you intend to pay for it.'

'Eh?' said Soap, and, 'What?'

'You quite upset the constable who was driving. He'll probably need to have counselling. But you won't have to pay for that, it's covered by the company.'

'The company,' said Soap, his shoulders sagging.

'Yes,' said Hovis, and his tone lacked not for bitterness. 'Everything is covered by *the company* nowadays.'

'You're not too keen,' said Soap, a-rubbing at his eyes.

'I'm an old style copper, me,' said Hovis. 'Haul 'em in and bang 'em up and throw away the key. But what do they get now? Fines is what they get. Every young copper is on a bonus system, all working hard for the company accountants.'

'Oh,' said Soap, now scratching at his head.

'And what do I get lumbered with?'

'I don't know,' said Soap.

'Stuff and nonsense. Weirdo stuff and nonsense. Here, come and take a look at this,' Hovis marched off to his desk and Soap rose carefully to follow.

He was quite taken with the looks of the Inspectre. The long lean frame, encased in a three-piece suit of Boleskine tweed. The stiff Victorian collar. The blue velvet cravat. The watchchains and the pince-nez and the spats. This fellow was a 'character' and that was fine with Soap.

'What do you make of these?' asked the character, gesturing all about his desk.

'Photos,' said Soap. 'You have hundreds of photos.'

'I have *thousands* of photos,' said Hovis. 'And all showing the same damn thing.'

'Why?' asked Soap. 'What are they?'

'Take a look for yourself.' The Inspectre pushed a pile in Soap's direction.

Soap took one and peered at it. 'It's a picture of a road,' he said.

'It's a picture of a motorway. The M25, to be precise. Taken by a police speed camera. So we can fine motorists who drive above the legal limit.'

'That's clever,' said Soap. 'How does it work?'

'I don't know how it works. It's digital, some computerized non-sense. It's triggered automatically to catch the registration plate of the offending motorist. Surely you've heard of the damn things.'

'Well . . .' said Soap. 'I've never actually owned a motorcar. In fact I've never actually been on a motorway. But I get the picture.'

'And what do you get from looking at *that* picture?'

'Well . . .' said Soap.

'Well, look at it, man, what do you see?'

'I don't see any motorcars,' said Soap.

'No,' agreed Hovis. 'No motorcars at all. But what about that?' and he pointed.

'Oh,' said Soap. 'It's a man in the middle of the road. A fat man. In a black T-shirt and shorts.'

'Yes,' said Hovis. 'And what is he doing?'

'He's walking along,' said Soap.

'Isn't he, though. And look at the little figures in the bottom left-hand corner of the photograph. The ones in miles-per-hour. Tell me what speed he's walking along at.'

'Oh,' said Soap, 'that can't be right. It says here he's walking along at one hundred and forty miles per hour.'

21

'Pretty spry for a fat bloke, don't you think?'

'There must be something wrong with the camera.'

'Would that there were,' said Hovis. 'But look,' and he pushed further photos at Soap. 'Here he is again, caught on another camera. And here again and here and here.'

'And he's in *all* these photographs?'

'Not all,' said Hovis. 'There's at least twelve different men involved. All dressed alike. Each of them strolling along the middle lane of a motorway at impossible speed in the early hours of the morning.'

'Avoiding the traffic.'

'Good point,' said Hovis.

'Thank you,' said Soap. 'So how's it done?'

Inspectre Hovis made a fearsome face.

'Sorry,' said Soap.

'Never mind. I have certain theories, of course. Or should I say, *had?*'

'And these were?'

'Well, firstly I thought that perhaps some whizzkid joker was hacking into the computer system and feeding these images in. But that won't wash because the cameras aren't linked to a central system and, before you ask, they haven't been tampered with. Secondly, I reasoned that it was some new form of automotive technology. A stealth car, perhaps.'

'Stealth car?'

'Like the stealth bomber that evades radar. This car evades speed trap cameras and throws up some kind of holographic after-image to take the piss out of honest policemen who are only doing their duty.'

'But it's not?'

'Certainly not. If such technology existed the police would have it first.'

'So where does that leave you?'

'It leaves me, Mr Distant, with a bloody great pile of photos on my desk.'

'Ah,' said Soap. 'But why *your desk?*'

'Because I am Brentford's Detective in Residence.'

'I don't think I quite understand.'

'No, and that is because there is something I neglected to mention. You see, we've plotted the routes taken by these moonlight strollers.

Plotted them out on a map. Would you care to take a look?'

'I would,' said Soap.

'Then be my guest.'

The map was a big'n and was blu-tacked to the bookcase behind the crowded desk.

Soap gave the map a good looking over. There were twelve lines drawn upon it. Each followed the route of a motorway or A-class road. They began at twelve separate points of the compass, but all met up at a single location.

That single location was Brentford.

'Oh,' said Soap.

'Yes, oh indeed. The photographs were taken two nights ago and there have been no further sightings. Whoever, or *whatever* they are, they're here. Right here in the borough.'

'Oh,' said Soap once more.

Bad Memory

By the bound Victorian gasogene.
By the black slate memory board.
By the swish French cooking calendar.
By the shutters I secured.
By the rows of hanging plantpots.
By the slightly dripping fridge.
By the wibbly wobbly worktop.
By the dust along the ridge.
By the rack of grey enamelware.
By the strangely angled shelf.
By the larder door that does not close
That I also fitted myself.
By the ceiling lights that don't light up.
And the dimmer that does not dim.
By the waste disposal unit
That bit my uncle Jim.
By the nasty Kenwood blender.
By the red tiles on the floor.
I'm obviously in my kitchen.

But what did I come in here for?

4

John Omally sat in his kitchen.

And a horrible kitchen it was.

It was a fetid kitchen. A vile kitchen. A foul and unkempt kitchen.

It was the kitchen of a single man.

Now, it might well have been argued that Omally's kitchen was also an anomalous and contradictory kitchen, given the scrupulous personal hygiene of its owner. Omally was nothing if not clean. His shirts were always laundered, his jackets showed no neck oil and as to his underpants, these were free of wind-smear. His clothes weren't new, but they were spotless and although he had never been a man of fashion, due to his ever-limited resources, he possessed a certain jumble sale chic that women found appealing.

So why the Goddamn horrible kitchen?

Well, when Viv Stanshall said 'Teddy boys don't knit' he was pretty near to the mark. Manly men don't do the dishes.

This may sound like male chauvinism, but it's not. In fact it is quite the reverse. It's all down to women and what women find attractive in a man.

You see, if a woman finds a man attractive, *really* attractive, more attractive in fact than any other man she knows, she will like as not wish to marry him. If she succeeds in doing so, her next task will be to domesticate him. Purge him of his nasty habits, mould him into a loving husband and caring father.

This on the face of it would seem reasonable enough. It makes perfect sense. But it has a tragic downside. It puts an end to their sex life.

Because a domesticated man is not a sexy man. A domesticated man, who does the dishes and cooks the dinners and hoovers the carpets and mends the fence and redecorates the house, is anything *but* sexy. There are few things less sexy than a man in a pinny.

And so while he might be very good about the house, his wife no longer finds him sexually attractive. Because he is not the man she married. He is a pale and domesticated shadow of the man she once found alluring.

And so while he is at home in the evenings, babysitting the kids and putting up a new spice rack in the kitchen, she is out at her amateur dramatics, being rogered rigid in the back of a Ford Cortina by her toyboy called Steve.

Steve lives in a grubby bedsit.

And Steve don't do the dishes.

Nice for the wife and nice for Steve, but what about the poor domesticated cuckold of a husband?

Well, he's having an affair with his secretary.

So it all works out fine in the end.

So there you have it, whether you like it or not. Manly men don't do the dishes, that is that is that.

Now, as well as dirty dishes, there are other things single men possess that married men do not. These are highly essential things and known as 'toys for boys'. They include such items as an expensive motorbike, an expensive sound system and an expensive electric guitar.

These items will vanish shortly after marriage.

The expensive motorbike will be traded in for a sensible family saloon. The expensive sound system will end up in the garage, having failed to survive the assault made upon it by a one-year-old child with a jam sandwich.

And the electric guitar?

Goodbye, Stratocaster. Hello, Flymo hover-mower.

That is that is that.

Omally possessed no toys for boys. He would have liked some, but, having never done an honest day's work in his life, for he valued freedom above all else, he knew not the joys of the chequebook or the loan that is paid back in monthly instalments.

He had his freedom, he had his health and he had his dirty dishes. But he dearly would have loved that Fender Strat.

When it comes to guitars, it can be said that it's all a matter of taste. But when it comes to taste itself, it's a matter of good taste or bad. And this is *not* a matter of personal preference. Some things simply *are* better than others, and some people are capable of making the distinction.

When it comes to electric guitars, the Fender Strat is king. For sheer elegance, beauty and playing perfection, the Strat has never known equal. When it appeared upon the music scene in 1954 musicians marvelled at its ergonomics, its sonic versatility, its tuning stability and its pure pure tone. The sleek new body form, developed from the original Telecaster, featured the now legendary double cutaway, or twin-horn shape. The advanced tremolo, allied to the three single-coil pickups, allowed the player greater playing potential. The Strat was capable of doing something new. And something wonderful.

One could spend all night singing praises to the Strat or indeed to composing paeans to its inventor, the mighty Leo Fender. That Mr Fender never received the Nobel Peace Prize during his lifetime and seems unlikely to be canonized by the church of Rome just goes to show how little justice there is in this world.

And that is that is that.

But Omally was Stratless. An air-guitarist he. Not that that fazed him too much, for, after all, he had no talent. He could strum a passable 'Blowin' in the Wind' without looking at his fingers, but anyone could do that and you don't do that on a Strat.

On a Strat you play rock. On a Strat you play the twenty-minute solo. And if you cannot play the twenty-minute solo you should not step onto the stage with a Strat strapped round your neck. Leave the Strat to Hendrix. Leave the Strat to Stevie Ray Vaughan*.

---

*Actually, Stevie Ray Vaughan got an even bigger sound out of his Strat by fitting it with heavier strings. Some even up to .013 gauge. (These things matter.)

So that's how John Omally left it. He left the Strat to the great rock legends, whom he joined onstage in his dreams.

But the point of all this, and there *is* a point, or else it would not have been mentioned, the point of all this was that Omally had recently heard tell of a rock band playing pub gigs in Brentford that owned to a Strat-playing fellow who could, in the words of one who'd heard him play, 'make that mother sing like an angel and grind like a thousand-dollar whore'.

Which is something you don't hear or see every day, especially in the suburbs of West London.

The Stratster's name was Ricky Zed, although his employers at the West Ealing Wimpy Bar, where he worked as the griddle chef, knew him as Kevin Smith. The band was called Gandhi's Hairdryer and they were playing tonight at the Shrunken Head. Which was why Omally now sat in his kitchen. He was polishing his winklepicker boots.

For Omally wished to look his best tonight. Omally wished to see this band and if they were all they were cracked up to be and indeed if Ricky proved to be the new Jimi, or the new Stevie Ray, Omally hoped to make them an offer he hoped they would not refuse.

An offer to manage them.

Because Omally had also heard that the Gandhis were looking for a manager.

Now the fact that Omally had never had a day job, nor indeed knew anything whatsoever about managing a band, did not, in his opinion, enter into the equation.

John felt deep in his rock 'n' roll heart that he was born to such a role. Wheeling and dealing, ducking and diving, bobbing and weaving and things of that nature were what he was all about. He was a man with no visible means of support who somehow managed to enjoy a reasonably comfortable lifestyle. Even if it didn't run to any toys for boys.

He was management material.

If cut from humble cloth.

No, if this band had potential, he, Omally, would realize this potential. And if he couldn't play the Strat he would bathe in the reflected glory of one who could. And also in the heated swimming pool into which he had driven his Rolls Royce*.

Omally buffed his boot and hummed a little 'Smoke On The Water'.

The kitchen clock had long since ceased to tick, but John's biological counterpart told him that opening time drew near. He took his boots upstairs, shaved and showered and put his gladrags on. They were slightly ragged, but they were extremely glad. Omally chose for this special occasion a Hawaiian shirt that his best friend Pooley had given him for Christmas, a dove-grey zoot suit he had borrowed from this selfsame Pooley, and the aforementioned winklepicker boots, which in fact were also the property of the also aforementioned Pooley. And which Omally had been meaning to give back. Examining himself in the wardrobe mirror, Omally concluded that he looked pretty damn hot.

'You, my friend,' he said, pointing to the vision in the glass, 'you, my friend, will really knock 'em dead.'

He teased a curly lock or two into a bit of a quiff, struck a pose and did the Townshend windmill.

'Rock 'n' roll,' said John Omally. 'Rock 'n' roll and then some.'

Ring ring went the front doorbell as John went down the stairs. He skipped up the hall and opened the door and greeted the man on the step.

'Watchamate, Jim,' said John.

'Watchamate, John,' said Jim.

The man on the step was Pooley. Aforementioned Pooley and John's bestest friend. Jim, like John, was 'unemployed', but where John did all that ducking and diving and bobbing and weaving, Jim applied himself to science. The science of horse racing. Jim considered himself to be a man of the turf and had dedicated his life to the search for the BIG ONE. The BIG ONE was the six-horse Super-Yankee accumulator bet. Which every punter dreams of and every bookie fears.

So far Jim had failed to pull off the six-horse Super-Yankee or, as future generations would know it, the *Pooley*.

But it was just a matter of time.

*This of course being *John's* heated swimming pool and *John's* Rolls Royce. For managers get twenty-five per cent.

Regarding the looks of Jim. They were varied. He was much the same stamp as John, and but for the obvious differences bore many similarities.

'Come on in,' said John Omally.

'Thank you sir,' said Jim Pooley.

'No, hold on,' said Omally. 'I was coming out.'

'I'll join you, then,' said Jim.

And so he did.

The two friends strolled up Mafeking Avenue and turned right into Moby Dick Terrace. Jim's face wore a troubled look which John saw fit to mention.

'What ails you, Jim?' asked John. 'You wear a troubled look.'

'I am perplexed,' said Pooley. 'I just ran into Soap.'

'Ah,' said John. 'I saw him at lunchtime. How did his interview go at the *Mercury*?'

'None too well by all accounts. Soap seemed very upset. He said that the world was going mad and it wasn't his fault.'

'Wah-wah,' said John.

'Wah-wah?' said Jim.

'As in wah-wah pedal. Go on with what you were saying.'

'Soap said that he'd expected things to change a bit while he'd been away. But he didn't see how they could have changed *before* he went away, without him noticing at the time.'

'I am perplexed,' said John.

'It was about the Queen being assassinated. And Branson being on the poundnotes.'

'Who's Branson?'

'The bloke whose face is on the poundnotes, according to Soap.'

'But I thought Prince Charles was on the poundnotes.'

'That's what I told Soap. I showed him a poundnote and I said, "Look, Soap, it's Prince Charles."'

'And what did he say?'

'He said, no, it was definitely Branson.'

'He's confusing him with that film star,' said Omally.

'Which film star?'

'Charles Branson. In the *Death Wish* movies.'

'I think you'll find that's Charles Manson,' said Jim knowledgeably.

30

'Oh yeah, that's the fellow. Wrote a lot of the Beach Boys' big hits and then went on to become a star in Hollywood.'

'You've got him.'

They reached the Memorial Library and sat down upon Jim's favourite bench. Early-evening sunlight filtered through the oak trees, sparrows gossiped and pussycats yawned.

Omally took out his fags and offered one to Jim. 'Soap will be all right,' he said. 'It's just all the excitement of getting back and everything. He'll soon sort himself out.'

'I hope so. Some of the stuff he was telling me was seriously barking. He said a policeman had showed him pictures of a fat man in a black T-shirt and shorts walking down the middle of a motorway at one hundred miles an hour.'

'Oh dear,' said John, lighting up.

'And he said that the more he thought about it the more he noticed odd little changes that didn't make sense. That things just weren't the way they should be.'

'He had been drinking a bit,' said John.

'He owned up to that.' Jim took John's lighter and lit his fag. 'I used to have a lighter just like this,' he said.

Omally stretched and yawned.

'And come to think of it,' said Jim, 'I used to have a suit like that and a pair of winklepicker boots.'

'They're only borrowed, Jim. And if all goes well tonight I'll buy you a dozen suits and a dozen pairs of boots.'

'Yeah, right. But I am rather worried about old Soap.'

'He'll be fine. It's just some temporary aberration. When I last saw him we drank a toast to Brentford and how what he liked about it best was that nothing ever changes here. I mean, look around you, can you imagine this place changing?'

Jim looked all around him. He saw the mellow-bricked library and the streets of terraced Victorian houses. He saw a crumbling wall plastered with movie posters, one of which, coincidentally, advertised Virgin Films' latest release. Charles Manson starring as Forrest Gump. And above and beyond, the highrise flats and the gleaming silver spires of Virgin Mega City.

'No,' said Jim. 'You're right, of course. Nothing ever changes round here.'

31

Stage-Struck and Later By Lightning

Terence the Thespian sat on his laurels.
People remembered his glorious years.
Bowing before the great packed auditorium.
Bowing and bowing to thousands of cheers.

Getting the knighthood and winning the Oscars.
Five nominations at least in a week.
Dodging the press at the gay dinner functions.
Opening fêtes, more or less, so to speak.

Posing for painters with R.A. credentials.
Saying 'Yum yum' to the products that pay.
Dancing with debs and the wives of new statesmen.
Getting a centre-page spread every day.

Buying up mansions and landaus and sofas.
Taking the lions for walks in the park.
People say, 'Oooh, he's not like you expect him.
Thought he was lighter, or thought he was dark.'

Terence the Thespian sat on his laurels.
Counted his royalties, counted his hair.
Terence the Thespian struck down by lightning.
Just goes to show he was mortal. So there!

5

When Terence the Thespian got his comeuppance and copped the old bolt from the blue, his children were left to divvy up the spoils.

The eldest, Alexander, or Sandy to his daddy, or Master Sandy to his private tutors, or just plain jammy bastard to the rest of us, found himself in the enviable position of being a teenaged millionaire.

Now, while it is certainly true that many a man of means owes his success in life to the labours of a deceased relative, it is also often the case that wealth that is suddenly come by is wealth that is suddenly gone.

This was indeed the case with Sandy.

Sandy dispossessed himself of wealth in truly Biblical fashion. He dallied in the fleshpots of Ealing, that modern-day Babylon, where, in his gilded youth, he drank deep of iniquity's wine and dined upon fruits forbidden.

And thusly did he squander his birthright upon many a libertine pleasure. Carousing with harlots and hedonists, sybarites and sodomites, debauchees, degenerates, wallowers and wastrels.

Very nice work if you can get it, but sadly few of us can.

And having squandered all, and somewhat more besides, Sandy was forced to flee the fleshpots and take unto his toes. And sorely did his creditors mourn for his departure. And greatly did they weep and wail and gnash their teeth and rend their raiments. Yea, verily! And many amongst them did swear mighty oaths and promise him the torments of the damned.

Sandy wandered wearily, footsore and sick at heart, a vagabond with all hope gone, a sad and sorry fellow. He walked alone for many days and covered many miles and, as you do on the road, had all kinds of exciting adventures involving Red Indians and pirates and highwaymen and knights in armour and wizards and witches and giants and goblins and beautiful princesses with long golden hair.

Because there's a lot more to life on the road than sleeping in shop doorways and drinking aftershave. As anyone who's been on the road will tell you.

Sandy tramped the highways and the byways for almost twenty years. Scouting for wagon trains, sailing on the seven seas and getting into all kinds of sticky situations involving the princesses with the long golden hair. But eventually he tired of it, cashed in some gold doubloons that he'd dug up on a coral island and bought the Shrunken Head.

The Shrunken Head had always been a bit of a dump. It lay at the bottom of Horseferry Lane, beside the River Thames. You couldn't actually see the river from the Shrunken Head, but you got a feel of it during the high spring tides when the cellar filled up with water.

When Sandy purchased the place it was a 'folk pub', where men with big bellies and beards, manly men who drank only real ale, howled out those horrible unaccompanied songs that always begin with 'As I walked out one morning' and end with graphic descriptions of genitalia being pierced by fish hooks.

Sandy, who had enjoyed the company of a good many long-legged women during his days in the fleshpots of Ealing, ousted the big-bellied beardies and turned the Shrunken Head into a proper music venue. One that would attract the right kind of punter. He stripped the barrels and beer engines from the cellar and opened it up as Brentford's answer to the Cavern.

Sandy catered to all tastes, bar 'folk', because all tastes bar 'folk' attract women. Good-looking women, that is.

The Shrunken Head became *the* place to go in Brentford, if you were looking to rock 'n' roll. Because Sandy did the job the way it should be done.

The Cellar, as it was imaginatively called, was small and damp and airless. The beer was served in plastic tumblers, warm and flat and overpriced. The bouncers were brutal, the bands played much too loud, junkies chased the dragon in the toilets and as for the smell . . .

John Omally loved the place.

Jim Pooley, however, did not.

'I would rather have my genitalia pierced by fishhooks than spend an evening there,' he said, when he learned that this was to be their destination.

'Come on, Jim,' said John, nudging his friend's elbow. 'If this band is as good as they say it will be a night to remember.'

'But the place is a hellhole and as for the guvnor—'

'Sandy the sandy-haired barlord?'

'The man is a twat,' said Jim.

'He's been about a bit, though, and tells an interesting tale.'

'I tell an interesting tale and I've never been anywhere.'

'But do you have a duelling scar?'

'No.'

'Or a bullet wound, or a scald on your arm where a dragon breathed on you?'

'No,' said Jim. 'I don't.'

'And do you know of any other barlord in Brentford who bears the marks of the stigmata?'

Pooley thought about this. 'Not off-hand,' he said.

'Or any other bar that attracts so many long-legged women?'

Jim thought about this also. 'There's the Brown Hatter in Fudgepacker Street,' he said.

'Those aren't women, Jim.'

They walked a while in silence.

'Look,' said John as they crossed the Kew Road. 'Just come in with me and listen to the band for a couple of numbers. If they're rubbish we'll both head off to the Swan.'

'I like the Swan,' said Jim. 'It's peaceful in the Swan.'

'It wouldn't be, except for me.'

'Whatever do you mean?'

35

'Well, who do you think sees to it that the brewery's jukebox remains forever out of service?'

'True enough,' said Jim. 'But if you love music so much, why do you do it?'

'Because the Swan is *not* the place for music. The Swan is a dignified establishment run by a dignified barlord. You go there to relax and enjoy the sparkling repartee and well-versed conversation of its patrons. *Not* listen to music. If you want music you want *live* music. And if you want live music you want it in a sleazy overcrowded stinking sweathole of a place. *Hell*hole of a place. Getting it right is everything, Jim. A place for everything and everything in its place.'

'Let's go to the Swan.'

'No,' said Omally.

Jim made a sulky face.

'Don't be a baby,' said John.

They arrived at the Shrunken Head at a little before six. The band was scheduled to play at nine, which in rock 'n' roll time meant ten. So why were they there so early?

'So why are we here so early?' asked Jim.

'Because we need to be. We need to grab a table near the door and hang on to it. I intend to make myself known to the band when they arrive and buy them a couple of drinks.'

Pooley whistled. 'Now that is something I would like to see. You buying drinks for complete strangers.'

'It's an image thing. And bands play better when they think there's a talent scout in the audience.'

'And if they turn out to be a load of old pants?'

'Then you will enjoy much laughter at my expense, telling the tale in the Swan.'

Pooley shrugged. 'It has that going for it, I suppose. You go on in, then, and I'll come back at around half past nine.'

'No, Jim. This job requires two. One to hang on to the table and the other to be up at the bar. Now, let's get inside before anyone else does.'

John pushed open the door to the bar and pushed Jim through the opening.

It was dim and grim in the Shrunken Head.

And it smelt like a wino's armpit.

The floor was of fag-scarred lino in a colour that has no
name.

The evening sunlight drew up short at the windows where
the grime held court.

The furnishings were dark and dank.

The curtains rotten and ragged and rank.

At the sight of it all Jim's heart sank.

For this pub knew no shame.

'Sheer poetry,' said John. 'Although of a difficult metre.'

Pale-faced in the gloom, Pooley shook his head and made the sign
of the cross, Spectacles–testicles–wallet–and–watch. 'This is truly the
Pub from Hell,' he whispered. 'When we die and go to the bad place
this is where we will drink out eternity.'

'Enough of that, Jim,' said John. 'You're making me all of a shiver.
Now you go up to the bar and get us in a couple of pints while I
choose us the table.'

'Me?' went Jim. 'But I—'

'Cut along now. Before the place fills up.'

'But,' Jim glanced all about the evil den, 'it's half full already.'

'Yes indeed, you're right.'

There were at least a dozen young men in the bar. Young men
wearing black T-shirts and shorts. They had been rabbiting away as
the two friends entered, but now they had grown silent and were
nudging one another and pointing somewhat too.

'They're looking at us,' whispered Jim. 'Why are they looking at
us?'

'Ignore them,' said John. 'They're fanboys. A good sign, that.
Means the band has already got a cult following.'

'Cult?' said Jim. 'I don't like that word at all.'

'Go to the bar,' John ordered. 'Go to the bar at once.'

Jim went up to the bar, doing the old 'Excuse me, please' as he
passed between the fanboys. But the fanboys weren't giving Jim a
second glance. They were all watching Omally.

Jim reached the bar counter and almost leaned his elbows upon it.
Almost.

He surveyed the unpolished surface. The butt ends and the beer

37

pools. A slight shiver ran through him. This was not his kind of place at all.

Sandy the sandy-haired barlord looked up from a nudie book and grinned a grin at him.

'If it isn't my old friend Pooley,' he said.

'You're quite right there,' said Jim.

'Your Irish mate winkled you out of the Swan, then, has he?'

'Something like that, yes. Two pints of whatever you have that passes for beer, please.'

Sandy lined up a couple of grubby-looking plastic tumblers and drew from beneath the bar a brace of those multi-pack cans of supermarket lager that're not supposed to be sold separately. 'Five quid,' he said.

Jim clutched at his heart.

'Wish I could do it cheaper,' said Sandy. 'But, as the music's free, I have to make a little on the beer.'

'Yes, I quite understand.' Jim's hand had found his wallet but seemed unable to drag it from his pocket.

'Come on, Pooley, tug a little harder. There's thirty-five quid in there.'

'Thirty-five . . .' and Jim's jaw fell.

'You just missed Bob the Bookie. He told me he'd given you a loan.'

'It's not a loan. I won it this afternoon on the horses.'

'Bob looks upon it as a loan. After all, he knows he'll get it back tomorrow.'

'He bloody won't,' said Jim.

'Quite right,' said Sandy. 'You spend it here. That'll show him.'

'I will.'

Having parted company with a five-pound note, Jim sought out Omally, who now sat at the table of his choosing.

John was not alone. Sitting across from him in the seat that should surely have been Jim's, was a fat man in a black T-shirt and shorts. He and John were chatting like buddies of old.

Jim placed a can and a tumbler on the table and sat down next to the fat man.

'Cheers, Jim,' said John, 'this is Geraldo.'

'Pleased to meet you, I'm sure,' said Jim, raising his cup of warm cheer.

'Geraldo is a big fan of the Gandhis.'

'The biggest,' said Geraldo.

'Nice,' said Jim, sipping his drink and making a face.

'Geraldo thinks that the Gandhis will be the biggest band of all time.'

'That I doubt,' said Jim.

'Oh, they will,' said Geraldo, in a voice that made Jim turn his head. For such a big fat man he had a very tiny voice. It seemed to come from way down deep inside him, as if he was calling up through a drainpipe. Or something. 'They'll be the biggest ever, you just wait and see.'

'They won't be bigger than the Beatles,' said Jim. 'No band could ever be bigger than the Beatles.'

'The Beatles have had their day,' said John.

'Oh, excuse me,' said Jim. 'And how many number-one hits have the Beatles had?'

'A couple of dozen, I suppose.'

'Fifty-seven,' said Jim. 'And the last one only a few months ago. To celebrate John Lennon's sixtieth birthday.'

'Exactly.' Omally pushed his tumbler aside and drank straight out of his can. 'And look at Lennon. Bald and fat. He should have turned it in years ago.'

'Stop a moment there,' squeaked Geraldo. 'John Lennon was sixty, did you say?'

'I bought the single,' said Jim. 'It had a holographic picture sleeve.'

Geraldo's jowls were all awobble. 'But John Lennon was shot in nineteen eighty,' he said faintly.

'Yes,' said Jim. 'But he was only wounded and if it hadn't been for the shooting, the Beatles would never have re-formed.'

'He should have died,' said John. 'He'd have become a rock icon if he'd died.'

'What a wicked thing to say.' Jim made tut-tut-tuttings. 'And if he had died and the Beatles hadn't re-formed, England would not have won the Eurovision Song Contest four years running. Nineteen eighty-two, nineteen eighty-three, nineteen—'

'Yes, I know all that.' Omally viewed his drink can with distaste. 'But what a sell-out that was. Eurovision Song Contest. That ain't rock 'n' roll.'

'Just stop! Just stop!' Geraldo waved his chubby paws about. His voice was faint but frantic. 'You're saying that John Lennon did *not* die in nineteen eighty?'

'Of course he didn't die.' Jim shook his head and rolled his eyes. 'That young bloke saved his life. What was his name, now?'

'They never knew his name,' said John. 'He just appeared out of nowhere and patched Lennon up. And then he vanished when the paramedics arrived. Lennon wanted to give him a million bucks but he never came forward to claim it.'

'Perhaps it wasn't a bloke at all,' said Jim. 'Perhaps it was an angel. Perhaps it was the Spirit of rock 'n' roll. Are you all right, Geraldo?'

But Geraldo wasn't all right. Geraldo was coughing and spluttering. 'It's not right,' he kept saying between convulsions. 'He should have died. It isn't right.'

'You're not right,' said Jim. 'Have you been drinking?'

'I've gotta go.' Geraldo rose shakily to his feet and stumbled off to join his fanboy cronies at the bar.

'What a very strange man,' said Jim.

'Perhaps he's a chum of Soap's.'

'Come again?'

'Well, Soap's got a bee up his bum that the Queen wasn't assassinated and Geraldo thinks that John Lennon *was*.'

'Nineteen eighty,' said Jim.

'What about it?'

'Nineteen eighty was when Lennon got shot and survived and the Queen was assassinated. Same year.'

'People get shot every year,' said John. 'It's a tradition, or an old charter or something.'

'Or something. But this is a bit of a coincidence, isn't it? Who is this Geraldo anyway, John? Where do you know him from?'

'I don't know him at all. He just came up and asked for my autograph.'

'Why would he want your autograph?'

'I think he thought I was someone famous. He was terribly polite and sort of—'

'Sort of what?'

'Reverential,' said Omally. 'That's the only word I can think of.'

'This is all very weird.'

'There is nothing weird about it.' John gulped down the contents of his can and tried to look happy for doing so. 'This is a music pub, Jim,' he said. 'And the folk who go to music pubs are not your everyday folk. Don't go getting yourself all upset.'

'I wasn't getting myself all upset,' said Jim, who clearly was.

'Well, don't. Soap is confused. Geraldo is confused.'

'Both of them?'

'Both of them. Lennon *did* survive, the Queen did *not*. That's history and you can't change history, can you?'

'Well . . .' said Jim. 'I suppose not.'

'You definitely can't. History cannot be changed.'

And That's Why I Live In a Tent

The invasion of the body snatchers.
The thing from Planet Z.
The big-eyed beans from Venus.
The fiend without an 'ead.

The wild wild women of Wonga.
Morris the human mole.
Loup Garou.
The man from the Pru.
The beast from the bottomless hole.

The phantom of the opera.
The lad from the Black Lagoon.
Vampires and umpires and pirates and poets,
The Scotsman who lives on the moon.

Turned up on my doorstep yesterday,
To say that they'd put up my rent.
I said, curse and damnation
(They had an Alsatian),
And that's why I live in a tent.

6

Norman Hartnell* once said that life would be a whole lot easier if it could be lived in little movies. The gist of this was that life nowadays is simply too complex for the average man to get his average head around. There's too much going on all at the same time. Too many plot-lines, if you like, weaving in and out and all round about. If you could live your life in little movies, each with a beginning, a middle and an end, you could concentrate on one thing at a time. Enjoy each for whatever it was and give of your best to each in turn.

And things of that nature.

Generally.

Norman considered that, ideally, each little movie would last for a week. You would begin whatever particular enterprise you chose to begin, on the Monday. Give it your absolute and undivided attention until Friday (by which time it would have been brought to a satis-factory conclusion), and then you'd have the weekend off to plan what you should do the following week.

Norman was what is called 'an Idealist'.

---

*He was never confused with the other Norman Hartnell, because no one could remember who the other Norman Hartnell was.

He was also a corner-shopkeeper.

And a single man.

Norman's shop was known to the good folk of Brentford as *The Sweetie Shop that Time Forgot*. Norman had inherited the shop from his father, Norman Hartnell Senior (whom many at the time had confused with the other Norman Hartnell), way back in the nineteen sixties and had done his best to keep it just the way it was.

This was not for the sake of nostalgia, or as some posthumous tribute to his daddy. It was simply that Norman liked the shop the way it was and could think of no sound reason for changing it. The shop served as Norman's base of operations, where he applied himself not only to living his life in little movies, but also to his hobby.

For Norman, Idealist, corner-shopkeeper and single man, was also an inventor.

England has proudly given birth to many a great inventor. It has also, almost without exception, failed to capitalize on this. Inventors have found themselves unable to raise finance to develop their ideas and have inevitably sold them abroad.

The reason for this, in Norman's opinion, was that those who sat in the seats of power, those big seats in Whitehall with red leather backs, tried to do too much at once and so did everything badly. They missed opportunities because they didn't live their lives in little movies.

Norman had written to them explaining this, but so far had received no reply.

Which, in his opinion, proved his point.

So Norman did not waste his precious time sending off details of his latest revolutionary invention to the big-seat-sitters of Whitehall. He applied himself to solving local problems. To improving the lives of those who lived around him.

Idealist, shopkeeper, single man, inventor and very nice fellow was he.

This week Norman was building a horse.

It was to be a surprise present for Jim Pooley, who was a good friend of Norman's. Jim was the only man that Norman knew of, other than himself, who actually lived his life in little movies. True, Jim's little movies were always repeats. In fact they were always the very same movie. The one about the bloke who spends all his time trying to win on the horses but always fails to do so. It was a very dull little movie and it didn't have a happy ending.

But Norman meant to change all that for Jim. He was doing what inventors do. Which is to identify the problem and provide the simple solution.

Over the previous weekend Norman had identified the problem. Jim never won much money on the horses, because they were not *his* horses, and so he could never know for certain whether they would win or not. Therefore the solution was to provide Jim with a horse that could be guaranteed to win.

The answer was therefore to build Jim a horse.

It might well have been suggested to Norman that the answer would be to *buy* Jim a horse. But Norman would certainly have pooh-pooed this suggestion.

Racehorses cost a fortune to buy. It was simpler all round just to build one.

Norman had recently come into possession of a scientific magazine, ordered in error by a customer. In this there had been a long and involved article about a sheep called Dolly, which had supposedly been cloned. This had set Norman thinking.

Like all manly men, all *truly* manly men, Norman had a love of science fiction. Not just a liking, but a love. And there was no short-age of novels dedicated to this particular subject. Norman had rootled about in his collection and come up with a couple of Johnny Quinn classics. *Crab Cheese* and *The Man Who Put his Head on Backwards*.

In *Crab Cheese* the eponymous detective (Crab Cheese) finds him-self on the trail of a serial killer of the vampire persuasion, who turns out to be a human clone. The cunning twist at the end is that the man does not have a soul. The theory being that you might be able to clone the man, but you *cannot clone the soul*.★

This gave Norman pause for thought. Did animals have souls? No one really knew for certain. But then if they did, and the one you cloned didn't, would it really matter? Norman wondered about Dolly. Had she shown any leanings towards vampirism? If she had, the scientific journal failed to mention them.

★Please bear this in mind.

The Man Who Put his Head on Backwards was a different kettle of genetics altogether. It involved rich people in the future who were cloned by their parents at birth. The clones were then carefully reared on special farms to provide spare parts and replacement organs for the originals. As and when required.

This led Norman into wondering whether he should perhaps clone half a dozen horses in case the first one broke a fetlock or something.

But he decided to scrub around that. He only had space in his back yard to graze one horse and he didn't want the neighbours complaining again.

What a fuss they'd made about his outside toilet. It had seemed such a good idea at the time, catering as it did to customers who were suddenly caught short in his shop. The world had clearly not been ready for the open-air female urinal.

So, over the aforementioned previous weekend Norman had set himself to planning how he might clone the greatest Derby winner of them all. It would need to have all the best features of all the best horses all rolled into one. But how to go about the task? How to acquire the necessary genetic material? You couldn't just knock at the door of some stud farm and ask to borrow a few skin scrapings. Well, you could, but . . .

Well, you *could* in a manner of speaking. You could certainly ask for *something*.

On the Sunday Norman drove off to Epsom in his Morris Minor. He set out early and sought the grandest-looking stables. Here he leaned upon the fence and watched the horses being groomed. He had brought with him two essential items. A breeder's guide and a bucket. These were all he needed to gain the *something* he required.

His technique proved to be faultless. Having selected from the breeder's guide a horse suitable for cloning, Norman shouted abuse at the stable lad grooming it. The stable lad replied to Norman's abuse in the manner which has been favoured by stable lads since the very dawning of time.

He hurled horseshit at Norman.

Norman gathered up the horseshit and put it in his bucket.

Having visited five stables, Norman had a full bucket, containing all the genetic material he needed.

He was even home in time for Sunday lunch.

On the Monday, Norman used whatever time he could between serving customers to slip away to his back kitchen workshop and extract the DNA from the horseshit. This was a rather tricky task, requiring, as it did, a very large magnifying glass, a very small pair of tweezers and a very steady hand . . .

By shop-close, however, he'd filled up a test tube. Now, there is, apparently, something of a knack to gene-splicing. It calls for some pretty high-tech state-of-the-art equipment, which is only to be found in government research establishments. Norman did not have access to these, so instead he gave the test tube a bloody good shake. Which was bound to splice something.

On the Tuesday, which was today, things had not gone well for Norman. He'd been hoping to at least knock out a test horse, but there had been too many interruptions.

People kept bothering him for things. Could he get them this? Could he get them that? Norman told them all that he certainly could not. And then there had been all the fuss about the videos.

He should never have started hiring out videos. It was a very bad idea. Norman couldn't think for the life of him why he'd started doing it in the first place. But then, for the life of him, he remembered that he could.

It was all the fault of John Omally.

Omally had come into Norman's shop a couple of months before, complaining bitterly that there was nowhere in Brentford where you could hire out a videotape.

Norman had shrugged in his shopcoat.

'There's a fortune waiting for the first man who opens a video shop around here,' said Omally.

Norman nodded as he shrugged.

'A fortune,' said John. 'I'd open one myself, but the problem is finding the premises.'

'Why is that the problem?' Norman asked.

'Because there aren't any shops to rent around here.'

'Which must be why no one has opened a video shop.'

'Exactly,' said Omally. 'And it's not as if you'd need a particularly large shop. In fact, when you come to think about it, all you'd really need would be a bit of shelf space in an existing shop.'

'I see,' said Norman.

Omally glanced around at Norman's shop. 'I mean, take this place, for instance,' he said. 'Those shelves over there. The ones with all the empty sweetie jars. Those shelves there could be earning you a thousand pounds a week.'

'How much?' said Norman.

'A thousand pounds a week.'

'Those shelves there?'

'Those shelves there.'

'Bless my soul,' said Norman.

Omally did a bit of shrugging. 'Makes you think,' said he.

'It certainly does,' Norman agreed. 'Of course, there would be the enormous capital outlay of buying all the videos.'

'Not if you had the right connections.'

'I don't,' said Norman.

'I do,' said John.

And it *had* seemed a good idea at the time. What with Omally knowing where he could lay his hands on five hundred videotapes for a pound each. It was only after Norman had parted with the money and Omally had loaded the tapes onto the shelves that Norman thought to ask a question.

'What are on these tapes?' Norman asked. 'None of them are labelled.'

'I don't know,' Omally said.

'But haven't you tried any out?'

'How could I try any out? I don't own a VCR.'

Norman's face came over all blank. 'But I thought you were bitterly complaining that—'

'There was nowhere in Brentford you could hire a videotape from. Yes, I was. But I was speaking generally. I didn't mean me personally.'

'Oh,' said Norman. 'I see.'

'Well, I'm all done now,' said John. 'So I'll be off.'

And with that said, he was.

It took Norman more than a week to go through the tapes. He had some very late nights. To his great disappointment, none of them turned out to be Hollywood blockbusters. All contained documentary footage. Of Chilean secret police interrogating prisoners.

Norman marvelled at the methods of torture employed, although he did think that some of the electrical apparatus used could have been improved upon.

'Although I won't waste my time writing to tell them,' Norman said to himself. 'Because they probably won't answer my letter.'

But now Norman realized that he had a very real problem on his hands. What was he to do with these videos? I mean, he could hardly hire them out.

Not without titles.

And when it came to little movies, these ones all had the same plot.

Norman put his mighty brain in gear. Snappy titles, that's what they needed. Norman at once came up with *OUCH!: THE MOVIE*. This was good because it allowed for *OUCH! II: THE SEQUEL*. And also *OUCH! III*. In no time at all Norman was into his stride.

He followed up the OUCH collection with the NOW THAT'S WHAT I CALL TORMENT series and he even managed to cut together a blooper tape of humorous out-takes. Torturers slipping over in the blood and accidentally electrocuting themselves and so on.

Norman toyed with the idea of calling this one CARRY ON UP MY BOTTOM WITH THE ELECTRIC CATTLE PROD.

But that was a bit too long.

Norman earned his money back on the videos and he made a bit extra besides. They didn't prove popular as family viewing, but they attracted a certain following amongst a certain type of male.

The police raid at lunchtime had come as a bit of a shock. He'd noticed the police presence, just up the road outside the Flying Swan, and when a couple of coppers came into his shop to buy sweets, Norman had asked them, in all innocence, whether they'd like to join his video club.

And now here he was in a police interrogation room at the Brentford nick. An interrogation room that looked strangely familiar. Norman sighed and shifted uncomfortably. The metal chair was cold on his naked bum. The electrodes were pinching his nipples.

Norman hoped that they'd soon let him go. After all, he'd

answered all their questions. Several times over. He'd said all the things they'd expected him to say. That he was an innocent victim of circumstance. That he'd bought the videos from a stranger he'd met in a pub. The policemen wouldn't keep him tied up around here much longer, would they? Sitting on cold chairs gave you the piles and Norman didn't want those.

And he had too much to do. He had to get back to his workshop and see how his horse was coming along. He'd left the DNA gently cooking in a nutrient solution on the stove, and although it was only on a low light, it might all end up stuck to the bottom of the saucepan if he didn't get back soon to give it a stir.

Norman sighed again and made a wistful face. If only there weren't so many complications, he thought. If only we could live our lives in little movies.

As chance would have it (or if not chance then fate, and if not fate then who knows what?), there was something closely resembling a little movie going on in Norman's kitchen workshop even as he thought and said these things.

It was a little *B*-movie, although the special effects were superb.

If there had actually been a script for this movie, it might well have begun something like this.

SCENE ONE
Interior: Norman's kitchen workshop.

Camera pans slowly across small and shabby room. We see bundles of newspapers and magazines. Cigarette boxes, cartons of soft drinks, all the usual stock of a modest corner shop. We see also a sink piled high with unwashed dishes and a work table. Here we find evidence of scientific endeavour, test tubes, retorts, a scientific journal open at a page about cloning, a box of Meccano.

Camera pans towards a filthy stove (1950s grey enamel), where we see an old saucepan. Its contents are boiling over, a thick green liquid is bubbling out. We follow the course of this liquid as it drips slowly down to the floor (ancient lino). Here there is movement, as of things forming and moving.

Camera pulls back rapidly, rising to view the room from above.

And we see them. Dozens of them. Racing round and round the kitchen floor. Leaping over discarded cans and flotsam. Tiny horses, no bigger than mice. Galloping around and around and around.

Music over: the Osmonds, 'Crazy Horses'.

Of course if it was a little B-movie it would need a title. It would have to be one of those *The Thing from Planet Z* or *The Beast from the Bottomless Hole*, or even *The Scotsman Who Lives on the Moon* sort of jobbies.

Norman could no doubt have thought of one. *Invasion of the Tiny Horses*, perhaps, or *Night of the Stunted Stallions*. That sounded better.

But as Norman wasn't in his kitchen, he wasn't going to get the chance.

So knowing not the wonder of it all, Norman sat in the steel chair in the interrogation room in the Brentford nick and fretted and fretted and fretted.

And in his kitchen workshop, the tiny horses galloped around and around and around and around.

And around.

The Alien Say

(Or, How Elvis Presley failed to heed the voice of Interplanetary Parliament and so condemned Planet Earth to destruction.)

To be sung in the voice of Early Elvis.

The alien say that the truth will make me free.
The alien say that he knows the inner me.
But I don't care what the alien say.
All I wanna do is rock 'n' roll all day.
Wop bop a loo bop wham bam hip hooray.

The alien say it's a karmic symbiosis.
Divinely inspired cerebral metamorphosis.
But I don't care what the alien think.
All I wanna do is take drugs and drink.
A wop bop a loo bop wham bam kitchen sink.

(*middle eight*)

The alien reckons that the future beckons
And the end is drawing near.
Throw away our bombs before the holocaust comes.
His message was loud and clear.

The alien say we're destroying the eco-system.
The alien say we should call upon cosmic wisdom.
But I don't care who the alien calls.
All I wanna do is screw young girls.
A wop bop a loo bop wham bam string of pearls.

(*another middle eight*)

The alien thinks that humanity stinks
And we've blown it all to hell.
The message is grave, but he can still save us
And he chose *me* to tell.

The alien say the galactic federation
Has condemned this world to a swift annihilation.
The alien said I should pass it on.
But I forgot his message when I went to the John.
Wop bop a loo bop – *Where's the planet gone?*

Thank you, ma'am.

7

Elvis should have called it quits way back in '77 when he had his first heart attack. He was never quite the same man after that. He wandered around Gracelands, clutching at his head and talking to himself and telling those who would listen that he was having revelations. Clearly the King was two strings short of a Strat.

His latest offering, a stream of semi-consciousness rambling over beefy drum and bass, pumped now out of Sandy's behind-the-bar sound system, making any form of conversation in the Shrunken Head just that little bit more stressful.

It was now almost nine of the night-time clock and Jim Pooley took another elbow to the ear.

'Ouch,' went Jim and, 'Mind out there.'

'Stop making such a fuss,' Omally told him.

'It's all right for you.' Jim shifted in his chair as another music-lover squeezed by him. 'You have the seat against the wall.'

'I have to keep watch on the door for the band. The place is filling up nicely, though, isn't it?'

Jim ducked another elbow. 'I hate it!' he shouted. 'It's horrid and stinks. Don't any of these blighters ever wash under their arms?'

'Men who wear black T-shirts rarely wash under their arms. It's a tradition, or an old charter or something.'

'I want to go home,' wailed Jim.

'Hold on,' said John. 'Big-hair alert.'

'What?'

'Men with big hair. It must be the band.'

Jim turned and caught an elbow in the gob. 'Ouch,' he went again and, 'Where?'

'There.' Omally pointed and there indeed they were. Above the motley mob and moving through the fug of fag smoke, big-haired boys were entering the bar.

'Big hair,' muttered Jim. 'What an old cliché that is.'

Omally was now on his feet and waving. 'Chaps,' he called. 'I say, chaps, over here.'

'*I say, chaps?*'

Omally hushed at him. 'It's an image thing,' he told Jim. 'Think class. Think Brian Epstein.'

'Ye gods,' Jim raised his beer can to his lips, thought better of it and set it down again.

'Chaps, I say.' Omally coo-eed and waved a bit more. 'I say, chaps. Hold on, come back.'

But the big-haired chaps were paying no heed, they were humping their gear towards the entrance to the Cellar.

'I'll give them a hand with their guitars,' said Omally. 'You hang onto this table.' He leaned low and spoke firm words into the ear of Pooley. 'And don't even think about slipping away,' he said.

'I might have to go to the toilet.'

'Hold it in.'

'But it might be number twos.'

Omally made fists. He showed one to Pooley. 'I am not by nature a violent man,' he said, 'but if you let me down on this—'

'All right.' Pooley raised the palms of peace. 'I'll hold the table for you. But I'm not going downstairs to hear them play. Absolutely no way. No siree, by golly.'

'All right, all right.' John struggled out of his chair and into the crowd. 'Just don't let me down, Jim. This really matters.'

Pooley shrugged and Pooley sighed and Pooley wanted out.

'Is anyone sitting there?' asked a voice at his ear.

'Yes,' grumbled Jim and, looking up, 'No. My friend's gone home. You can sit in his chair if you want to.'

'Thank you, I will,' she said and she did.

Jim watched her as she settled onto Omally's chair.

She was beautiful. Simply beautiful.

In fact it would be true to say that she was the most beautiful woman Jim had ever seen in his life. And considering that Brentford is noted for the beauty of its womenfolk, that is really going some.

And then some more.

She was the size known as petite. Which isn't the size known as little or small. And there was a symmetry about her features and a delicacy about her entire being that made Jim do a double double-take. To Pooley she seemed perfect, and perfect can be just a little fearsome.

With his jaw now hanging slack and his eyes glazing over, Jim took in the poetic wonder of her face.

Her eyes were large and green and fringed with long dark lashes.

Her nose was small and tilted at the tip.

Her mouth was wide, and there, inside, her teeth were lightning flashes.

A tiny blue moustache was glued above her upper lip.

Jim's face took on that drippy gormless expression that is so often worn by men who have fallen suddenly and hopelessly in love.

'Are you all right?' asked the beauty.

'Oh,' went Jim and, 'Mmm.'

'Pardon?'

'I'm fine,' shouted Jim.

'That's good. I thought you were going to chuck up.'

'No, I'm fine,' Jim shouted some more. 'No, hang about. How do you do that?'

'I usually put my fingers down my throat.'

'No, I don't mean that. I mean how do you do what you're doing now?'

'What am I doing now?'

'There!' shouted Jim. 'You did it again.'

'What?'

'Well, I'm having to shout above all this racket, but you're just speaking normally, and I can understand every word you're saying.'

'It's just a way of projecting your voice. My brother taught me.'

'Wonderful,' shouted Jim. 'I'm Jim, by the way.'

'I'm Litany,' said Litany.

56

'Have you come to see the band? Are you here with your, er, boyfriend?'

'You don't have to shout. I can understand *you*. And I'm with the band and I don't have a boyfriend.'

Groupie, thought Jim.

'And I'm not a groupie.'

'Of course you're not.'

'I'm the lead singer.'

'I've been really looking forward to seeing your band,' said Jim. 'I'll be right down at the front.'

'Oh, really?'

'Absolutely. Can I get you a drink or something?'

'No, thank you.' Litany shook her perfect head. Her perfect hair, of a colour somewhere between this and that, moved all around and about. It wasn't exactly big hair, but it had many big ways. 'The beer's rubbish here. I'd much prefer a pint of Large.'

'I could run to the Swan and bring you one back. Or we could perhaps go together.'

'I have to play. There's a lot of fans here tonight.'

'Yes.' Jim now made a somewhat thoughtful face. Which was a great improvement. 'How come . . .'

'How come what?'

'How come you're not being mobbed? How come you're just sitting down here with me and no one's bothering you? How come there's not a big mob of adoring fans gathered about this table?'

'Would you like there to be?'

'No. But . . .'

'It's something else my brother taught me. I'll tell you about it some time. Over a pint of Large, perhaps.'

'Oh yes,' said Jim. 'Oh yes, indeed.'

'I like you, Jim,' said Litany. 'You're everything I hoped you'd be.' And on that mysterious note, she rose from Omally's chair, smiled at Jim and melted into the crowd.

Pooley lifted his can of beer and emptied the contents down his throat. And just for a moment, only for a moment, mind, the thin warm ale took on the taste of a cooling pint of finest Large.

And then a great cheer went up from the mob, as the mob became

57

aware that Litany was among them and Jim got another elbow in the ear.

And then John Omally returned.

'Bastards,' he said, reseating himself.

'Pardon?' shouted Jim.

'Bastards,' shouted John.

'Any particular bastards, or just bastards in general?'

'Big-haired bastards, they wouldn't speak to me.'

'Perhaps they didn't take to your old chaps routine.'

'They mocked my suit.'

'*My* suit?'

'Your suit, then. But mock it they did.'

'Well, it is a really horrible suit. Which is why I've never asked for it back.'

'I've a good mind not to manage them now.'

'That'll teach them!' bellowed Jim.

'You might as well push off, then.'

'No, that's all right, John. You push off, I'll stay a bit longer.'

'What?'

'I think I'll stay and watch the band.'

'What?'

'Just a couple of numbers.'

'What?'

'Did you get her autograph?' It was Geraldo, the big fat fellow in the black T-shirt and shorts. His tiny voice squeaked very loud, in order to make himself heard.

'What?' said Jim.

'That's my line,' said John.

'Litany's autograph. That was her talking to you, wasn't it? I didn't recognize her until she got up.'

'What?' went John.

'He was talking to Litany,' squeaked Geraldo.

'Who is Litany?' John bawled back.

'Just a friend,' said Jim.

'What?'

'She's the Gandhis' lead singer. Your mate was chatting her up.'

'I never was.'

'You were *what*?'

'Oh, all right. I was talking to her. She does this really clever thing when she speaks, she—'

'Bastard!' shouted John. 'I turn my back and you're diving in to steal my job.'

'It wasn't like that. She came up to me. I didn't know who she was. I think she fancies me and—'

'Blue moustache tonight.' The big fat fellow pointed to his face. 'Always a blue moustache on Tuesdays.'

'What is he going on about?'

'She was wearing a blue moustache.'

'A woman with a moustache?'

'Blue one,' Jim shouted. 'A Clark Gable, I think.'

The big fat fellow shook his big fat head. 'A Ramon Navarro.'

'Did he wear a moustache?'

'On Tuesdays he did. A blue one.'

'You're mad!' shouted John. 'The pair of you. Stone bonkers.'

'I think I'll just slip down to the Cellar.' Jim made down-a-ways pointings. 'I'd like to get up close to the stage.'

'I'll come with you,' Geraldo squeaked as loudly as he could. 'I don't want to miss the incident.'

'What incident?' Jim asked.

'The famous incident, of course. That's what we've come to see.'

And on *that* mysterious note, the fat fellow did his bit of melting into the crowd.

'Oi, wait for me,' cried Jim, attempting to melt but failing dismally. 'How do they do that?' he asked John.

'It's all in the elbows. Here, I'll show you.'

'Wait for me, then, oh damn.'

Jim did not get up close to the stage, although, given the dimensions of the Cellar, nowhere was particularly far from the stage. But Jim was about as far away as it was possible to be. He was last man in, which also meant he would be first man out and first man to the bar come the intermission, but that afforded little or indeed any pleasure at all to the aspiring fanboy. He squeezed himself against the wall and held his nose against the pong of unwashed armpits.

He bobbed up and down for a bit, hoping for a glimpse of Omally, but gave that up when a chap in front threatened to punch his lights out.

'I hate it here,' said Jim to himself. 'I hate it, hate it, hate it.'

And then all the lights went out and then the voice of Sandy one-twoed through the mic and said, 'Ladies and gentlemen, they're here, your own, your very own, Gandhi's Hairdryer.'

And there was a scream of feedback, a great dark howl from the crowd, the lights burst on and the band burst into action.

Jim could manage a bit of a 'Whoa' as the sight and the sound hit him bang in the face.

On stage stood Litany, surely taller, surely even lovelier, and flanked by fellows in black. She wore white and they wore black and they had great big hair. And they had really fab guitars and they did all the right movements and the drummer at the back beat seven bells of shit out of the old skins and the speakers pumped out mighty decibels and the music and the song and the heat and the smell.

And Jim came all over funny.

He could see them moving up there on the tiny stage and he could feel the rhythm as the big bass notes jumbled up his stomach and rumbled in his skull, but he seemed to hear and taste and sense and smell much more.

And it was all so much and all at once. It didn't build up slowly. It didn't rise to a crescendo. It was just right there. Instantly. In your face. In your bowels. In, right in.

At once.

All together.

Altogether.

Jim shook his head and pinched at his nose and sucked in very small breaths. Whatever this was, and it certainly was something, it was all too much for him. He tried to ease himself away from the wall but found to his horror that he couldn't. The seat of his trousers appeared to be welded to the brickwork. His feet were glued to the floor.

And it couldn't have been thirty seconds into the first number before the lead guitarist went into a solo. And yes, it was the most blinding guitar solo Jim had ever heard in all of his life and somehow Litany sang with it. Not words but sounds, musical notes, utterly pure, utterly precise. Rising and rising until the band cut short and

60

there was nothing, nothing but the sound of her voice, a note, a single note, that seemed to enter into Pooley through the very pores of his skin and—

What?

'Cleanse,' whispered Jim. 'I am being cleansed.'

'Thank you, Brentford, and goodnight.'

And all the lights went out.

And when they came back on again, the Gandhis were nowhere to be seen.

But what there was to be seen was something quite extreme. Blokes were clutching at themselves and weeping. Weeping men, and manly men too. Some were fingering at their heads and going 'My barnet, it's back' and others were feeling at their faces, saying 'All my spots are gone.' And others still were patting private places and mumbling things like 'Me piles have vanished' and 'Ye pox is no more.'

Jim blinked and boggled and sighed and took deep breaths. Men in black T-shirts were sniffing at their armpits and each other's. 'Nice,' was their opinion. 'Very fragrant.'

Jim found that he was sniffing too and nodding as he sniffed. And he felt so well. So healthy. He felt as if he had just spent a week at one of those places the toffs go to, where they cover you in mud and feed you lettuce and suchlike. Whatever that felt like. Good, is what that felt like. Incredibly good.

'What about that, then, eh?' A tiny voice spoke in his earhole.

Jim turned to see the fat bloke in the black T-shirt and shorts.

But.

The fat bloke wasn't such a fat bloke any more.

'Four bloody inches,' the fattish bloke said. 'Four bloody inches off my waistline.'

'How?' whispered Jim. 'I mean, what happened, how?'

'It's her voice. I knew it was true. The others didn't believe me. They said it was just a rock legend. But I talked them into coming. I knew it was true, you see. I'd read all about the Gandhis and their Apocalypso Music.'

'Slow down,' said Jim. 'I don't understand.'

'This was the incident. The one that started it all. And now I can say I was there. And if no one believes me' – the fattish bloke plucked at his trousers – 'they'll believe this, won't they? My mum will be dead pleased. She's always going on about me losing weight.'

'You knew this was going to happen.' Jim fought to make sense of it all. 'You knew. How did you know?'

'Looked it up on Porkie.'

'What's Porkie?'

'Its real name is SWINE. Single World Interfaced Network Engine. It pretty much runs the whole planet. Or did.'

'I'm losing this,' said Jim.

'Of course you are. But even if I told you all about it, you'd never believe me.'

'I'd give it a go.'

The fattish bloke turned to his friends, who were blissfully sniffing their armpits. 'What do you think?' he asked them. 'Should I tell him?'

The armpit-sniffers shrugged. One of them said, 'What does it matter? We'll all be off tomorrow.'

'Off?' said Jim.

'We're going to Woodstock.'

'Woodstock?'

'Yeah. But never mind about that. Do you want me to tell you, or what?'

'Please tell me,' said Jim. 'Tell me how you knew and tell me just what happened.'

'All right, I'll tell you it all. I know I really shouldn't, but as you tipped me off about John Lennon, I'll tip you off about something in return. You might do us all a bit of good by knowing.'

'Geraldo,' said Jim. 'It is Geraldo, isn't it?'

'Was the last time I looked.'

'Geraldo, what do you mean about John Lennon?'

'You tipped me off that he didn't die.'

'But he didn't die.'

'No, but he should have done. And if he didn't, it means that Wingarde's been interfering again.'

'Curiously,' said Jim, 'you've lost me once again. Who, in the name of whatever I hold holy, is Wingarde?'

'He's a flash little hacker with a better rig than mine.'

'All becomes clear.'

'Does it?' asked Geraldo.

'No,' said Jim. 'It does not.'

'Yeah, well don't you worry about Wingarde. He might think he's been really smart. But now that we know what he's done, we'll sneak back and put it right.'

'Put it right?' said Jim.

'See that John Lennon bites the bullet, as it were.'

'Eh?' said Jim, and, 'What?'

'Well, we can hardly leave things as they stand, can we?'

'Can't you?'

'Certainly not. And wasn't that Elvis I heard on the barman's sound system?'

Pooley nodded. 'It was,' he said.

'Bloody Wingarde again,' said one of Geraldo's cronies.

'Look,' said Jim. 'Just stop. Just stop right there and here and now. Just tell me simply and in a manner that will not confuse me.'

'What?' Geraldo asked.

'Just who the frigging hell you are.'

'We're fanboys,' said Geraldo. 'Surely you can work that out.'

'Fanboys,' said Jim. 'You're just fanboys.'

'Well, not *just* fanboys. We're rather special fanboys, as it happens.'

'And just how special might that be?'

'We're fanboys from the future,' said Geraldo.

Not with a Bang, or a Whimper, But a Quack

Don was a dead or dying duck.
The last of the final few.
The fowl of the air
Weren't anywhere,
And there weren't no rabbits too.

There were not even tiny frogs,
Nor jumping moles and that.
There barked no dogs
Or 'ollered 'ogs,
Nor sang no sing-song cat.

What now of your jovial toad?
Or ferret so fecund?
The pig on the road
Has done his load,
Like the swans on the village pund.★

All alone was Dead Eye Don
Whom quacked for all him worth.
And out somewhere
In that final air
The last quack on the Earth.

Bye bye, Don.
Goodnight, everyone.
Goodnight.

★Poetic off licence

8

Being the professional he was, Neville took it like a manly man. He didn't flinch and he didn't tremble. He didn't even break out in a sweat.

He would later admit in his bestselling autobiography, *Same Again: The Confessions of a Full-Time Part-Time Barman*, that the incident had shaken him severely and that he was never the same man ever again, be that manly or not.

It had shaken others who'd witnessed it, but none so deeply as Neville, who'd had to slip away afterwards and sit down quietly and dab his wrists with lemon juice and pray.

But then it *had* come as a terrible shock and the more Neville thought about it, the more inclined was he to believe that it couldn't actually have happened at all.

But it had.

It really had.

Jim Pooley *had* walked into the Flying Swan in the company of twelve sweetly smelling young men in black T-shirts and shorts and he really-truly–really–really-truly *had* stood them *all* a round of drinks.

Thirteen pints of Large and all purchased by Pooley.

No wonder Neville would wake up in the night, all cold sweats and screaming.

And it wasn't just the matter of the purchasing of all those pints. It was that in the shock of it all, Neville had committed a cardinal sin. He had forgotten about the Swan's dress code, which forbade the wearing of shorts in the saloon bar. He would never live *that* down at future Lodge meetings. The brothers of the *Sacred Order of the Golden Sprout* would make him the butt of many a bitter joke.

But it had happened.

It really truly had.

'Cheers, Neville,' said Pooley, accepting his change and, to the part-time barman's further horror, thrusting the coins straight into his pocket without even bothering to count them.

Neville slipped off for that quiet sit-down. Pooley led Geraldo to a table.

'It's a nice pub, this,' said the fattish bloke, seating himself upon a comfy cushion. 'Very quiet, very sedate.'

'And the finest beer in Brentford.' Jim raised his glass and sipped from it. 'Which is to say, probably the best beer in the world.'

'It's not at all bad.' Geraldo took a mighty swig. 'Although last week I had a beer in a New Orleans bar with Robert Johnson—'

'*The* Robert Johnson?'

'*The* Robert Johnson.'

'Who died in nineteen thirty-seven.'

'You know your bluesmen, Jim.'

'And so, apparently, do you. But listen, Geraldo. I've bought you the beer and so I'd like to hear the story. On the understanding, of course, that it is now beyond the ten o'clock watershed.'

'What is the ten o'clock watershed?' Geraldo asked.

'It is that time of the night when men in bars who have sufficient alcohol inside them begin the telling of tall tales, which generally conclude with the words "and that's the God's honest truth, I'm telling you". This is considered acceptable social behaviour in bars. It's a tradition, or an old charter—'

'Or something,' said Geraldo. 'I get the picture.'

'And,' Jim continued. 'Those who listen to such tall tales never ever respond by saying, "You are a lying git."'

'Even if they are?' Geraldo asked.

'Even if they are.'

'Very civilized,' Geraldo said. 'But what I'm going to say is the God's honest truth, I'm telling you.'

'You're supposed to say that at the end. But never mind, just please tell me your story.'

'Right.' Geraldo took another pull upon his pint and finished it. 'I'd like another one of these,' he said.

'*After* you've told your tale.'

'Right.' Geraldo set down his empty glass and rubbed his podgy hands together. 'Where to start. OK, I'll start at the end, because that's where it all began.'

Jim sighed inwardly. So far not so good, he thought.

'*The end*,' said Geraldo, 'came about at precisely ten seconds after the ninth minute of the eighth hour of the seventh day of the sixth week of the fifth month of the year four thousand, three hundred and twenty-one. The scientists at the Institute confirmed this and that made it OFFICIAL.

'Ten–nine–eight–seven–six–five–four–three–two–one. That was zero hour, you see.'

'I don't,' said Jim. 'But I do see a flaw in the calculations.'

'Then well spotted, Jim. The scientists didn't spot it, however. But whether that has any bearing on how things worked out I'm not sure. Now, I'm going to tell you what happened in the form of a story. I'll do all the voices and when I describe each character I'll do it in verse.'

'Why?' Jim asked.

'Because I'm a bit of a poet.'

Jim sighed outwardly this time.

'And I wasn't actually there when it all happened. But I watched and heard it all, because I'd hacked into the closed-circuit surveillance video at Institute Tower. I was hooked into Porkie, you see.'

'The Single World Interfaced Network Engine?'

'The very same. So just sit back and drink your beer and I will tell the tale.'

And so saying, Geraldo told Jim the tale. Doing all the voices and describing the characters in verse.

The tale had chapters and titles and everything.

And this is how it went.

1
ALL PORKIE'S FAULT

It was a conclave and a cabal. A council and a conference.

They were a synod of scientists. A bothering of boffins.

Top of the tree, these fellows were, in the fields of their endeavour. The back-room boys with the front-room minds and the lofty aspirations.

The year was 4321. It was early on a Sunday morning. It was rather later than it should have been in May.

The conclave and the cabal was held in the big posh high-domed solar lounge at the top of Institute Tower.

The tower itself was a monumental cylinder of pale pink plastiglass, which thrust from the Earth like a raging stonker and buried its big knob end in the clouds. It was a testament to technology, a standing stone to science.

It was an architect's vision.

The architect was a man.

The scientists were all men, of course. There had never been a lot of room for girlies in science. And so, on this very special day, there were four of them present and these were the last men who worked in the tower. These were the final four.

A thousand years before, when it was first constructed, the tower had housed hundreds of the buggers. Buzzing around like albino bees, with their white coats and their clipboards in their hands. They scratched at their unkempt barnets with the butt-ends of Biros. Chalked calculations on bloody big blackboards. Drank lots of coffee from styrofoam cups and wore those atrocious ties with little cartoons of Einstein, which folk always give to scientists for Christmas and scientists always wear to show what jolly chaps they are.

Those had been the days, my friends.

But those days were all gone.

Now there were only four of them left and soon these four would be gone, like the days had been gone. So to speak.

It was all down to knowledge, you see. For it was knowledge that had brought about THE END.

The director of the Institute was Dr Vincent Trillby. He was a man of considerable knowledge and, as it was he who had called the conclave into being, he was the first man to speak.

> Though not as tall as bigger men
> He didn't lack for height.
> His chest was trim
> And his hips were slim
> And there wasn't a pimple in sight.
>
> His eyes were grey
> As a cloudy day,
> And he carried himself in a confident way.
> He was dapper and sleek
> And when *he* rose to speak
> He was rarely obscure. He was never oblique.

'Gentlemen,' said Dr Vincent Trillby, rising from his antique chromium chair and casting a grey'n over his three colleagues, who sat about the black obsidian-topped table. 'Gentlemen, we all know why we're here. It's a regrettable business, but we all knew it had to happen eventually. The final papers are in. The calculations cross-check. The big clock on the wall is counting down and when the long hand reaches the tenth second past the ninth minute that will be it. THE END.

And that's OFFICIAL.'

The three men mumbled and grumbled and shifted in their chairs and drummed their fingers on the tabletop. They didn't like this at all. But they all knew that it had to happen one of these days and they all knew that the calculations had to be correct.

After all, the calculations were Porkie's and Porkie's calculations were always correct.

'Gentlemen, the clock.'

The three men turned their eyes towards the clock and watched the final seconds tick away, tick tick tick, the way those seconds do. The long hand crept around the face, reached the tenth second past the ninth minute.

And then stopped.

'So that's it,' said Dr Vincent Trillby. 'THE END. Not with a bang, nor even a whimper, just with a big full stop. And not even a big one. But that's it, gentlemen, our job here is done and I'm away to the golf course. Don't forget to clear your desks before you go and the last man out please switch off the lights.'

Following a moment of rather bewildered silence, a plump hand rose shakily into the air-conditioned air.

'Blashford,' said Dr Vincent Trillby. 'You have some apposite remark you wish to favour us with?'

'Something like that, sir, yes.'

'Onto your fat little feet then, lad, spit the fellow out.'

Blashford rose, a podgy youth.
A lover of women, a lover of truth.
The top of his class in advanced trigonometry.
Branches of physics and snappy geometry.
Though rather sweaty down under the arms
He was popular due to his eloquent charms.
And his optimism.

'Dr Trillby,' he said, in a polite and measured tone. 'Dr Trillby, I am aware, as we all are, that this is THE END. There is no room left for doubt. If I might, perhaps, liken science to a lady's silken undergarment. I, for one, would not expect to find the skidmark of error soiling its gusset. We, as the last men of science, know that everything that could possibly be achieved has now been achieved. That science has finally advanced to a point beyond which it cannot go. That all that can be done has been done. That—'

'Is there some point to this, Blashford?' Dr Trillby mimed golf swings. 'Because I can hear the fairway calling.'

'Dr Trillby.' Blashford toyed with his tie. It had little cartoons of Einstein all over it. 'Dr Trillby, sir. I do have to ask you this.'

'Well go ahead, lad, do.'

'Dr Trillby, what does it mean?'

'Mean, lad? Mean? It means that it's THE END. That's what it means. Mankind has come to a full stop. There can be no further progress. You said it yourself. All that can be done has been done. Everything.'

'If I might just slip a word in here.'

70

Clovis Garnett rose to speak.
Clovis with his fiery mane.
Clovis with his ruddy cheek.
Clovis with his ankle chain.

Clovis with his bright red blazer.
Clovis with his bright red tie★.
Clovis sharp as any laser.
Fixed them with his cherry eye.

'I think, sir, what Fatty Blashford is trying to ask—'
'Oi!' cried Blashford. 'Enough of that fatty talk.'
'What our esteemed and magnificently proportioned colleague
is trying to ask—'
'That's more like it,' said Blashford. 'Nice tie, by the way.'
'What he is trying to ask,' said Clovis, 'is: what happens next?'
'Nothing,' said Dr Trillby. 'Nothing happens next. That's the
whole point of THE END. Nothing happens after it. Nothing *can*
happen after it.'
'You'll be playing golf,' said Blashford. 'That will be happening.'
Clovis sniggered. 'There's nothing very happening about golf,'
said he. 'Golf was never a happening thing.'
Dr Trillby sighed. 'All right,' he said. 'I know it's Sunday and I
know it's early in the morning and I know this is all very upsetting
for you. So, as a special favour, I will run through it all just the one
more time and then I am off to play golf.'
Three pairs of eyes, two pairs blue and one pair red, fixed upon
Dr Trillby. Dr Trillby spoke.
'We have all read the Holy Writ of Saint Charles Darwin,' he
said. '*On the Origin of Species* has been taught in every classroom
and preached from every pulpit for nearly two thousand years.
Mankind evolved, through the Will of God, by means of natural
selection. Had natural selection continued, mankind would have
continued to evolve. Into what? Who can say. A race of gods, perhaps. But the point is moot. Mankind did not continue to evolve.
And for why? Because of science.

★The one with the cartoon Einstein motif.

71

'During the latter part of the twentieth century and the earlier part of that following, natural selection ceased. Advances in medicine, food production, welfare, genetic modification, *science*, saw to it that *all* survived. Not just the fittest. But *all*.

'No more survival of the fittest. No more evolution.

'So, as human evolution had ceased, it became inevitable that the human race would one day reach a cut-off point. When mankind had finally achieved everything it was capable of achieving; when every book had been written, every piece of music composed; everything capable of invention invented; everything that could be accomplished accomplished. The lot. The entire caboodle. All. There is now nothing that anyone can think of that hasn't been thought of before. It has all been done. Everything. We have reached THE END.

'And with that all said, *again*, would any of you now redundant fellows care to join me for a round of golf?'

'I have a question,' said Blashford.

'Perhaps you do, lad. But not one that hasn't been asked before.'

'But what if *I* thought of something new?'

'You can't, lad. There is nothing new that can be thought of.'

'It's preposterous,' said Blashford.

'I know, lad, I know.' Dr Trillby mimed a winning putt. 'It had to happen eventually and now it has. And that's OFFICIAL.'

'So what *will* happen next?'

Dr Trillby sighed once more. 'Nothing, lad. Go home and put your feet up. Watch some old rerun on the television.'

'I could write a new TV series,' said Blashford. 'Put a new spin on an old idea.'

'Been done. Every new spin that could be spun has been spun. We have been watching reworkings of reworkings of reworkings for more years than I care to remember.'

'But there will be news. New news.'

'News of what? There is no more crime, there are no more wars, there is no more sickness. Due to genetic modification, we all live to be exactly one hundred and seventy-five years old. The world is governed and run by Porkie and is as near to Utopia as it can possibly be. And that's OFFICIAL too!'

'Space travel,' said Blashford. 'What about space travel?'

72

'We have reached the limit of scientific achievement regarding space travel. No further developments are possible.'

'Nothing is impossible to science,' said Blashford.

Dr Trillby offered up what he hoped would be the final sigh of the day. 'There was a time,' said he, 'when that was probably true. The time of St Charles Darwin. At that time everything seemed possible and perhaps was possible. But that time has now passed. All that science can achieve has been achieved. Do I need to have this engraved upon a mallet and beat you over the head with it?'

'I'll hold him down if you want,' said Clovis.

'That won't be necessary. Now, I've said all I intend to say on this matter. All, indeed, that can be said. I am off to tog up in my Fairisles. Goodbye, gentlemen, and thank you very much.'

'I'll join you, then,' said Clovis. 'I always beat you anyway.'

'Only because you cheat, Clovis. Only because you cheat.'

'Dr Trillby, sir.'

A reedy little voice spoke up. The doctor in his turn looked down.

'Ah,' said Dr Trillby. 'Fourth Man Tripper, experts' expert. What have you to say?'

> Fourth Man Tripper gained his feet
> And tiny feet they were.
> Small boys mocked him in the street
> Because he dressed in fur.
>
> Fourth Man Tripper ran his thumb
> Through golden head of hair.
> Fourth Man Tripper, rarely dumb,
> Pushed aside his chair.

'For a chap with only three days to live,' he said to Dr Trillby, 'Your calmness does you credit.'

Dr Trillby consulted the lifespan chronometer he wore upon his wrist. 'Your calculations are somewhat amiss,' he told Fourth Man Tripper. 'I have another one hundred and five years, four months, three days, two hours and one minute to go before my clinical death, my next recloning and rebirth. I shall be around for many

73

centuries to come. Such are the perks of being a scientist.'

'You will die in three days' time,' said Fourth Man Tripper, reedily. 'And you will not be recloned again or reborn. I have rechecked all the calculations and I can assure you there are no bum stains on *my* knickers.'

'What are you on about, Tripper?'

'Inevitable consequences, sir. The inevitable consequences of THE END. It was all in the report that I left on your desk. Perhaps you did not get around to reading it.'

'Perhaps I did not.'

'Pity, sir. But it's definitely three days. The projections suggest that you die on the golf course. The mob beats you to death. Someone rams a number nine iron right up your—'

'Hold it right there, Tripper. Is this some kind of joke? Because if it is, then I can tell you it's not a new one. All jokes have been done. And most by the end of the twentieth century.'

'It's no joke, sir. Clovis here dies. Blashford dies. The mob will slay us all. The figures do not lie. They're Porkie's figures, after all.'

'Good old Tripper,' said Blashford.

'Eh?' said Clovis.

'I said, good old Tripper. He's come up with something new. It's not THE END at all. No, hang about. Me too? I die too? Why should I die? What have I done?'

Fourth Man Tripper thumbed some more at his goldy locks. 'It's not so much what you have done. It's more a matter of what you can no longer do. Would you like me to explain? Would you like me to tell you what is going to happen and why it's going to happen?'

'If you must,' said Dr Trillby, casting wistful eyes towards the window. 'But if this *is* a joke—'

'What will you do? Sack me?'

'Just say your piece.'

'Thank you, sir.' Tripper flicked imaginary dust from a furry cuff. 'Everyone on the planet has known for months that THE END was coming. There aren't any secrets any more, much as we would like there to be. Every home has a terminal, every terminal is linked to Porkie. Information is currency and all are mighty rich.'

'Good line,' said Blashford. 'New line?'

'No, it's not,' said Dr Trillby. 'Get on with it, Tripper.'

'Everyone knows,' said Tripper, 'we are on Porkie's camera even as we speak. The details of this meeting are already being processed to be broadcast worldwide on the mid-morning news. That the end has come will be broadcast. All the world will know. What do you suppose will happen next?'

'A mad rush to the golf course,' said Dr Trillby. 'But happily I will have finished my round by then and be enjoying the hospitality of the nineteenth hole.'

'No,' said Tripper. 'You really should have read my report. What will happen next is this. Everyone will sit about in bewildered silence, taking in the enormity of it and then they will say to themselves and to others, "No, this cannot be," and "It can't be THE END," and, "You can't tell me we now know everything there is to know and have done everything there is to be done." And then they will all rack their brains and try to come up with something new. But they won't be able to, because there's nothing new to come up with. And then do you know what they'll do?'

'Play golf?'

'No, they won't play golf. They'll look for someone to blame. That's what they always do. You see, the man in the street might hate change, but he always wants something new to enjoy. Nature of the beast, I suppose. And when the man in the street can't get what he wants he looks for someone to blame.'

'Now just hold on,' Dr Trillby raised his hands. 'You're not suggesting that the man in the street will blame *us*?'

'Who else would he blame? Scientists have been running this planet for thousands of years, supplying the needs of the people. Improving life. That's what scientists do, after all.'

'Some say,' said Clovis.

'Shut up, Clovis,' said Dr Trillby. 'But blame us, Tripper? Blame us? After all we've done for the man in the street?'

'*Done*, is the word,' said Tripper. 'We can't *do* any more. The mob will rise up and slay us all.'

'Are you sure about this? Are you sure about the calculations?'

'They're Porkie's calculations.'

75

There was a moment of silence. Each man alone with his own thoughts.

And then they all spoke.

Together. Well, three of them, at least.

'It's all Porkie's fault,' they said.

Tripper shook his head. 'And who built Porkie? Scientists, that's who. I'm afraid, gentlemen, that we are in the shit here. If we can't come up with something to please the man in the street very very fast, we are in the shit.

'And *that's* OFFICIAL!'

2

PORKIE TO THE RESCUE

'Anyone for golf?' asked Dr Trillby.

'Golf?' said Tripper. 'Golf?'

'And why not?'

'I would have thought that was patently obvious.'

Dr Trillby made a breezy face and spoke in an airy manner. 'We cannot stop what cannot be stopped. We are scientists and as scientists we must adopt a detached attitude. Even to our own extinction.'

'Bollocks to that,' said Clovis.

'I tend to agree with Clovis on this occasion,' said Blashford.

'And so do I,' said Dr Trillby. 'But then I have known Tripper for more years than our cat's had an interesting disease that I programmed into its genes to entertain my daughter. Look at that big smug smile on his face. You know a way out of this mess, don't you, Tripper?'

'I may do.'

'Then we're all saved!' Blashford cheered. 'Tripper's got a new idea. Three cheers for Tripper.'

Tripper fondled his cuffs. 'It's not a new idea,' he said. 'In fact it's a very old idea. But I think it's going to do the trick.'

Dr Trillby glanced towards the window. 'The sun rises higher,' he said. 'I shall be late for my round.'

Blashford grinned at Tripper. 'Tell us all about it, old buddy,' said he.

76

'You creep,' said Clovis. 'You fatty fatty creepy creepy creep.'

'And it's not *my* plan,' said Tripper. 'It's Porkie's plan. But if all goes successfully, as I'm sure it will, I will have no hesitation in taking all the credit.'

'And if all goes poo-shaped?' asked Dr Trillby.

'As I said, it's Porkie's plan.'

'I thought we'd agreed that we couldn't blame it on Porkie,' said Blashford.

'Do shut up, lad,' said Dr Trillby. 'Let's hear what Tripper has for us. It's going to be very good, isn't it, Tripper?'

'Very good indeed, sir, yes.'

'Then go on, lad. Let's have it.'

'Thank you, sir.' Tripper preened at his lapels. 'The answer to all our problems can be found in two words,' he said.

There was a moment of hushed expectation.

'Time travel,' said Tripper.

There was a moment of terrible groaning.

'We're all doomed,' said Dr Trillby. 'I really should have guessed.'

'Please hear me out.' Tripper knotted tiny fists. 'I know what you're going to say.'

'That time travel is impossible? Well there, I've said it. I've said it before, if I recall.'

'But it's not, sir.'

'But it *is*, Tripper. Time travel *is* impossible. If it hadn't been impossible we would have come up with it before THE END.'

'But we did, sir. *I* did, sir. Well, *Porkie* did, sir.'

'Porkie did *what*?'

'If you'd read my report, sir. It was all in there. Porkie's final innovation. His final gift to mankind, before THE END. He must have been working privately on it for centuries. Having projected precisely when THE END would come and what the consequences would be, our murders and his own destruction—'

'Porkie's destruction?'

'The mob, sir. When the mob has done with us, they do with Porkie too.'

'But if they destroy Porkie, that will be the end of mankind.'

'So many ends all in a single week, sir. I don't think it can be coincidence, do you?'

'Charlie's beard!' said Dr Trillby.

'Language, sir,' said Tripper.

'So you're telling me that Porkie has come up with a method of travelling through time?'

'That's what Porkie says.'

'And how does it work?'

'Ah,' said Tripper. 'Well, Porkie wouldn't tell me that.'

'He'll tell *me*,' said Dr Trillby. 'I'm the director of the Institute.'

'*Were*, sir. We're all out of a job now. Don't you remember?'

'But I . . . but I . . .' Dr Trillby huffed and puffed.

'There's really no problem, sir. Porkie has agreed that one of us can test the system to make sure that it's safe, before he puts it online for everyone.'

'Everyone?' Dr Trillby clutched at his heart. 'Everyone?'

'The man in the street,' said Tripper. 'Time travel will keep the man in the street happy for centuries to come. For ever, probably.'

'No no no!' Dr Trillby sank into his chair and fanned himself with an unread report. 'This is madness, madness.'

'Why, sir?'

'Because, because, oh, come off it, Tripper. You know why because. How many books have been written on the subject of time travel? Thousands, millions. Not to mention theoretical papers. Not to mention plays and movies. How many *Terminator* sequels have there been?'

'Several hundred,' said Blashford, 'and all of them killers. Although they have tended to get a bit samey over the past few years.'

'My point is this,' said Dr Trillby. 'We all know the drill. If someone from the present was to go back into the past, anything they did, anything at all, would affect the future. The very fact of them being there would affect the future. And that's just one person. Think about those geeky fanboy types who sit all day at their home terminals discussing old music with their online cronies. Imagine what damage even one of them might do.'

'That's why it has to be tested, sir. To make sure it's safe. But Porkie says that it is safe. According to Porkie, the past is fixed. It cannot be altered.'

'And if Porkie is wrong?'

'Perhaps the mob would settle for Blashford.'

'What?' said Blashford.

'Just my little joke. But I trust Porkie, sir, and frankly I don't think we've got any choice.'

Mournful sounds issued from the face of Dr Trillby. They came through his mouth and they quite upset his colleagues.

'Come on, sir,' said Tripper. 'Porkie's planned it all out. One of us makes the trip and attempts to make a tiny alteration to the past and—'

'Hold on there,' said Dr Trillby. 'It has just occurred to me that we keep talking about the past. What about the future?'

'Can't be done, sir. Porkie says that the past is fixed and nothing exists beyond the present.'

'But Porkie has already managed to predict the future. The number nine iron up the . . . and suchlike.'

'Those are just projections, sir. Of what will happen given certain circumstances. The future is not fixed. Only the past.'

'It all smells,' said Dr Trillby. 'But go on with what you were saying. Someone attempts to make a tiny alteration to the past.'

'Yes, sir, and then returns to the present and we all check to see whether anything has changed.'

'And what if it has? What if there are disastrous consequences?'

'Then that same person returns to the past and undoes what he has done. Arrives back a minute earlier than the time before, waits for his original self to arrive and then tells him not to do the thing he was originally going to do.'

Clovis rolled his rosy eyes. 'Now what could possibly go wrong with a plan like that?' he asked.

'Nothing,' said Tripper. 'Trust me.'

'Hold on again.' Dr Trillby raised his hands again. 'What is all this, trust *me*? You are not under the mistaken apprehension that *you* will be making this trip, are you? If anyone is going to make this historic journey that someone will be me.'

'Your bravery is an example to us all, sir. That's settled, then.'

'Hold on, hold on, hold on.' Dr Trillby flapped his hands about. 'You're not putting up much of a struggle.'

'Why should I, sir? Once you've proved it's safe, which is to say once you've survived the journey with mind and body intact, I'll have plenty of opportunities to take as many trips as I like.'

'Hm.' Dr Trillby made the face of thought. 'Perhaps it would be better if *you* made the first journey,' he said. 'After all, it is *your* project.'

'That's settled, then.'

'Eh?' said Dr Trillby.

'Snookered,' said Clovis.

Blashford said, 'Perhaps we should put it to a vote.'

Dr Trillby shook his head. 'Let's just get on with it,' he said. 'How do you propose to run this test, Tripper?'

'Very simply and very safely, sir.' Tripper rootled in his furry briefcase. 'I have here today's newspaper.'

'Anything new in it?' Blashford asked. 'Any new news?'

'None whatsoever.' Tripper held the paper up for all to see. Its headline read. NO NEWS AGAIN: AND IT'S OFFICIAL.

'Are you thinking of changing that, then?' Dr Trillby asked.

'No.' Tripper returned the newspaper to his briefcase and placed his briefcase on the table. 'My intention is to travel just two hours into the past and waylay the newspaper boy before he delivers the newspaper to my house. If I return from the past with the newspaper in my hand, then it will mean that the past *can* be changed and we shall have to abandon the whole thing.'

Dr Trillby nodded. 'Seems safe enough,' he said.

'I see a flaw in this,' said Blashford.

'Shut up, lad. Go on, then, Tripper, explain the mechanics of the thing. Is there a time machine you travel in?'

'Time machine!' Clovis rolled his rosy red'ns again.

'It's all done with this.' Tripper displayed the lifespan chronometer on his scrawny wrist. 'Porkie will download the program into the chronometer. All I have to do is set the coordinates and the time and date and press "send". Simple as making a telephone call.'

'What are these coordinates?' Dr Trillby asked.

'Of the place where I wish to materialize in the past. I can't just materialize here, can I? Two hours ago the Earth hadn't reached this spot in space. The coordinates have to be absolutely precise for the journey there and the journey back. Porkie has worked it all out. It's all in the program.'

'Porkie thinks of everything,' said Blashford. 'But—'

'No buts,' said Dr Trillby. 'How do you download the program, Tripper?'

'Simple as can be. I just type into my chronometer the words DOWNLOAD TIME TRAVEL PROGRAM and wait thirty seconds.' He did so and they waited. 'There,' said Tripper. 'I'm on line. So now I type in time and date and projected location.' He did this also. 'And I'm ready for the off.'

'Will you vanish in a puff of smoke?' Clovis asked.

'Don't be sarcastic,' Dr Trillby told him. 'This is a historic moment.'

'It won't work,' said Clovis. 'This is all a wind-up.'

'Ignore him, Tripper,' said Dr Trillby. 'Go on, do your stuff.'

'But, sir.' Blashford made pleadings. 'Please listen, sir. There is a serious flaw.'

'Do it, Tripper,' said Dr Trillby.

And do it Tripper did.

Geraldo paused in his tale and rattled his empty pint glass on the table.

'Don't stop,' said Jim. 'What happened next?'

'Well,' said Geraldo, 'what do *you* think happened next?'

Jim thought about this. 'That's a tricky one,' he said. 'If he did come back with the newspaper, that would have proved that the past could be changed, so they would have had to abandon the project. But if they had, then you wouldn't be here. But you are here. *But* according to you, the past *can* be changed . . .'

'Go on,' said Geraldo.

'Well,' Jim continued, 'if he *didn't* come back with the newspaper that would have proved that the past *couldn't* be changed. So they would have gone ahead with the project. Which they must have done, because otherwise you wouldn't be here.'

'But the past can be changed,' said Geraldo.

'So did he come back with the newspaper, or didn't he?'

'Both,' said Geraldo. 'Or possibly neither.'

'Both, or possibly neither?'

'Things got a little complicated. Allow me to explain. You see, Tripper travelled back into the past and tried to get the newspaper.

81

But the newspaper boy wouldn't give it to him. In fact he punched Tripper on the nose. So Tripper returns to Institute Tower with a bloody nose and no newspaper. He explains what's happened and Dr Trillby says he's a stupid boy and to go back and try again. So Tripper travels back into the past again, making sure that this time he arrives a bit earlier, so he can sneak up on the paper boy from behind. And he's just doing this when he sees his original self materialize in front of the paper boy.

'This is the Tripper who got the bloody nose,' said Jim.

'That's right. We'll call him Tripper number one.'

'So the other one is Tripper number two.'

'And so on.'

'And so on?'

'Allow me to explain. Tripper number one sees Tripper number two creeping up behind the paper boy and he thinks, Ah, this must be the plan I worked out in case something went wrong. This is myself coming back to tell me not to get the newspaper. So Tripper number one backs off, resets his chronometer and zips into the future. Meanwhile Tripper number two has grabbed the newspaper when the paper boy isn't looking and is about to zip into the future when Tripper number three arrives on the scene.'

'Who's Tripper number three?'

'He's Tripper number one, who's returned from the future where Dr Trillby has told him that he's a stupid boy too, and to go and have another try at the newspaper.'

'And does he have the bloody nose?'

'No, because he never got punched.'

'But if he didn't get punched—'

'He does get punched. By Tripper number two.'

'Why?' asked Jim.

'Because he tries to grab the newspaper off him. And that's when Tripper number four gets into the fight.'

'Who's Tripper number four?'

'He's Tripper number three, who goes back further into the past to find a stout stick to defend himself against Tripper number two. Are you sure you want me to go on with this?'

'No,' said Jim. 'I don't. How many Trippers were there in the end?'

'Dozens. Coming and going and going and coming. I counted at least six of them fighting in the solar lounge at one time. But, do you know, I never did see whether any of them had the newspaper.'

'So I assume that the time travel project was abandoned.'

'Sometimes it is,' said Geraldo. 'And sometimes it isn't. Things have become a little unstable in the future.'

'But they did put it online?'

'Oh no,' said Geraldo. 'They never actually put it online.'

'This is all beyond me.' said Jim. 'If they didn't put it online, how did you get here?'

'I nicked it,' said Geraldo proudly. 'As I said, I watched and heard everything, because I had hacked into Porkie. So when Tripper explained how to download the program, I hastily downloaded it as well.'

'But after you saw all the chaos, how could you even think of using it?'

'Wouldn't you have done the same?'

'Well,' said Jim, 'the prospect of time travel is very appealing. I could certainly win a lot of money on the horses.'

'Yeah, and screw up the future. We took a vow to change nothing. We're fanboys and all we wanted to do was travel back to the twentieth century and see all the great bands play. All the originals.'

'Like the Beatles, for instance?'

'Exactly. We agreed to meet up at different gigs. But Wingarde never showed up here, and now I know why. He's been travelling about through time, saving famous rock stars from early deaths.'

'It's a very noble thing to do,' said Jim.

'It's chaos,' said Geraldo. 'And it's all my fault. I should never have trusted him.'

'You weren't to know,' said Jim.

'Yes, but I should have known. It's in his genes, you see. He can't help the way he is. His father was the same and his grandfather before that. All trying to live down the family name.'

'Why?' Jim asked.

'Because they had an ancestor in the twentieth century who made a fortune.'

'What's so bad about that?' Jim asked.

83

'It was the way he made it. He cheated and so his name became a household word, meaning a dirty rotten scoundrel.'

'Oh,' said Jim. 'It wasn't Branson by any chance, was it?'

'No,' said Geraldo. 'It was Pooley. The scoundrel who pulled off The Pooley.'

Old Sea Shanty

Sing us your old sea shanty, Ted.
Said crowds of little nippers.
As ancient Ted sat in his shed
Cooking his ancient kippers.

Well, said Ted, there's one I know
Of days on masted brigs.
With scupper hold and casks of gold
And outboard schooner rigs.

Eh? went the nippers, levelling bricks at him.
Ted sang his shanty.

'Twas in the year of 'fifty-two
Aboard the black ship Didgery Doo,
With Captain Rolf and his mutinous crew
That I went out a-whaling.

We left the port five days behind
Out west the great white whale to find.
We waved at Drake on the *Golden Hind*
As he leaned over the railing.

At last with rations running low
And Rolf boy running to and fro,
We spied a whale off the starboard bow
And shouted, cool and groovy.

And Captain Rolf put down the mate
And came across on a roller skate,
And said, I think we'll have to wait,
I'll miss the midnight movie.

So after we had watched the show
We lowered little boats to row,
And got our harpoons out to throw.
But by that time the whale had buggered off.

'And?' said the nippers. 'What happened next?'
'Nothing,' said Ted. 'That was it. I did see a mermaid on
the way home. But I'll tell you all about that another day.'
The nippers entered into a brief discussion, arrived at a
consensus agreement and, without further ado, stoned
old Ted to death.

9

'Stone me,' said Jim Pooley.

'And that's the God's honest truth, I'm telling you,' said Geraldo, rattling his empty glass once more.

Jim considered the phrase 'You are a lying git' but dismissed it as redundant. The tale simply *had* to be true. He had never told anyone about The Pooley. Certainly all who knew him knew of his quest for the six-horse Super-Yankee. But he had wisely refrained from mentioning the name he intended to give it.

Jim finished his pint and set down his glass. The health-farm glow had fled from his cheeks and he felt far from well.

'I need the bog,' he said.

'Then give me the cash and I'll get in the round.'

Jim fumbled in his pocket and dragged out a oncer. 'Take it,' he said. 'Get a pint for yourself and a vodka for me.'

'Fair enough. No, wait just a minute.'

'I can't,' said Jim, making haste to his feet. 'I think I'm going to be sick.'

'But this poundnote. Is it all right? Who's this bearded bloke on the front?'

Jim took to flapping his hands as he ran to the bog. Generally in moments of acute agitation he flapped his hands and turned around in small circles. But this time he had to flap on the hoof.

'I hope it wasn't something I said.' Geraldo took his empty glass to the counter.

Within the bog of the Flying Swan, Jim made for cubicle three. And here he emptied the contents of his stomach into the white china bowl.

'Oh my God,' went Pooley. 'Oh my God.' And he reached for the chain to flush away the horrors.

'Don't pull that,' said a voice from above.

'Oh my . . .' and Jim's hand hovered.

'God,' said the voice. 'This is God.'

'God?' said a pale and trembling Jim, glancing all round and about. The bog was empty but for himself. But for himself and—

'God?'

'Don't pull that chain,' said God once more. Jim's hands began to flap.

'And don't flap your hands,' said God.

'I'm sorry, sir,' said Jim, who was now on the point of collapse.

'And down on your knees when you're talking to me.'

'Oh, yes, sir, I'm sorry.' Jim knelt down in the cubicle, his nose too near to the horrors. This was all he needed! A telling-off from God!

'Pooley,' said God.

Jim shuddered at his name.

'Pooley, I am displeased with you,'

'But it isn't my fault,' said Jim to God. 'I haven't done anything wrong.'

'What, never?' God asked.

'Well, sometimes,' said Jim. 'But you'd know all about those.'

'You're a bad man, Pooley,' said God.

'But I don't mean to be. I'd never knowingly do harm to anyone. I can't be held responsible for things that happen in the future.'

'What are you on about?' God asked.

'The future, sir, what happens in the future.'

'So you want to know what happens in the future, do you?'

Pooley nodded dismally.

'Is that a yes or a no?'

'It's a yes, sir,' said Jim.

'It'll cost you,' said God.

'What?'

'The information will cost you.'

'Do you want me to put money in the poor box at St Joan's?'

'No, you can leave it here on the floor. I'll see that they get it.'

'Eh?' said Jim.

'Are you querying God?'

'Oh, no, sir, I'm not.'

'Then I will give you a name and an address and you will give me a fiver.'

'I don't think I have a fiver left,' said Jim. 'It's been a very expensive evening.'

'What about the fiver you keep in your left boot for emergencies?'

'You know about that fiver?'

'Everybody knows about *that* fiver.'

'Oh,' said Jim.

'Well, whip it out.'

Still in the kneeling position, Jim fought to remove his boot.

'You want to wash your socks a bit more often,' said God.

'Yes, sir, I'll do that.' Pooley placed the crumpled fiver on the floor.

'Right,' said God, 'So this is what you do.'

And God spake unto Pooley and did tell him of a woman who dwelt in a terrace called Moby Dick. That she was possessed of great powers concerning the foretelling of the future, for she was a Penist and could read the willies of men. And God named this woman and gave Jim the number of the house and also the telephone number, which could, if he forgot it, be also found in any one of the local telephone boxes upon certain coloured cards affixed to the walls with blu-tack. And then God instructed Pooley that he should bugger off at the hurry up and be grateful that he hadn't got a thunderbolt up the bum for being such a bad fellow and also that he should, in future, give money to people smaller and less fortunate than himself, if asked for it.

'And so, on your bike,' said God. 'And sin no more, you bastard.'

And Pooley, having heard the word of God, did hasten from the bog.

And God, having heard the door slam behind him, did hasten

from his hiding place in the cistern of cubicle three. And did shin down the chain and snatch up Pooley's fiver.

'Thank you very much, Jim,' said Small Dave, tucking it into his pocket.

It was a pale and shaking Jim that returned to the saloon bar. A Jim that had had enough for one night and many nights yet to come.

A Jim that—

'Whoa!' went Jim. 'Where are they?'

An equally pale-faced Neville was loading empties onto a tray. 'Who?' he asked, without enthusiasm.

'The chaps I came in with. The chaps in the black T-shirts and shorts.'

'The shorts!' growled Neville. 'The shorts!'

'But where are they? Where've they gone?'

'Buggered off,' said Neville, 'and good riddance, too. Shorts in my bar. You're a bad man, Pooley.'

'No,' mumbled Jim at the terrible phrase. 'I'm not a bad man, I'm not. But I have to speak to Geraldo. Why did he go? Did he say where he was going?'

'No, he didn't, and *I* didn't ask. He came up to the bar just after you'd rushed off to the bog, and if you've been sick on my tiles you're in bigger trouble. He came up to the bar and I said, "What's the matter with Pooley?" and he looked at me and said "Pooley?" in that silly little voice of his and then all his friends started saying "Pooley?" and looking at each other and then they all rushed out of the door.'

'Oh no!' Jim's hands were flapping once again.

'And don't do that in here,' said Neville. 'It fair gives me the willies.'

'The willies,' said Jim. 'The willies, that's it.'

'Go home and sleep it off, Pooley.'

'I'm not drunk. I only wish I was.'

'Well, you're not drinking any more in here tonight.'

'No,' said Jim. 'All right, I'm going.'

'Good,' said Neville. 'Goodnight.'

Jim wandered, lonely, through the night-time streets of Brentford. He was all in a daze and a dither and he didn't know quite what to

90

do. Although Norman admired Jim for living his life in little movies, the truth of the matter was that this was the only way Jim could live his life. One thing at a time was all the lad could ever deal with. Two or more and it was goodnight, Jim.

The rain was falling once again and Pooley turned his collar up. 'I *am* sorry, God,' he said to the sky. 'You don't have to rain on my head.'

A rumble of thunder came down from above and Jim put more spring in his step.

He would greatly have preferred to have gone round to Omally's. The Irishman was his bestest friend and Jim felt that he would have known what to do. But, as he hadn't seen John since before the Gandhis' remarkable performance, and had no idea whether he would even be home, *and*, as he really didn't want to get on the wrong side of God, Jim pressed on towards Moby Dick Terrace.

It as growing late now, after eleven, and Jim had no way of knowing whether the reader of willies would still be open for business. Nor was he exactly certain why God had sent him to seek out this woman anyway. Surely God knew all about the future, didn't he? He could have just told Jim about it there and then.

But, then, God knew his own job best, of course.

And who was Jim to argue?

And he *had* paid out five quid for the information.

And he *was* really desperate to get this thing sorted.

And it *was* getting late.

And he *was* in a state.

And that *was* a tiny little horse that just ran across the road up ahead.

'No, it wasn't,' said Jim, to no one but himself. 'I'm sure it really wasn't.'

Most of the houses in Moby Dick Terrace were bed and breakfasts, catering to the needs of the many tourists who poured in throughout the seasons to visit Britain's best-loved borough. There was always a holiday feel to the terrace, no matter the time of the year.

But at night time there was something more. A strangely nautical feel. Many might have put this down simply to the name. After all, this was the terrace where the legendary Captain Ahab was born. But there was more to it than that.

91

Certain streets have their own personalities, which they often keep very much to themselves and which you may only catch by chance. And then only in the middle of the night.

Moby Dick Terrace was one of these. A B and B'er's paradise by day it might have been, but by night, with the rain coming down and the wind in the right direction, you could almost smell the briny deep and hear the flap of sailcloth.

It no longer seemed to be land-locked suburbia. Now it was harbour lights and fishing floats and crabbing pots and whalebone uplift bras.

As Jim marched along through the wind and the rain he fancied that he heard the sirens singing. Seeking to lure him to his doom in front garden ponds. Or onto rockeries, where the ghosts of drowned sailors searched in vain for their hats.

Beat beat beat went the rain on Jim's head.

And Jim beat a path to the Penist's door.

It was a bright-blue door, as it happened. Blue as the deep blue sea. The house was called Ocean View, as were many of the others, but the number was right. It was twenty-three.

Jim ducked into the shelter of the porch.

'Any old porch in a storm,' said Jim.

And gave the house a good looking-over.

It was your standard two up, three down Victorian masterpiece. With a *No Vacancies* sign in the front window. It was as nice or as nasty a house as suits your personal taste. In his present mood, Jim was in no fit state to judge.

He stood on the doorstep and dithered, damned by doubt and direly desirous of deep deliberation. He didn't want to go through with this. He really, truly didn't.

The more he thought about seeing the Penist, the less he liked the idea. Jim was a sensitive soul. He wasn't one of those blokes who whip their old chaps out at the slightest excuse. And certainly not in front of a lady.

Jim would never even have considered displaying his private parts to a lady, unless they had been properly introduced (Jim and the lady, that is. Not the private parts), shared a romantic candlelit dinner for two and both got so out of their faces on wine that they probably wouldn't remember in the morning.

But this lark wasn't for him. This was for the likes of John Omally. Or Small Dave. He was always pulling his tadger out and waving it all over the place.

'I'm not doing this,' said Jim.

Crash went the thunder and flash went the lightning.

And press went Jim's finger on the bell.

There was one of those little intercom things and this gave a sudden crackle and a lady's voice said, 'Can I help you, please?'

Jim sighed a deep and heartfelt. 'I've come to see Madame Crowley,' he said.

'In you come, then, dear.' The door buzzed and clicked and Jim pushed it open. 'And please wipe your feet,' said the voice.

Jim wiped his feet upon the mat. Shook what rain he could from his shoulders and head and closed the front door behind him. He was standing in a pleasant little hall, which had all the usual guesthouse how-do-you-do. The hall stand with the raincoats and the waders and galoshes, the buckets and spades and the shrimping nets, the coloured brochures advertising the beauties of the borough and where to go to get the best tattoos. There were the house rules. No sheep in the rooms after nine p.m. and suchlike. And so forth.

And there was something more.

The left-hand wall was covered in masks. Carnival masks. Dozens of them. Masks of clowns and public figures, film stars old and new. In the very midst was a sign.

And this is what it said.

CLIENTS OF A MODEST DISPOSITION OR OTHERWISE DESIROUS OF ANONYMITY MAY CHOOSE AND DON FROM THIS COLLECTION BEFORE HAVING THEIR WINKIES READ.
                              Courtesy of the management.

'Very thoughtful,' said Jim, wondering what he should choose.

He passed on the Bill Clinton. It looked rather worn out and over-used. And he gave the Hugh Grant a miss too. The Dalai Lama seemed hardly appropriate and exactly what Sister Wendy was doing there—

Jim settled for a rather dashing domino, which lent him, he

thought, the look of the Scarlet Pimpernel. Or Batman's Robin, at a push.

And having posed a bit before the hall mirror and wrung what rain he could from his hair, Jim squared up his sagging shoulders and knocked on the living-room door.

'In you come, dear,' said the lady's voice and Jim put his best foot forward.

He found himself in a room that might have been anyone's. It might have been his Aunty Norma's, or his Aunty May's. It was an aunty's room that looked just the way that aunties' rooms always do.

Jim squeezed past the stuffed gorilla and stepped over the stripped-down Harley-Davidson. His shoes made sucking noises on the latex rubber carpet.

'Hold it there, dear, if you will.'

Jim held it there and sought out the owner of the voice. His gaze fell upon an ancient white-haired lady of respectable good looks, who wore more lace than a Southern belle and sat at a table littered with all the usual tools of the duff clairvoyant's trade. The crystal ball, the tarot cards, the magnifying glass, the KY jelly and the stirrup pump.

And the pair of surgical gloves.

'Good evening,' said Jim nervously. 'Are you Madame Crowley?'

'I am she. Now just hold still for a mo, if you will, dear.'

Jim held still for a mo and Madame Crowley gazed thoughtfully towards his trouser fly.

If it's X-ray eyes, I suppose I don't mind, thought Jim.

'Well,' said the elderly mystic. 'I can tell that you're not a bad man.'

'You can?' said Jim. 'You can?'

'I can,' and the old one nodded her head. 'You "dress" on the left, that's always a good sign.'

'Is it?' asked Jim. 'I mean, what?'

'The side you dress. The side your penis hangs.'

Jim shivered. Somehow the word penis always sounded ruder than any of its slang counterparts.

'The left side is the right side. Which is odd when you think about it, because the left-hand course is the wrong course, of course.'

'Of course,' said Jim. Do what? he thought.

94

'Never mind, my dear. Never mind. Would you care to take a seat?'

'Thank you,' said Jim. 'I suppose you want me to take off my trousers first.'

'I sense that you're not very keen.'

'I'm not very keen at all, as it happens. Do you think we could do it some other way?'

The mystic cocked her head on one side. 'I am versed in many forms of divination,' she said. 'I can read all parts of the body. The penis, of course, is the easiest to read. Men think with their penises, you know.'

'I've heard that said,' said Jim. 'But only by women, if I recall.'

'Women are the more intelligent sex.'

'I've heard them say that too.'

'Well, as you please, dear. I can see that you're deeply troubled. Let us take a little look at your palm and see what might be done.'

'Splendid.' Jim sought out the nearest chair. It was constructed from the bones of sheep, but the cushion looked quite soft.

He drew up the chair to the table and placed his soggy bum upon it. 'Which hand would you like to see?' he asked.

'The left one, dear. The left one is the right one. Which is curious when you come to think about it, because—'

'The left one it is, then.' Jim stretched his paw across the table.

Madame Crowley took up her lens and peered at Pooley's palm. She peered at it once and she peered at it again and then she shook her ancient head and peered at it once more.

And then she turned it over and took to peering up Jim's sleeve. 'Could you draw back your shirt cuff?' she asked.

Jim drew back his shirt cuff.

'Up to the elbow.'

Jim drew his shirt cuff up to the elbow.

'Utterly remarkable,' said Madame Crowley, sinking back into her chair. 'I have never seen anything quite like that before.'

'Is it bad?' Jim asked, examining his palm.

'I really don't know if it is,' Madame Crowley beckoned back the palm of the peering Pooley. 'You see,' she continued, pointing at it with her thumb, 'you have two lifelines.'

'Two?' Jim leaned forward for a squint.

'Two. Here and here. This one,' and she pointed once again, 'comes to a rather sudden halt.'

'Oh dear,' said Jim.

'But this one, this one runs right round to the back of your hand and vanishes up your sleeve.'

'Oh,' said Pooley, without the 'dear' this time.

'Remarkable,' said Madame C. 'Remarkable indeed.'

'But what does it mean?' Jim asked.

'It means—'

But now a knock came at the door.

'Mrs Crowley,' came a young man's voice. 'Can I come in, please?'

'No, sorry, dear, I'm with a client. What was it you wanted?'

'A clean towel, is all.'

'There's new ones in the airing cupboard at the top of the stairs. Please take as many as you like.'

'Thank you, Mrs Crowley,' said the young man's voice.

The mystic listened to the young man's footsteps on the stairs. 'I'm sorry about that,' she said to Jim. 'It's just the young gentleman who's lodging with me for a couple of days.'

'Tourist?' Jim asked.

'I don't think so. He says he's here on family business, trying to locate an ancestor. Trace records, I suppose. He says he has a loose end he needs to tie up. I offered him a reading – I do the past as well as the future – but he said no. He said he had to deal with it himself.'

'To tell the truth,' Madame Crowley whispered, 'I didn't much like the way he said it. But he keeps himself to himself, and I *do* need the money.'

Pooley shrugged an 'it takes all sorts' sort of shrug.

'But let us address ourselves to your magical palm.'

'Just tell me what it means,' said Jim.

'It means the impossible,' said Madame Crowley. 'It means that you will die very soon. But also that you'll live for ever.'

Jim shook his sodden head. 'That isn't helping much,' he said. 'But can you tell me this? Is it possible for a man to cheat his own fate?'

'Could you be a little more specific, dear?'

'Well,' said Jim, 'I have it on very sound authority that I will do something in the future that will affect a great many lives. And not in a good way. Can I avoid doing this?'

'Indeed,' said the mystical lady. 'If you have been granted the knowledge of what the thing is, the power is yours to avoid it. Is it something that *can* be avoided, dear?'

'It can,' said Jim. 'But it would mean me giving up my life's ambition. My chance to be rich.'

'Then if that is the price you must pay, you must pay it. To cheat one's fate one must pay a heavy price.'

'So I must throw away my dreams,' Jim gave out with a sorry sigh.

'The choice would seem to be yours. The two lines are there upon your palm. The choice of which you choose is yours.'

'But which line is which?' Jim asked.

'I think that will all become clear, dear. I think that will all become clear.'

'All right, then,' said Jim. 'If the choice *is* mine, I will make it.'

'Splendid, dear, then that will be five pounds.'

Pooley left the house of Madame Crowley five pounds lighter, but with head held high. He would make the right choice, he knew that he would. He would give up betting on the horses. It was the only way and Jim knew it. If he gave up betting, he could never win The Pooley. And if he never won The Pooley, then generations of Pooleys yet to come would have no name to live down and one of them would not come back into the past and bugger it all about.

'Dealt with,' said Jim. 'And sorted too.'

And off he marched into the night.

Madame Crowley padded up her stairs and knocked upon her guestroom door. 'I'm off to bed now, dear,' she called. 'Was there anything further you wanted?'

'No thanks,' called back the young man's voice. 'I'm off to sleep myself now. I have to be up early in the morning.'

'Tracing that ancestor of yours?'

'Precisely,' said the voice.

Madame Crowley, her ear to the door, thought she heard a clicking from within. To her it was just a clicking sound and nothing more at all.

To a munitions expert, however, one trained to recognize the distinctive sounds of weapons being cocked, it would have been quite another matter.

Had such an expert heard that click, he (or she) would have recognized it at once as the sound of an AK47 being cocked.

'As long as everything's all right, then, dear,' called Madame Crowley.

'It will be soon,' the voice called back. 'Goodnight, Mrs C.'

'Goodnight, Wingarde dear,' said Mrs C.

Green Tweeds

The green tweeds of spring, with the first cuckoo's note.
That calls through his beak, having come up his throat.
And it's out with the rod and the line and the boat.
The green tweeds.
The bonny green tweeds.

The green tweeds of summer are calling me back.
The green tweeds I share with my brother called Jack.
Who lives in a box and peers out through a crack.
The green tweeds.
The bonny green tweeds.

The green tweeds of autumn, the nights drawing in.
The green tweeds are putrid and make the nose ring.
So it's down the dry-cleaner's and Elvis is King.
The green tweeds.
The bonny green tweeds.

The green tweeds of winter and Yuletide and that.
With old Father Christmas, all merry and fat.
And firesides and puddings and cheerful and chat.
The green tweeds.
The bonny green tweeds.

Let us drink and make merry
And raise up a glass.
And laugh and shout 'Good-oh' and 'Yippee'.
For I'll wear those green tweeds
As my father before me,
Cos no bugger calls *me* a hippy!

Mad, yes.

10

'Green tweeds,' said Jim to John. 'You're back to your old green tweeds, I see.'

'They mocked the zoot,' said John to Jim. 'So it's back to the old green tweeds for me.'

It was the morning of the following day and they were in Omally's kitchen. The kitchen looked much as it had done before. Though possibly just a tad worse.

'I'd offer you coffee,' said Omally, 'but, as you know, I have just the one mug and it's grown a mite furry of late.'

'No matter,' said Jim brightly. 'I had a little water from my tap and it's only an hour until opening.'

John looked his companion up and down. 'You seem very chipper this morning,' said he. 'Very chipper indeed.'

'I am chipper,' said Jim. 'I have made a momentous decision and I want you to be the first to hear about it.'

'I am honoured,' said John. 'So what is it?'

'I've given up betting on horses,' said Jim.

'Well, that's highly commendable.' John nodded thoughtfully. 'Hang on there, what did you say?'

'I've given up betting on the horses.'

John looked at Jim.

And Jim looked back at John.

'Oh, very funny,' said Omally. 'You really had me going there.'

'No, John, I'm deadly serious. I've really given up.'

'You've given up on The Pooley?'

Pooley's face fell. 'How did you know I called it that?' he asked.

'Because you talk in your sleep. Remember that night on the allotment when we were too drunk to walk home and we slept in my hut?'

'Not in any great detail,' said Jim.

'Well, you talked in your sleep and kept on and on and on about The Pooley.'

'Hmm,' said Jim, running his finger over the tabletop. 'But that's what I've done, John. Given it up for good. I have to do it, although I won't explain why, because you'd never believe it.'

'I don't believe it now, Jim. Betting's in your blood. You could never give it up.'

'I can and I have,' said Jim.

'Nonsense,' said John. 'You won't last till the end of the day.'

'I bet you I will,' said Jim.

Omally shook his head. 'If you're absolutely serious,' he said, 'I'll stick by you . . .'

'Thank you, John, I appreciate that.'

'But you won't tell me why you're doing it?'

'Maybe some time. If everything sets itself aright.'

'That's fine by me,' said Omally.

'So tell me, John. How did things go for you last night?'

'Not so well as they might have done. Did you see the Gandhis play?'

'Yes, I did.' Pooley's finger was now glued to tabletop goo. 'It was incredible, wasn't it? Like some religious revival meeting or something. People getting cured of the clap and having their hair grow back.'

'It was that good, was it, eh?'

'It was amazing. But didn't you watch them yourself?' Pooley struggled to release his gummed-down finger.

'I didn't get to see or hear them.' John made a very bad face. 'I followed one of the big-haired bastards into the downstairs bog and tried to tune him up about management. Do you know what he did?'

'No,' said Jim. 'I don't.'

'He chinned me,' said John. 'He knocked me unconscious.'

'You have to be kidding,' said Jim. 'Could you give me a hand here? I seem to be glued to your table.'

John took to tugging with Jim. 'That's what happened,' he said as he tugged. 'I missed the entire gig. But I'll have my revenge. As soon as I'm managing that band. I'll sack the big-haired bastard.'

'What, even if he's the Stratster?'

'It wasn't the Stratster. Stratsters don't punch people. It was the drummer, I'm sure.'

'Sack him,' said Jim. 'Get in Ringo. If things go the way I hope they will, Ringo might well be out of a job quite soon.'

'Ringo it is, then,' said John.

'But what makes you think they'll let you manage them?'

'I have this,' said Omally, rooting in the pocket of his old green tweeds.

'And what is that, might I ask?'

Omally displayed a cassette tape. 'A bootleg of the gig is what it is.'

'But how—'

'Sandy always bootlegs the gigs. He makes copies and sells them.'

'I told you I disliked him.'

'Yes, well, I availed myself of the master copy, out of his deck when he wasn't looking.'

'You stole it.'

'I'd like to say relocated. Shall we call it a long-term loan?'

'If that pleases you. Am I going to be glued to this table for the rest of my life, do you think?'

'I'll get some paint-stripper,' said John.

'You bloody won't,' said Jim. 'But listen, John. Geraldo said last night that the Gandhis were going to be very big and I believe him. If you could get to manage them, I think your fortune might be made.'

'I'm not entirely certain I should base my future on the word of a fat bloke with sweaty armpits.'

'Make an exception for me, then. Apocalypso music will be the next big thing.'

'What is Apocalypso music?'

'It's what the Gandhis do, apparently. It's something about the way Litany sings. Something in her voice. That's what did the healing and stuff. This is big, John. This is very big.'

'You suddenly seem most enthusiastic.'

'Yes, well, I would.' Pooley wrenched his finger free. 'I heard her sing and as I'm no longer a betting man I'm looking for a job.'

'A job?' said John doubtfully. '*You* are looking for a job?'

'I am,' said Jim. 'I am.'

'And what sort of job did you have in mind?'

'Oh,' said Jim. 'I thought perhaps something in the music industry. You see, I met this woman in a pub. She's the lead singer of a band and she said that I was everything she hoped I'd be. I thought I might go into management.'

'What?!' roared John, appalled.

'*Joint* management,' said Jim. 'After all, you have the tape and I have the inside connection.'

John gave this a moment's thought. 'All right,' he said slowly. 'Joint management it is. The music industry is a tricky old business and it would be good to work with someone you know you can trust.'

'Yes,' said Jim. 'I do suppose it would.'

'So, we'll shake on it. Fifty–fifty down the line, all profits, all expenses.'

'I can't see how I can lose on that.' And Jim shook John by the hand.

'And so to business,' said Omally. 'The first thing we have to do is get some copies made of this tape.'

'I don't have a deck,' said Pooley.

'And nor do I,' said John. 'But all is not lost by any means, for I know a man who does.'

The man who does and the man who did went by the name of Norman.

Norman had been up since five, when the day began for him with the numbering up of the papers. Having done all this and sent young Zorro* out on his rounds, Norman was left with a few hours to think before he opened his shop.

---

*As a matter of interest, it would be one of Zorro's descendants who, as a paper boy himself, would one day punch Tripper number one upon the nose.

103

Norman, this day, had done some heavy thinking. He'd had a very rough evening, had Norman, and one he would sooner forget.

The policemen had finally set him free, having confiscated all his tapes and fined him the clothes that he would have stood up in, if he'd been given them back. Norman had been forced to jog home in his underwear, which had been, to say the least, a trifle wet and chilly.

The sight that had met his weary eyes upon his return to his kitchen, however, had given him quite a thrill. It hadn't been quite what he'd hoped for. But it was something pretty damn special.

Norman had looked on in awe, as the tiny horses raced before him, round and round and round.

Round and round the horses went. And round and round and round.

Norman had watched them, thrilled by their beauty. Their grace and their form and their wonder.

Round and round they continued to go and then out through the door he'd left open.

And that had been the last Norman saw of his tiny horses. He'd tried to run after them, but a neighbour, looking out of her bedroom window, had screamed and Norman had been forced to retreat to his shop. And that had been it for his night and Norman had slept very badly indeed.

It was now ten o'clock in the morning. The shop bell tinged and Norman looked up from his dusting.

In walked Jim and in walked John, and Norman viewed them with a bitter eye. Here were two men he'd rather not have seen. For each of them had got him into one kind of shit or another. Although only one was truly to blame and that one had to pay.

'Get out of my shop, Omally!' Norman shouted. 'And never darken my counter again.'

'Hi-de-ho,' said John merrily. 'So what ails you, my friend?'

'And don't you "my friend" me, you bastard. Take to your heels at once.'

John picked up a Snickers bar and fiddled with the wrapping.

'And put that back,' said Norman.

Omally put it back.

'And now get out.'

104

'Hold on there.' John raised calming palms. 'Something is wrong. I can sense it.'

'Look at my shelves,' Norman gestured to his shelves. 'Empty. You see that?'

'I see that,' said John. 'Have you been robbed?'

'The police. They confiscated all the tapes and you owe me five hundred pounds.'

'They took your tapes?' said John. 'Why did they take your tapes?'

'Because they were illegal. Snuff movies, they called them. You've ruined my standing in the borough. I will never be able to hold my head up at the next Lodge meeting. The brothers will make mock of me.'

'I'm terribly sorry,' said John. 'But I had no idea that the tapes were illegal. As I told you myself, I hadn't played them.'

'Yeah, but you must have known what they were.'

'Hardly,' said John. 'I am as much an innocent victim of circumstance as you. I bought them in good faith from a bloke I met in a bar.'

'The police now have a tape of me saying that. Strapped to a chair with electrodes on my nipples.'

'Nasty,' said Jim.

'Handy,' said John. 'Surely you'd own the copyright. You could rent out copies of that.'

'Wait there,' said Norman, 'while I find a stout stick to beat you with.'

'No, just hold on.' And John's palms went aloft again. 'Good friends like us should not fall out over such a matter. Happily I am now in the position to make full recompense. If you will perform a simple service for me, all will be put to rights.'

'Eh?' said Norman.

John pulled out his cassette. 'I just need a couple of copies of this.'

'More tapes!' Norman sought his stick.

'He seems most upset,' said Pooley. 'Perhaps we'd better go.'

'He'll be fine,' said John. 'He's all talk, Norman is.'

Norman returned with a gun. He pointed this at John.

'All talk?' Pooley said.

'Out!' shouted Norman. 'Or I shoot you dead.'

'Where did you find that gun?' Omally asked.

105

'Someone hid it under my dustbin yesterday.' Norman worried at the trigger.

'It doesn't work,' said John. 'The firing pin is missing.'

'Give me half an hour and then come back. I'll have it fixed.'

'There is really no need for any of this,' said Omally.

'Lean your head forward,' said Norman. 'I'll club you to death with the thing.'

'No,' said John. 'Now stop stop stop. I will pay you back the five hundred pounds and give you another one thousand besides. All you have to do for me is make two copies of this cassette.'

'Strange as it may seem,' said Norman, 'I don't believe what you say.'

'Have I ever lied to you?' Omally asked.

Norman thought. 'No,' he said slowly, 'you haven't. You have merely neglected to tell me the truth.'

'Just make two copies of this tape. Give me one back with the original and keep the other for yourself. It will soon be worth an awful lot of money.'

'Why?' Norman asked.

'Because it is a rare collector's item. The first recording of a band that is soon to be famous.'

'What about my fifteen hundred quid?'

'I'll give you that within the week.'

'Within the week?' said Norman.

'Within the week?' said Jim.

'Within the week, I promise.' Omally crossed his heart.

'You saw that, Jim,' said Norman. 'You saw that with your own two eyes. He swore and crossed his heart and everything.'

'And I'll shake on it too,' said John, sticking out his hand.

Norman shook Omally's hand and Norman's mouth was open.

'Within the week,' said John. 'Now take the tape and make the copies. I'll be back within the hour.'

John and Jim walked up the Ealing Road.

'You promised him fifteen hundred pounds,' said Pooley. 'You promised it to him and you shook his hand.'

Omally shrugged. 'It sounds a lot,' said he.

'It *is* a lot,' said Jim.

106

'Not when you split it in half, it's not.'

'I suppose it wouldn't be,' said Jim.

'I'll tell you what,' said John. 'The best thing for you to do would be to pay my half as well. I can owe you the difference.'

Jim drew up rather short in his stride. 'What are you saying?' he asked.

'Oh, come on now, Jim. Don't say you've forgotten already. We shook on it, didn't we? Half the profits, half the expenses, we agreed. I hope you don't intend to renege on our deal.'

'What?' went Jim. 'What?'

'Look upon it as a kind of negative investment. We'll be making millions soon. What's a mere fifteen hundred to you?'

Jim Pooley shook his disbelieving head. 'I have only been in the music business half an hour,' said he, 'and already I've been done up like a kipper.'

'The day is yet young,' said John to Jim. 'We haven't got started yet.'

Anthem to the Griddle Chef

Of all the noble men at arms
And Casanova's love-nest charms.
And knights of old with painted spears.
Or pirates on the chandeliers★.

No fellow that did e'er draw breath
Could aught compare to the griddle chef.

No long-dead earl of Arran's Isle,
Who might have won some maiden's smile,
By striking down that dragon bad.
Nor even Tom the farmer's lad.

Could ever, though, in noble death
Compare at all to the griddle chef.

The griddle chef.
The griddle chef.
A hero bold and true.
'Two Wimpy Brunch,' goes up his cry.
'One with no onions, too.'

★Douglas Fairbanks, probably.

11

'All right, then,' said Jim to John. 'I assume you have some kind of a plan.'

'And then some,' said John to Jim. 'When it comes to a plan, I am ever your man.'

They stood in the sundrenched Ealing Road. Right outside the business premises of Bob the Bookie. The graffiti-spattered brickwork glittered in the sun, and the red and white plastic slash curtain at the doorway moved gently in the breeze, swaying sensuously, it seemed to Jim, bidding him to enter.

Jim bit his lip and folded his arms and turned his back on temptation. 'Speak to me, John,' he said bravely. 'Tell me of your plan.'

'It's simplicity itself. I'll get the tapes from Norman and I'll make some important phonecalls. You'll hasten at once to West Ealing.'

'West Ealing?' Jim gave his lip another small chew. 'Now why would I, or indeed anyone, wish to go to West Ealing?'

'Because that is where the Stratster works. His name is Ricky Zed and he is the griddle chef at the Wimpy. You will visit him and employ your charms. I assume that the lead singer did not give you her telephone number.'

'You assume correctly.'

'Then you chat up Ricky, see if you can get it from him.'

'Will this involve lying?' Jim asked. 'I'm not very good at lying.'

'Tell him the truth, then. Tell him that we wish to manage the band and tell him that they can expect a record contract by the end of the week.'

'And that would be the truth, would it?'

'Jim, I intend to have a record contract sorted by lunchtime.'

'Right,' said Jim in a thoughtful tone. 'Right. By lunchtime. I see.'

'Well, there's no sense in hanging around, is there?'

Jim shook his head. 'I suppose not,' said he.

'Then off on your way, Jimmy boy. Make me proud of you.'

'All right,' said Jim. 'I'll give it a go. Because, after all' – and he jingled the meagre change in his pocket – 'I really have nothing to lose.'

They shook hands in a professional manner, agreed to meet later in the Swan and went their separate ways.

Now Jim was no Marco Polo, and the lands which lay beyond the boundaries of the great Brentford Triangle★ were mostly terra incognita to him. Normally the thought of such a journey would have filled Jim with dread and he would have done anything within his limited powers to avoid it. But he was on a mission here. Two missions, in fact. The first being to avoid the bookies and evade the dreaded Pooley. The second to succeed at something. He had never succeeded at anything, hadn't Jim, and this, perhaps, would be his opportunity.

So he girded up his loins and put his best foot forward and stuck his hand out boldly at the bus stop.

'You should wait until you see a bus coming before you do that,' said a lady in a straw hat. 'And get to the back of the queue or I'll punch your lights out.'

Jim got to the back of the queue.

The journey was for the most part uneventful. No terrorists hijacked the bus. The driver did not fall asleep at the wheel, nor did he become lost. No Red Indians attacked and there wasn't a highwayman to be seen.

★For those few who might be unaware of the fact, the borough of Brentford is enclosed within the boundaries of a triangle, formed by the Great West Road, the Grand Union Canal and the River Thames. Things do go on outside this triangle, but not things of very much interest.

110

A couple of pirates did try to get on at the traffic lights, but the bus conductor blocked their passage and firmly tossed them off.

At length Jim found himself in West Ealing, outside the Wimpy Bar. It was everything he'd hoped it would be, and just that little bit more besides. Delicious odours wafted from within, and through the window Jim could make out beautiful people in elegant clothes, discoursing, no doubt, upon intellectual topics whilst tucking into their brunches.

Jim sighed a sigh and dreamed that dream we have all dreamed. That one day he might own a Wimpy Bar.

He then took a deep, preparatory breath, pushed open the door and went in.

Gentle music played from hidden speakers. Subtle lighting touched upon the tasteful decor. The beautiful people looked up from their brunches and eyed Jim with suspicion.

Pooley sat down at the nearest table and cast his eyes over the menu.

It was a gorgeous colourful gatefold affair, printed upon paper, yet sealed within a transparent plastic shell through some method of technological wizardry that was beyond Jim's understanding. Jim viewed the photographic portraits of the toothsome viands. Here was a double cheeseburger with *all* the trimmings and here a saveloy known as a Bender. On the back page was the ice cream selection. The now legendary Brown Derby and the Jamaican Long Boat. Each of these could be had as it came or with a choice of cream or maple syrup.

Pooley's mouth began to water. It was all too much.

A waiter approached his table and stood looking down upon him. He wore the traditional red and white livery and the jaunty paper cap. This perched somewhat perilously upon a mighty hive of hair.

'Do you wish to order, sir?' asked the waiter. 'Or have you just come in to dribble on the table?'

Jim looked up and went, 'Oh!'

'Oh?' said the waiter.

'Oh,' said Jim. 'Aren't you Ricky Zed?'

The waiter nodded his big-haired head. He was long and tall and lanky and lean, all cheekbones and dark sunken eyes. Jim was taken at once by his curious hands, each finger of which had three knuckle joints instead of the usual two.

111

'I thought you were the griddle chef,' said Jim.

'I am,' said Ricky. 'But we have a change-around each week. It's company policy. One week on the griddle, one on the tables, one on the washing-up and one on the cash register.'

'That must be exciting.'

'No,' said Ricky. 'It's shite.'

'Oh,' said Jim.

'Yes, oh,' said Ricky. 'Now what did you want to order?'

'Well, actually I didn't want to order anything. Well, that is to say, obviously I would like to order everything. I mean, who wouldn't? But I came here to see you. About your band.'

'It's not *my* band. It's *our* band.'

'Right,' said Jim. 'Well, I saw you and the band play last night at the Shrunken Head and it was one of the most incredible experiences I have ever had in my life.'

'So what do you want? My autograph, is it?'

'No,' said Jim. 'I want to manage you.'

Ricky looked Jim up and down. 'Fuck off, mate,' he said.

'No, please,' said Jim. 'Just listen to what I've got to say.'

'And what *have* you got to say?'

'Well, my partner says that he can get you a record contract within the week.'

'Won't happen,' said Ricky. 'Can't happen.'

'Why not?' asked Jim.

'You wouldn't understand.'

'Then try me, please.'

Ricky shook his big-haired head and his cap fell off. He did not stoop to retrieve it, he simply waggled a finger at Jim.

'Do you have any idea just what happened last night when we played?' he asked.

'No,' said Jim. 'All I know was that it was something marvellous. Something wonderful and something that the whole world should hear and experience.'

'The whole world will never experience it.'

'Oh yes it will,' said Jim. 'Apocalypso music will be the biggest thing ever.'

'What did you call it?'

'Apocalypso music.'

112

'That's a good name,' said Ricky. 'I like that.'

Pooley made a hopeful face.

'But it won't happen. It won't be allowed to happen.'

'Why?' asked Jim. 'Who would want to stop it?'

'Record companies,' said Ricky. 'Record companies would stop it.'

'Why?' asked Jim once more. 'That doesn't make sense. Litany's voice can heal the sick. I saw it happen. I heard it and I felt it too. Any record company would pay millions to own an artiste like that.'

'No, they wouldn't,' said Ricky. 'And I'll tell you why. There are no independent record companies any more. They've all been bought up by the huge corporations. And the huge corporations don't just market music. They market everything. Cars and food and weapons and telecommunications and technology and chemicals and pharmaceuticals. All these companies interlink and a few people at the very top control everything.'

'Scientists,' said Jim.

'Businessmen,' said Ricky. 'And the House of Windsor. So imagine what would happen if all you had to do when you were sick was to put on a music CD and be cured.'

'It would be brilliant,' said Jim. 'And everyone in the world would want that CD.'

'And then they would all be well and free from sickness.'

'Brilliant,' said Jim.

'Brilliant for them, perhaps. But not so brilliant for the mega-corporations that make zillions of pounds every day from producing and marketing pharmaceuticals. It's like the everlasting lightbulb and the motorcar tyre that doesn't wear out. These things exist, but they'll never see the shop counter. The mega-corporations see to that.'

'Bastards,' said Jim.

'Exactly,' said Ricky. 'But that's the way things are. That is the way society has evolved.'

'Ah,' said Jim. 'Evolution.'

'Evolution,' said Ricky. 'Would you like me to tell you all about that?'

'Well,' said Jim. 'Actually—'

113

'Everything evolves,' said Ricky. 'Everything. And not just living things. Inanimate objects, too.'

'Eh?' said Jim.

'Take cars,' said Ricky. 'The way cars have evolved.'

'Cars?' said Jim.

'Cars,' said Ricky. 'Take the Ford Escort, for example. The Ford Escort of today bears almost no resemblance to the Ford Escort of twenty years ago. And why is that?'

'Because it's been redesigned,' said Jim.

'No,' said Ricky. 'That's what they'd like you to think. The Ford Escort has evolved by itself, with no help from human beings.'

'What?' said Jim.

'I'm telling you the truth. I used to work for Ford at Dagenham. I worked on the production line, putting the rattly bits in the doors.'

'I often wondered who did that.'

'Well, it used to be me, but I left because I couldn't take all the pressure. But do you know how long it takes to set up a production line? Make all the tools that make the parts and the moulds and templates and so on and so forth?'

Pooley shook his head. He didn't know.

'Years,' said Ricky. 'Four or five years. So imagine this. There are no spare production lines standing empty. All the production lines work non-stop turning out cars. Seven days a week they work, and fifty-two weeks of the year. And if you stop a production line for even five minutes it costs the company thousands of pounds in lost production. So they just rumble on and on and on.

'But notice this. Every year the cars that roll off that production line look a bit different. It's the same model of car, but it's not quite the same. It's evolved.'

'But how could that be?' asked Jim.

'Don't ask me. I'm not God. But it can be and it is. The production line itself evolves. In Germany some production lines have evolved so much that they don't need humans to run them any more. They're all robotic.'

'Incredible,' said Jim.

'And it's not just cars. It's everything. Radios and televisions and telephones. And what about records? They used to be big black things made out of plastic. Look at them now.'

114

'And you think they're all evolving by themselves, without people to help them?'

'It's all part of the big conspiracy. All these so-called new developments. It works by natural selection. But it's the men at the top who do the selecting and they do it for their own gain. That's why you won't see the everlasting lightbulb and that's why you won't hear the Gandhi's Hairdryer CD.'

'I see,' said Jim. 'Well, when you explain it all to me like that, it all makes perfect sense.'

'Evolution,' said Ricky. 'And natural selection, and it will all go on and on like that for ever.'

'Oh no, it won't,' said Jim.

'Oh yes, it will.'

'It won't,' said Jim. 'And I will tell you why.'

And Jim told Ricky why. He told Ricky everything that Geraldo had told him. All about how natural selection in human beings would come to an end and mankind would not evolve any further and how this would eventually lead to THE END in a world that was run by scientists. He didn't go into all the details and he didn't do any of the voices or do the descriptions in rhyme, and he didn't mention the time travelling. But he laid it all out for Ricky and when he was finished the Stratster sat down and stared and stared at Jim.

When Ricky finally found his voice, all he could say was, 'Wow.'

'So there you go,' said Pooley.

'Wow,' said Ricky once again. 'It all makes sense to *me* now.'

'It does?' said Jim.

'Oh yes, it does. You see, there was just one thing I could never get my head around.'

'Just the one?' said Jim.

'Just the one. About the Stratocaster. You see, it evolved from the Telecaster, but its evolution stopped in the nineteen fifties and I never could understand why. I thought it should go on and on. That it would keep on evolving. But it can't, can it? It has evolved as far as it can. Because it's perfect. It has reached THE END as far as guitars are concerned.'

'I suppose it must have done,' said Jim.

'You're a fucking genius, mate.'

'Well, I don't know about that.'

'You are,' said Ricky, and he reached a curious hand across and patted Jim on the shoulder. 'You and me, we think the same way. We've both got different parts of the big puzzle. But they fit together. We could do things, think things.'

'Work together?' said Jim. 'As in music?'

'As in Apocalypso music, yes. You've got it all figured out, haven't you?'

'Not all,' said Jim.

'But you really think that the Gandhis could be the next big thing?'

'I know that for a fact,' said Jim.

'Then I trust you, mate. Put it there.'

And Ricky put out his curious hand and Pooley gave it a shaking.

Omally's hand was shaking too. Both of his hands were shaking, in fact, and most of the rest of him also. Omally sat hunched at the bar counter of the Flying Swan. The time was but a little past five-thirty opening, but John had already put three pints of Large inside himself, and looked in the mood to put down several more.

Neville watched John as he pulled him the pint. And Neville did not like what he saw. He had known Omally to have the occasional off day, but he had never seen him look as grim as this. Neville passed the pint across and took himself off for some polishing.

And then the door to the bar swung wide and in breezed Pooley. Omally looked up and let out a groan and sank once more to his pint.

'Evening, John, evening, Neville,' said Jim. 'Two more of those, please, I think.'

Neville hastened back to the pumps and John sank a little bit lower.

'So, then, John,' said Jim. 'How did the day go for you?'

'Oooooooooooooooooh,' went Omally.

'Not too well by the sound of it.'

Omally shook a dismal head. 'I don't know what to say,' he said. 'It doesn't make sense, it just doesn't.'

'No luck with the record companies?'

'Madness,' said John. 'Absolute madness. Norman copied the tape

116

and we played it together. It's incredible, just like you said. You know that horrible wart thing Norman had on his neck?'

'Oh yes,' said Jim. 'Very nasty, that.'

'Cured,' said John. 'It vanished away. And his bald spot's thatched over.'

'The music does that. It's in her voice.'

'I know, I heard it, and I've spent half the day playing the tape down the telephone to record company executives.'

'And they weren't keen?'

'They said that they'd heard stuff like it before. That every so often a singer turns up who can do this sort of thing.'

'But they weren't interested.'

'No. None of them. It doesn't make any sense. Here we have something that's worth millions of pounds and no record company will touch it.'

'Well, never mind,' said Jim.

'Never mind? Have you gone mad?'

'It doesn't matter,' said Jim.

'Doesn't matter? But we could have made a fortune.'

'We still can,' said Jim. 'Because I have this.' And he whipped out a grubby sheet of paper.

'And what is that?' Omally asked.

'Contract,' said Jim proudly. 'Signed by each of the Gandhis and giving us exclusive rights to their music.'

Omally took the contract from Jim and examined it. 'You got them all to sign,' he said. 'You worked so hard. I'm so sorry, Jim.'

'You don't have to worry, John. It'll be better this way.'

Neville passed the pints across.

'I'll get these,' said Omally. 'I owe you that at least.'

'No, I'll get them,' said Jim. 'I've got plenty of money.' And with that he pulled out a roll of twenties that had Omally gasping.

'How?' went John. 'Where?'

'Investment capital,' said Jim. 'The Gandhis all wanted to buy in.'

'You got money *from* the band?'

'Money up front to pay for recording time.'

'But none of the record labels will touch them.'

'Brentford Records will.'

'Brentford Records? There is no Brentford Records.'

'There is now,' said Jim. 'And we are they. As it were. None of the big companies will touch the band, John. So Ricky and I came up with an idea. We'll set up our own independent record company and market the music ourselves. Beat the big boys, eh?'

Omally's mouth fell hugely wide. 'You are a genius, Jim,' he said. 'A fu—'

'I'll settle for just a genius. But that's what we're going to do. Have a pint on me, Neville.'

Have a pint on me? Neville's face folded in horror. If last night hadn't been bad enough, *have a pint on me!*

As Neville fought to find some words, Omally had plenty to say. 'You've done it, Jim,' he cried. 'You've pulled off the big one.'

'Pretty smart, eh?' said Jim. 'And I never went near the bookies. I just set my mind to the task in hand and I came up with a solution.'

'We must drink to this,' said Omally. 'Drink to this historic moment. At some future time, when Brentford Records is the biggest record company in the world, we'll look back upon this hour and say that this was the turning point in our fortunes. This was the moment when everything fell into place.'

'Let's not get too carried away,' said Jim.

'Nonsense,' said John. 'You did it and you'll take the credit. History will record this day as the day you pulled off The Pooley.'

Neville finally found some words. 'Why has Jim fainted?' he asked.

The Boys from the Brown Stuff

Cab-Arthur Roper
Loved cantilever bridges.
And the sound that the wind made
When it blew down chimneys.

Cab-Arthur Roper
Could call up spirits.
Ask them questions
And write down their answers in a small black book.

Cab-Arthur Roper,
Some called him mad.
Some called him master.
Some even said he was not of this world.

Duck-Barry Martin
Had twenty-three pistols,
And a cellar full of mushrooms
That no one was allowed in.

Duck-Barry Martin
Lived with two women,
And breathed into their nostrils
Which made them obey him.

Duck-Barry Martin,
Some called him Baz.
Some called him Duck Boy.
Some even said he was Jesus come back.

Wild-Norman Peacock
Opened safes for robbers.
Let free pigeons from their lofts
And spoiled babies' Christenings.

Wild-Norman Peacock
Never worked for a living.
Was registered as a charity.
Received a grant from the Arts Council.

Wild-Norman Peacock.
Some call him clever.

I, for one!

12

Now, although Jim's day had been hot on success, it hadn't been big on adventure.

Jim was not an adventurous type. He was more your chit-chat-in-a-bar-and-get-things-sorted kind of body. As opposed to, say, your macho-manly-man-gung-ho-abseil-into-the-embassy-shoot-all-the-terrorists-rescue-all-the-hostages-and-shag-six-chicks-before-tea-time blokish sort of bloke.

Not that Jim wasn't a manly man. He was. He lacked not one jot for manly mannishness. He just wasn't big on adventure.

But, then, who is?

Life, as we have seen from this small slice in Brentford, is mostly composed of conversation. Few people ever actually *do* very much. And if they do *do* anything, it is rarely of an adventurous nature.

There are exceptions, of course. There are always exceptions. There will always be one or two folk in every community who positively thrive on action and adventure. But you will rarely, if ever, get to meet these people. Because they will be off somewhere else, getting into action and having adventures.

In fact, the only time you will get to meet them is when they are home for a while between adventures and you have a conversation with them in a bar. And if it's past the ten o'clock watershed, you probably won't believe anything they tell you anyway.

But they do exist and every community, no matter how small, can usually boast at least one.

Brentford could. And Brentford did.

If you were looking for an action man in Brentford, for a man who combined the courage and adventurousness of Indiana Jones, the true grit of John 'The Duke' Wayne, the chandelier-swinging skills of Dougie Fairbanks Jnr, the 'I-ain't-got-time-to-bleed' toughness of Jesse 'The Body' Ventura and the big-cock action of Long Johnnie Holmes, that man would be—

Soap Distant.

At least in *his* opinion it would.

Although those who knew Soap well might have questioned certain aspects of this character assessment, they would have agreed that any man who had journeyed to the centre of the Earth was deserving of certain respect. And if he chose to spice up his CV somewhat, he should be forgiven.

And when he told people about things he had actually done and things he had actually seen and how he himself knew that things that shouldn't have changed *had* changed, he should be believed.

But he wasn't. The Lord of the Old Button Hole had pegged him as a loony and his conversation at the Brentford nick with Inspectre Hovis had only complicated matters further and made him more confused than ever he had been.

So what was Soap to do?

He certainly didn't want to sit about in bars and chit-chat. He wanted action and he wanted it at once.

What did he want?

Action!

When did he want it?

Now!

And so it came to pass, upon that evening previous, that Soap Distant had taken his leave of Inspectre Hovis in a suitably action-packed fashion.

'I'm leaving now,' said Soap.

'You're not,' said the Inspectre.

'I am,' said Soap. 'There is much I need to know and, interesting as this conversation has been, I feel it is now time for action.'

Inspectre Hovis leaned across his photo-crowded desk. 'I'm arresting you, sunshine,' he said.

'Arresting *me*!' said Soap.

'For harbouring a wanted criminal and aiding and abetting him in the course of his escape from justice. Such crimes incur considerable fines and if you do not have the wherewithal to pay, you may well find yourself in one of the Virgin workcamps, manufacturing the rattly bits that are put in Ford Escort doors.'

'What?' cried Soap. 'What?'

'David Carson, the cannibal chef.'

'Small Dave?' said Soap. 'But how—'

'The thing about police surveillance cameras,' said Inspectre Hovis, gesturing variously round and about, 'is that they are simply everywhere. Everywhere. A few years ago people were outraged by them. They complained that they violated human rights. That it was Big Brother. But people don't complain any more, do they? Not since the police force put a little spin on them with the aid of television crime shows. Now people watch their TVs and see the crims caught on camera and have a chance to phone in and grass them up. People just love surveillance cameras now. They make the man in the street feel that someone is watching over them. And that's always a comfort, don't you think?'

'I'm sure it is,' said Soap. 'But I'm innocent of all charges and I'm off. Goodbye.'

'Not so fast,' said Hovis. 'There's something I'd like you to see.'

The Inspectre rootled around amidst the photos on his desk and unearthed a video cassette. This he slotted beneath a small portable television type of a jobbie, the screen of which he turned in Soap's direction. 'Tell me what you think of this,' he said.

Soap watched as the screen lit up, and stared at the image displayed. It was a view of the Flying Swan's front doorway, evidently filmed from one of the flat blocks opposite.

Soap watched as the onscreen pub door opened and he and Omally came out and walked away.

'That is a violation of human rights,' Soap complained.

'Those who are innocent have nothing to fear from the law,' said Inspectre Hovis.

Soap looked at Hovis.

123

And Hovis looked at Soap.

'Sorry,' said Hovis. 'It just slipped out.'

'And I should think so too.'

'However,' said the Detective in Residence, 'this particular doodad has more than one trick up its sleeve. The footage you have just seen was taken this very lunchtime, when the forces of the law were surrounding the Flying Swan in the hope of arresting the cannibal chef. But he somehow sneaked past us. Now how might that have been?'

'How should I know that?' asked Soap, making the face of all innocence.

'Let's see what the doodad has to show us.' Hovis tinkered at the television jobbie. Soap's image reversed and froze and expanded to fill up the screen. And then it went all multi-coloured.

'Oh,' said Soap. 'Whatever is that?'

'Thermal imaging,' said the Inspectre. 'Clever, isn't it? We use it to track criminals from helicopters. That makes good television, too. The crims try to hide in dustbins, but their heat signatures give them away. Lots of laughs all round.'

'I'm not trying to hide in a dustbin,' said Soap.

'No, and at least you'll know better than to do so in future. But tell me,' Inspectre Hovis pointed to the colourful Soap on the screen. 'What would you take *that* to be?'

'What?' Soap asked.

'This area here. Up the back of your coat. Surely that is the heat signature of a tiny man, all crouched up, isn't it?'

'No,' said Soap. I'm nicked, he thought.

'You're nicked,' said Hovis. 'I have you bang to rights.'

'Now look,' said Soap. 'I can see that this doesn't look too good for me at the present and I can see that on the evidence it would seem that you have a case. But, as dearly as I love justice, and I do love it dearly, don't get me wrong, I'm afraid I can't stay around here any longer. I have important things to be doing and I—'

'Have to stop you there,' said Inspectre Hovis. 'Have to give you the necessary caution. Must keep things all legal and above board.'

'Would you take a bribe?' Soap asked.

'Certainly not,' said Hovis.

124

'Well, could you pass my case on to an officer who would take a bribe?'

'Nice try,' said Hovis. 'Novel suggestion. But I think I'll just bang you up in the cells until the accounts department can work out just how much you owe us in fines. Now, do you want to go quietly, or will I be forced to summon in a couple of constables to rough you up a little?'

'I am a Buddhist,' said Soap, 'and I abhor violence. So—'

And here at last Soap got his chance for some action.

He gathered up his hat and goggles, thrust them on and with no thought for anything but the said action, rushed the Inspectre's office and flung himself through the plate-glass window.

If this courageous deed had been captured on camera it would have been well worth a play on *Crime Watch*. Viewers would no doubt have taped it for their private collections and played it in slow motion, and freeze-framed on the good bits and even run it in reverse, which is always good for a laugh, if you're suitably sad and lonely.

But it wasn't, so they couldn't, so to speak.

For there were no surveillance cameras trained on the Inspectre's window. Not that there weren't any trained on the building. There were, loads of the buggers. But these were all aimed at the ground floor.

And Inspectre Hovis's office was not on the ground floor.

Inspectre Hovis's office was on the twenty-third floor.

A bit too high up to merit surveillance.

Now it came as some surprise to Soap that, having smashed through the plate-glass window, he did not land immediately upon the ground. He had assumed, incorrectly as it proved, that he *was* on the ground floor and the spectacular rooftop view of Brentford★ that met his eyes for a mere split second was pleasing to behold. But the pleasure was fleeting and tempered by a feeling of alarm and, as he began the rapid rush downwards, alarm in turn became terror.

'Aaaaaaaaaaaaaaaaaaaaaaaaaaaagh!' went Soap Distant, the way that you do when falling to your death. 'Aaaaaaaaaaaaaaaaaaaagh!' and, 'Look out, below.'

★The very same view pictured on the ever-popular postcards.

125

There is, apparently, a mathematical calculation that can be worked out, regarding the speed of a falling object. Soap did not know this calculation, and even if he had known, and indeed known that it would take him precisely 3.4256 seconds to make contact with the ground below, it is doubtful whether he would have shown a lot of interest.

But a lot can happen in 3.4256 seconds, as anyone who knows such things will tell you.

But you have to know, of course, precisely which 3.4256 seconds to choose.

'Aaaaaaaaaaaaaaaaaaaaaaaaaagh!' continued Soap, using up 1.3849 seconds.

'Aaaaaaaaagh!' went he a little more, which was part of the very same 'Aaaaaaaaaaaaaaaaaaaaaaagh!'

And then he stopped aaaaaaaaaaghing, because he ceased falling, which must have meant that he'd made impact.

As indeed he had. Though not with the ground.

Soap suddenly found himself hanging in the air. Just hanging there, suspended, so to speak. Some three good yards above the pavement and perched on a cushion of air.

And looking up from directly below him was a lad. A lad in a black T-shirt and shorts. A lad who looked strangely familiar.

'What's your bloody game?' asked the lad. 'You could have killed me falling down like that.'

Soap took to floundering up upon high. Boggle-eyed behind his goggles, open-mouthed beneath. Hovering on nothingness, defying gravity's law.

'It's a good job I'm wearing this,' said the lad, pointing to a complicated wristwatch affair. 'Personal lifespan chronometer, incorporating personal defence mechanism. Activated by a wide-band polarizing field that detects rapidly approaching objects. Do you have any idea of the speed you were travelling?'

Soap managed a 'No' and shook his head a little.

'Well, I can work it out on my chronometer. Look, here comes your hat.'

Soap's black hat came fluttering down and landed on his head.

'Well caught, that man,' said the lad.

'What?' went Soap. 'How?'

'How does it work? Simple. The wide-band polarizing field detects the approaching object, calculates its mass and causes a cohesion to occur in the surrounding air, effectively joining the oxygen molecules to create a spherical barrier that is virtually impenetrable. Go on, poke it with your finger if you don't believe me.'

Soap didn't bother. He did believe him.

'Trouble is,' said the lad. 'It takes it out of the batteries. So if you don't mind I'll just step aside and switch it off.'

This he did, and Soap crashed to the pavement.

'Are you all right?' the lad asked.

Soap sat up and felt at his limbs. He seemed to be all in one piece.

'Well, if you're not, it will just serve you right for falling on people. If you must jump out of high windows, try to do it when no one's around. And look at all this glass, someone could cut themselves on that.'

Soap nodded numbly.

'Goodbye,' the lad said.

'No, wait, please.' Soap climbed painfully to his feet.

'What is it?' said the lad.

'You saved my life. I want to thank you.'

'I didn't do it on purpose. In fact I didn't do it at all.'

'Well, thank you anyway. My name is Soap Distant. Might I ask you yours?'

'Soap Distant?' the lad thought for a moment. 'No,' he said. 'That name doesn't ring any bells.'

'But it will,' said Soap. 'I will soon be very famous.'

'No,' said the lad. 'If you were to be, I'd know.'

'Eh?' said Soap.

'Goodbye,' said the lad.

'No, hold on, please. At least tell me your name.'

'My name is Wingarde,' said the lad. 'My surname I'd rather not mention.'

And with that he walked away, leaving Soap to wonder.

But he didn't stand and wonder very long. Because all at once alarms began to clang out from the police station.

Which proved, at least, that Soap did ring *some* bells.

★

127

Soap fled the scene of his falling and saving and spent the evening and the night stalking around and about. He rarely, if ever, slept nowadays. Ten years beneath had altered him in many ways.

Soap stalked along the streets of his youth, passing the houses of friends he'd once known. Cab-Arthur Roper, Duck-Barry Martin, Wild-Norman Peacock and all of the rest. Soap paused at times to lurk in alleyways, where, with the rain beating down on his hat, he viewed people's various doings.

He saw Norman Hartnell in his underwear returning to his shop. He saw Pooley★ enter the Penist's house and he made a mental note of the address. And he saw other things that were strange and mysterious. Things that you only see late in the night.

By the coming of the new dawn, Soap had formed a plan of action. Determined as he was to discover exactly what was going on and how history could have changed while he'd been belooooow, he was equally determined to remain at liberty and out of the clutches of the Virgin police.

Nine-thirty of the morning clock found Soap upon the steps of the Memorial Library. Hardly an action-packed kind of a place, you might think, but appearances can be deceptive.

Soap's appearance this morning, for example, was one that he hoped might deceive.

Soap no longer wore his broad-brimmed coal-black hat, his coal-black coat and boots of coaly blackness. Instead, Soap sported a Hawaiian shirt, a dove-grey zoot suit and a pair of white winkle-picker boots. He had acquired these during the night, but from where was anyone's guess. Soap cut a dashing figure in this get-up and one that he hoped would allow him to move about the borough unrecognized by those who viewed through street surveillance cameras.

When the Keeper of the Borough's Books made the ceremonial opening up of the door, Soap hurried into the library, marched across the marble-panelled vestibule and presented his similarly acquired credentials at the desk.

★Lest the discerning reader think to spy a monstrous plothole looming, yes, Soap did run into Pooley earlier in the evening. Just after he'd made his escape from the police station. Which was just before Jim reached John's house. Which was when he told Jim about Branson being on the poundnotes.

The clerk on duty looked over the credentials and then the clerk on duty looked at Soap.

'This library ticket is out of date, Mr Omally,' said the clerk.

'Then kindly furnish me with a new one.'

'These things take time. If you'll call back in a week or two.'

Soap Distant took to the shaking of his head. 'It is time for action,' he said. 'Kindly direct me to the reference section.'

'Oooooooh,' went the clerk. 'The reference section. Are you sure you can handle it?'

'Just lead me to it,' said Soap.

'Well, then, it's through that door over there.'

'That door?' said Soap.

'No, *that* door,' said the clerk.

'Aren't they both the same door?' asked Soap.

'It depends what you mean by "the same", I suppose.'

'I suppose it does,' Soap agreed.

The reference section came as a bit of a shock to Soap. It didn't have any books. All there was now was a neat row of desks, each of which held up a television jobbie attached to a typewriter keyboard. Soap sat down upon a chair at the nearest and stared at the TV screen.

WELCOME TO THE WORLD OF KNOWLEDGE
To access please touch any key.

Soap sought the key marked 'any'.

'Assistance, please,' called Soap.

The clerk from the desk came bustling in. 'What do you want?'

'I want action,' said Soap. 'And I want it now. Where are all the books, please?'

'All the books are now on the Web.'

Soap's thoughts returned to the offices of the *Brentford Mercury* and the woman who was worrying at wires. She had mentioned the Web, and she had mentioned it proudly.

'What exactly is the Web? asked Soap.

The clerk explained all about it.

Now it doesn't take long to explain about the Web, and the average person can grasp all the essentials and gain a good working

129

knowledge in less than a lifespan. Soap listened patiently for at least five minutes.

'So I just touch *any* key,' he said.

'Yes,' said the clerk and departed.

And so Soap Distant, voyager to the realms belooooow, became a surfer of the Web. The Web, the Web, the wonderful Web, from which all knowledge flows.

It's all there on the Web, you know. The whole wide world and then some.

Of course, you do have to know *where* to look.

Soap had no idea, but he got straight down to the action.

He typed in QUEEN ELIZABETH II and was quite amazed by what flashed up before him. And then he typed in ASSASSINATION OF.

And then he sat right back and stared.

According to the Web, Queen Elizabeth had been shot dead while on stage during a Beatles concert at Wembley Stadium in nineteen eighty.

'A Beatles concert in nineteen eighty?' Soap called up THE BEATLES.

And according to the Web it was true. The Beatles *had* played Wembley in nineteen eighty. The show had been organized by John Lennon, who had apparently become something of a royalist after receiving a visit from Prince Charles while he lay in hospital recovering from the shooting incident.

'Shooting incident?' said Soap. 'But Lennon should be dead.'

Soap called up JOHN LENNON: SHOOTING and learned to his amazement how the great one's life had been saved by a mystery man who never came forward to claim the fortune Lennon offered him. All that was known of the mystery man was that he wore a black T-shirt and shorts.

'Oh ho,' said Soap. 'Oh ho.'

But as 'oh ho' didn't help a lot, Soap continued his search.

He backtracked to the Wembley gig and boggled at the list of support bands. Not only had The Doors played there. But also the Jimi Hendrix Experience. *And* Janis Joplin.

'Methinks I see a pattern here,' said Soap.

'Would you please keep the noise down,' said the clerk, poking a clerkish head around the door.

'I'm sorry,' said Soap. 'But could you help me here?'

The clerk sighed and plodded over. 'What is the trouble now? I do have things to be doing.'

'All the bands listed here,' said Soap. 'They all really played at Wembley in nineteen eighty, did they?'

The clerk perused the list. 'Yes. It was a legendary gig. The video of that gig has outsold any other.'

'Really?' said Soap. 'And this would be a Virgin video, would it?'

'What other make of video is there?' asked the clerk.

'Just checking,' said Soap. 'Now go away, please.'

'Well, really!' said the clerk and went away.

Soap surfed the Web until lunchtime. It was all action stuff. Well, at least it was sometimes. Well, perhaps it wasn't really, to be honest. No, in fact, actually, it wasn't all action at all. It was just sitting at a TV screen and typing at a keyboard, and although there are ways of putting a spin on that kind of thing and making it sound really interesting—

IT ISN'T!
IT'S CRAP!!!
GET A LIFE!!!!!!!

By lunchtime Soap had had his fill of the Web. He had learned from it all he could learn from it. This hadn't been all that he'd wanted to learn, but he *had* learned the Web's evil secret.

And the evil secret of the Web is this, my friends.

That all you can ever learn
from The Web is what the
people who put the stuff onto
it want you to learn.

'Right,' said Soap. 'Well, that's quite enough of that. Time for a bit of action, I think.'

And right on cue (for there is no other way) came that good old police loudhailer voice.

'John Omally,' it called. 'John Omally, this is the Virgin Police Service. We know you're in there. Come out with your hands held high.'

131

'Oh,' said Soap, to no one but himself. 'John Omally, what?'

'You have been positively identified from a frame of surveillance footage as the man aiding Soap Distant to assist a wanted criminal in his escape from justice. To whit, one David Carson, also known as the Cannibal Chef and Brentford's Most Wanted Man.'

'Oh,' said Soap once again to himself. 'But how?'

'In case you're wondering how we know you're in there, our police crime computer is linked into every other national computer and it has just registered your library ticket being fed into the Memorial Library system for renewal.'

'Some of a gun,' mumbled Soap. 'That's clever.'

'Well, actually,' the loudhailer voice continued, 'in case you were thinking how clever that was, I have to own up that it's not how we tracked you down. You see, the clerk at the library desk just telephoned us to say that you have a library book outstanding on your card. *How to Play the Stratocaster.* And you should have returned it fifteen years ago. There's a two-thousand-pound fine to pay.'

'It never rains but it pours,' said Soap in a philosophical tone.

'So come on out now, or we'll come in and get you.'

'Very tricky,' said Soap.

'And get a move on,' called the voice. 'We want to have our lunch.'

'Righty-right.' The man from belooow considered his options. He could try and bluff his way out. Say that he wasn't John Omally but had just popped into the library to renew John's ticket for him. Soap shook his head at that. It lacked the action he sorely craved. Some other way out, then.

Soap looked up and all round and about. There was only the one door into the reference section and this led from the vestibule and the front entrance. Outside which, the police were no doubt waiting.

But there was also the window. And he was on the ground floor this time. Soap considered the window. It was a most splendid window. A stained-glass window, bequeathed to the borough by its most famous son, the author P.P. Penrose. It featured scenes from the adventures of Lazlo Woodbine, the most popular fictional detective of the twentieth century, the creation of P.P. Penrose.

Soap considered the window some more. How would Lazlo have

132

got out of this? He would have pulled off some ingenious stunt. But a stunt that had plenty of action.

Soap squared up before the window. 'Time for action,' he said.

The police gave Soap five minutes and then they rushed the building. They burst into the vestibule with big guns drawn, visors down and tear gas at the ready.

The clerk at the desk looked up at them. 'He's in the reference section,' said the clerk. 'Lying face down on the floor, unconscious.'

'Unconscious?' said a constable, a-cocking his big gun.

'He tried to jump through the window. But it's made of vandal-proof Plexiglas. He knocked himself unconscious.'

The constables chuckled as constables do and went in to pick up the body.

'Not that door,' said the clerk. 'It's the other one.'

The police went in through the other one and the clerk went off for lunch.

The clerk was several streets away before he stopped walking and started to laugh.

'I'm sorry I had to do that,' said Soap Distant, for the clerk was he. 'But if I hadn't bopped you on the head and changed clothes, I might really have had to jump through that stained-glass window.'

And Soap Distant went off on his way, secure at least in the knowledge that P.P. Penrose was not turning in his grave for the loss of his window. The great writer would surely also have admired Soap's cunning escape. For although it lacked for action, it certainly was ingenious.

Two by One
(or, The Carpenter's Friend)
A song about wood to be sung in the music hall style.

Oooooooooooooooooooooh . . .

The two by one, the two by one,
That's the stuff for you, old son.
It makes your DIY such fun,
You can't go wrong with the two by one.
I would not lie, I kid you not,
It's the greatest of them all.
The four by two is much too large,
And the one by one's too small.

Oooooooooooooooooooooh . . .

I've sawn this and I've sawn that,
I've reeved and grieved and sworn and spat.
I've dug my bradawl to the hilt,
I've chiselled 'til I could have kilt.
I've planed away for hours on end
Through knotholes and through planks that bend.
But finer work I've never done
Than working with the two by one.

Oooooooooooooooooooooh . . .

The two by one, the two by one,
That's the stuff for me, old son.
The war and battle, both are won,
When working with the two by one.
I would not lie, I could not lie,
It's the greatest of them all.
The four by two is much too large,
And the one by one's too small.

Oooooooooooooooooooooh . . .

I've banged nails, what times I've had
With a two-inch cut and an oval Brad.
A size-ten clout, a three-inch wire,
Whacking at the obo 'til we all perspire.
And screws, by God, I've known each twist,
Damaging the muscles on my right wrist.
But I'll keep on 'til I am done,
As long as I can do it with the two by one.

Ooooooooooooooooooooh . . .

The two by one, the two by one,
The finest wood on Earth, my son.
I'd raise my trusty elephant gun
To him who'll say a word against the two by one.
I would not lie, no faker I,
This stuff is on the ball.
The four by two is much too large,
And the one by one's too small.

Ooooooooooooooooooooh . . .

It's clean and white and dry and cut, and you buy it
    by the grain.
In a curious manner, so to speak, it's not unlike cocaine.
It comes in many handy lengths, just ask at your supplier,
And you can use the odds and ends left over for the fire.
So when I get to heaven, when my time on Earth is done,
And Saint Peter asks me what I'd like, I'll tell him . . .

All together now . . .

The two by one, the two by one,
etc, etc, etc . . .

Dances from stage to monstrous applause . . .

Thank you and goodnight.

13

'Wake up, Jim. Wake up there.'
Smack.
'Wake up, Jim. Wake up.'
Shake, shake.
'Loosen his collar,' said Neville.
'I'll loosen his wallet instead,' said John. 'I think the weight has pulled him over.'
Smack, smack, shake and *loosen.*
'Get off me. Get off me. Oh.' And Jim returned to consciousness. Omally helped him onto a stool. 'Whatever happened?' he asked.
Jim took his pint in a shaky hand and sucked upon his ale. 'Don't *ever* mention that again, John,' he said. 'Don't ever mention The Pooley.'
'The Pooley?' asked Neville. 'What is The Pooley?'
'It's nothing.' Pooley flapped with his pintless paw. 'It's nothing and it isn't what I've done and it isn't what I'm going to do ever.'
'Well, I'm glad we've cleared that up,' said Neville. 'Now kindly get out of my pub. You're barred.'
'Excuse me, please?' Jim spluttered into his pint.
'Coming into my bar last night, buying a round of drinks for twelve young louts in shorts—'

'A round for twelve?' and John did splutterings too.

'He did,' said Neville. 'And now "Have a pint yourself, Neville."
What are you trying to do, Pooley? Push me over the edge?'

'But—' said Jim.

'But me no buts. I've heard about bars where the patrons offer to
buy the barman a drink. "Have one yourself, barlord," they say. But
twenty long years I've run this establishment and not once, not once,
mind, have any one of you tight-fisted bastards *ever* offered to buy *me*
a drink.'

'Not *once*?' said Jim. 'I'm sure I—'

'Not once. And now you've ruined it. I was hoping to get into
the *Guinness Book of Records*.'

'Were you?' John asked.

'No, of course I bloody wasn't. But I'm warning you, Jim. One
more. One more of anything and you are out of this pub for good.'

Omally raised his ever-calming palms towards the barman. 'I'll see
that he behaves,' he said, steering Jim away from the bar and off to
a quiet corner table.

John sat down and Jim sat down and John stared hard at Jim. 'You
bought a round for *twelve*?' he whispered. '*You*, a round for *twelve*?'

'I don't wish to talk about it, John.' Jim took another pull on his
pint. 'It was a very trying evening. I'd rather just forget all about it,
if you don't mind. But you must promise me this. Never, *ever*, speak
of The Pooley again. Do you promise?'

'I promise,' said John. 'If it means so much to you.'

'It does and I thank you. And so.'

'And so?' asked John.

'And so down to business. I have arranged for the band to meet us
here at seven o'clock. To celebrate the founding of Brentford
Records. Which gives us a bit of time before they arrive, to work
out our business plan.'

'Business plan.' Omally gave approving nods. 'Very professional,
Jim.'

'Thank you, John. Now the first thing we're going to need is a
recording studio. There are some vacant units on the old industrial
estate down by Cider Island. There's one called Hangar Eighteen
that I like the look of. We'll rent that and fit it out and—'

'Have to stop you there,' said John.

137

'Oh yes, and why?'

'Why? Do you know how much it costs to fit out a recording studio? All the equipment you need?'

'Haven't a clue,' said Jim. 'Which is why I'll leave that side of it to you. Ducking and diving and wheeling and dealing is what you're all about.'

'Yes I know, but—'

'Come on now, John. Pull your weight.'

'It's not a matter of pulling my weight. It could cost at least half a million quid to fit out a recording studio. Probably much more than that.'

'Fortune favours the brave,' said Jim. 'Now, regarding the look of Hangar Eighteen. I think we should go for something really distinctive. Something eye-catching. I have a vision of a huge hairdryer up on the roof. Or, even better, a dirigible shaped like a hairdryer, moored to the roof and floating in the sky and—'

'Stop!' said Omally. 'Stop stop stop.'

'You're not keen on the dirigible?'

'I'm not keen on any of it. We don't *need* a recording studio, Jim. It isn't necessary.'

'It isn't?' said Jim. 'But how can we make records if we don't have a recording studio?'

'We'll record the band when they play live. On a portable mixing desk.'

Pooley gave this a moment's thought. 'That's brilliant,' he said.

'And we'll get Norman to turn out as many copies of the tapes as we want. We'll pay him a retainer, or two bob a tape, or something.'

'That is also brilliant,' Pooley said.

'And then we'll distribute them to the record shops.'

'That is not so brilliant,' Pooley said.

'Not so brilliant? Why is that?'

'Because the record shops won't take them. I've discussed all this with Ricky. The shops are all owned by the big record corporations. They won't sell tapes that are independently produced.'

'They're bastards,' said Omally.

'I agree, and that's why we'll beat them. Brentford Records are going to have their own retail outlets. A chain of independent record shops.'

'What?' went John. 'What?'

138

'A chain of small shops up and down the country.'

John Omally shook his head in a weary kind of a way. 'Jim, Jim, Jim,' he said to Jim. 'And where will the money come from?'

Pooley smiled a broad and cheery smile. 'Ah,' he said. 'I was wondering about that myself. But as you've just saved us half a million quid on the recording studio, we can use that money.'

Omally buried his head in his hands and Jim got another round in.

The arrival of the Gandhis at precisely seven o'clock came as a bit of a surprise. And if their punctuality glared into the face of rock 'n' roll, their appearance positively gobbed in its eye.

The Gandhis looked—

Respectable.

The four male members wore matching dark grey business suits. Their big hair had been slicked back and tucked down the collars of their white shirts. White shirts! And these white shirts were buttoned at the neck. And these white shirts had *ties*!

Litany, grey moustached but make-up free, favoured a demure beige two-piece number over a white cotton blouse. She wore sensible shoes on her feet and she looked like a lady librarian. She even had a briefcase!

'Jesus Jones!' said John Omally.

'By the prophet's beard!' said Jim.

'Good evening, madam, good evening, gents,' said Neville the part-time barman.

Litany smiled upon Neville and Neville pinked up at the cheeks. 'I've heard you draw the finest pints of Large in Brentford,' she said.

Neville's pigeon chest came swelling up his shirt front.

'Then five pints, please,' said Litany. 'The gentleman there will be paying.'

Neville glanced at the gentleman there. The gentleman there was Jim.

'Hmm,' went Neville, his pigeon chest falling. 'The gentleman there. I see.'

The gentleman there had his mouth hanging open. The gentleman with him had too.

'Is that really them?' whispered John.

'It is,' Jim whispered. 'It is.'

'But why are they—'

139

'Dressed like that? Because I asked them to, John. I didn't want Neville getting all upset, so I asked them to dress down a bit.'

Omally shook his head. 'Well, we can't just sit here staring. Let's give them the big hello.'

Pooley made the introductions. John shook hands all round, lingering somewhat longer than was perhaps necessary on the shaking of Litany's.

Litany smiled up at John.

And John smiled down at Litany.

And whatever thoughts were now going through John's head, he kept very much to himself. But had these thoughts been set to music and brought out on a CD, it is a certainty that the CD would have needed one of those labels that says PARENTAL GUIDANCE: EXPLICIT SEXUAL CONTENT.

'Can I have my hand back, please?' asked Litany.

'Oh yes,' said John. 'Won't you all come over and join us at our table? Jim will take care of the drinks. Won't you, Jim?'

'I will,' said Pooley. 'I will.'

Neville brought a tray out and loaded up the pints. 'Now that's more like it, Jim,' he said. 'A bit of class in the bar. Estate agents, are they? Or accountants?'

'Something like that,' said Jim, fishing out his wad and peeling off a ten-spot.

Neville held it up to the light. 'This better be kosher,' he said.

'But it's the change you gave me from the last round.'

'Exactly,' said Neville. 'So watch it.'

Pooley struggled across with the tray and set it down on the table. 'Don't I get a seat?' he asked.

'Bring one over, Jim,' said John, who was sitting next to Litany. 'I'd give you my seat, but I'm sitting here.'

Pooley dragged a chair across and squeezed himself in between Gandhis.

A description of the Gandhi men might be useful here. But sadly there is little to be said. In their suits and with their hair dragged back, they all looked much of a muchness. Tall and lean, with sticky-out cheekbones, big on sunken eyes. Very much like brothers, they looked. But not at all like the Osmonds.

There was Ricky Zed, on lead guitar. Dead Boy Doveston on

140

bass. Matchbox Finial on rhythm guitar and occasional keyboards, and Pigarse Peter Westlake on drums. There would no doubt have also been Adolf Hitler on vibes and Val Doonican as himself had this been the Bonzos' *Intro and the Outro*. But it wasn't, so there wasn't.

So to speak.

Jim pushed pints around the table, smiling all round and about.

'Now, before we begin,' said Litany, 'there is something that Pigarse wants to say. Isn't there, Pigarse?'

'I have a morbid fear of identical twins,' said Pigarse.

'No, not that,' said Litany.

'My father once pushed a Barbie doll up his bottom for art,' said Pigarse.

'No, not that either.'

'I'm very sorry for punching you last night in the Shrunken Head, Mr Omally,' said Pigarse. 'It was rock 'n' roll madness and it won't happen again.'

'Yes, that's it,' said Litany.

John, whose eyes had hardly left her for a single moment, said, 'That's all right, Pigarse, forget it.'

'Stone me,' said Jim.

'Forget it,' said Omally. 'I thought I'd wait until the band got really big before terminating Pigarse's contract and chucking him out on his ear.'

'Most amusing,' said Pigarse.

'Glad you think so,' said John.

Litany took a sip at her Large and drained an even half-pint. 'This is very good stuff,' said she. 'So shall we get right down to business?'

John, who had never actually seen beer vanish quite as fast as that, even when it was going down his own throat, said, 'Yes, that would be fine.'

Litany opened her briefcase and took from it papers which she laid on a spare bit of table. 'It is imperative,' she said, 'that from the word go we all know where we stand, legally. We have signed a contract with Jim, giving Brentford Records exclusive rights to our music and we have each put up five hundred pounds to make us shareholders in the company. This is to ensure that we have absolute artistic control over our music and an equal share in all profits.'

'Absolutely,' said John.

141

'Absolutely,' said Litany. 'Jim and I discussed this during the afternoon and I have had these legally binding contracts drawn up to ensure your commitment to us. That you will fulfil your side of the bargain. Do what is expected of you. So forth and suchlike. Do you understand?'

'Absolutely,' said John once again.

Litany took up the contracts and passed them over the table. One to Jim and one to John. 'Please read them carefully,' she said. 'We must get this right from the start. I don't want us all fighting later. I have no wish to get screwed by a bunch of solicitors and end up coughing into their pockets.'

Omally tried to picture that, but his thoughts took a deviant sexual turn so he set to reading the contract.

'This part here,' he said.

'Which part is that?' asked Litany.

'The party in the first part of this contract will be known as the party in the first part.'

'What about it?' asked Litany.

'I don't like it,' said John.

'Nor do I,' said Jim. 'It's out of an old Marx Brothers movie.'

'Ignore that bit, then,' Litany said. 'And just read through the rest.'

Jim read and John read and Jim turned pages.

John turned pages too and Jim read some more.

John turned a page then and Jim turned another one.

And then they turned some pages back. They weren't entirely sure.

'Happy with it?' Litany asked.

'It has a certain poetry,' said John. 'But what it says, in essence, is that Jim and I are entirely liable to all expenses incurred by the band. That we finance it ourselves, but all costs are defrayed against record sales and all profits split seven ways.'

'That's it,' said Litany.

'Well, I'm happy,' said John. 'What about you, Jim?'

'The sanity clause worries me,' said Jim. But as few around the table were big Marx Brothers fans, the remark received the contempt it deserved.

'All right,' said John. 'We'll sign.'

'Does someone have a pen, please?' asked Jim. 'I lent mine to Pigarse and he never gave it back.'

'I've lent it to my dad,' said Pigarse. 'He's using it for art.'

'I'll buy another tomorrow,' said Jim.

Litany took from her briefcase a slim black leather box. In this was an elegant silver stylus. 'You may use this,' she said. 'But there is just one thing.'

'And that is?' John asked.

'You have to sign it in blood.'

'Blood', said Norman of the corner shop, 'is what it's all about.'

He didn't say this in the Flying Swan, however, because he wasn't in the Flying Swan. Norman said it in his kitchen workshop, where he was working on his horse.

Now it might have been a coincidence that he said the word 'blood' at the very same moment as had Litany. Or it might have been a synchronicity, or even a fateful foreshadowing.

But say it he did and he said it again. 'It's all in the blood,' said Norman.

As this was Wednesday half-closing, Norman had had the entire afternoon to work on his horse. And he had been putting consider-able effort into it. Unaware that Pooley had given up the horses, Norman continued with his project, determined to have it finished by Friday, in keeping with his life-in-little-movies principle and looking forward to turning up on Jim's doorstep on the Saturday to give him his big surprise.

But it had been a difficult afternoon for Norman. What with all the magnifying glass work and the tweezer work and the splicing the genes together with really small bits of sellotape work. But the saucepan was back on the stove now and the contents were bubbling nicely.

Norman had also done some splicing with his copy of the Gandhis' tape. He'd spliced it into a loop, so he could play it con-tinuously while he worked. The magical music just made him feel so well, so alive, so healthy. It made him feel ready to take up any challenge and win win win win win.

He wiggled his bum in time to the tune and gave the saucepan a stir. 'I think I'll just pop up and have a bath,' said he, 'while this lot comes to the boil.'

Norman went over to switch off the tape and then thought better of it. It would be nice to hear the music while he bathed. He turned up the Gandhis full blast and danced out of the kitchen.

'This time,' he said, 'I'll make me a winner. This time I'll go for the big one.'

'We're going for the big one this time,' said Litany. 'And it's a rock 'n' roll statement.'

'Ozzy Osbourne did it,' said Pigarse.

'War Pigs,' said John.

'War Pigarse,' said Pigarse.

'Yes,' said Jim, 'but blood. Real blood. *My* blood.'

'Only enough to sign your name,' said Pigarse. 'My dad once squeezed blood out of his piles and onto a canvas for art. Saatchi bought it for his collection.'

'Your dad has an enterprising bottom,' said Jim, 'but I don't know much about art.'

'Do it for me,' said Litany, smiling at Jim. 'You're not afraid to, are you?'

Jim took the stylus. 'I'm not scared,' said he.

The actual thumb-pricking and the wincing and the fussing and the coming all over faint and the dipping the stylus into the blood and the puffing, the blowing and the gulping at pints afterwards wasn't all *that* rock 'n' roll. But eventually the task was completed. The contracts were signed and Litany tucked them away in her briefcase.

And then she raised her glass. 'To success,' she said.

'To rock 'n' roll,' said John.

'To Apocalypso music,' said Jim.

'To art,' said Pigarse.

'To Jim,' said Ricky.

And so on and so forth.

'And now,' said Litany. 'Let's talk business.'

'Yes,' said John. 'Let's do.'

'Oh, just one thing before we start,' said Ricky. 'I have to give you this.' He handed John a folded piece of paper.

'What is this?' John asked, unfolding it.

'It's the bill for these clothes. Jim told us to dress down a bit. No

144

leather strides and so forth. So we all went out and bought these God-awful suits. If you could let us have the money back out of petty cash it would be helpful.'

'Oh,' said John and, 'Ah.'

'And I'm going to need a new amp,' said Ricky. 'Mine's really fucked.'

'And a whole new wardrobe of stage clothes,' said Pigarse. 'And designer stuff, not rubbish. And I need a new set of skins for my drums.'

'And I need a new mic,' said Litany. 'And our van's knackered too.'

'A proper tour bus is what we need,' said Matchbox Finial. 'Mercedes do a great one. I've got a catalogue here.'

'Right,' said John and, 'Yes, indeed.'

Litany smiled once more upon John. 'I know that we're going to work really well together,' she said. 'I'm sure we'll grow very close. It's such a relief to be signed up with professionals. You wouldn't believe the idiots who've offered to manage us in the past.'

'You're right there,' said Pigarse. 'Remember that moron who thought he'd get away with recording us live on a mixing desk and knocking tapes out in his mate's back kitchen?'

Litany laughed and Ricky laughed and Dead Boy laughed as well.

'Whatever happened to that bloke?' Matchbox Finial asked.

'I took him for a little drive into the country,' said Pigarse. 'They haven't found all of him yet.'

Gandhi members laughed some more.

'Most amusing,' said John Omally.

'Glad you think so,' said Pigarse.

Gladness was the rage in Norman's bathroom. Kit was off, the tub was full, the bubbles overflowed. Norman had his own personal brand of bubble bath. He had created it himself.

The bubbles smelled great and they really got the dirt off, though it didn't do to soak in them too long. Norman had once forgotten to pull the plug out after bathing and the next morning he had discovered that the bubbles had eaten through the enamel of the bath and right down to the iron.

But, with the bubbles gnawing him clean and the music belting up the stairs and filling the room with good vibrations, Norman sank into the scented water and felt most glad all over.

Down in the kitchen workshop the brew made bubbles of its own. Great big bubbles heaved and popped in time to the Gandhis' music. Really beautiful bubbles, they were. Really really beautiful.

'Really beautiful strings,' said Ricky, back in the Swan. 'I saw them in Minn's Music Mine the other day, but I couldn't afford to buy them then. I think you should get me three sets, John. Just to be on the safe side.'

'And I need to get my roots dyed,' said Pigarse. 'And my dad needs a new seat for his Honda. Perhaps we could make that tax deductible.'

Jim looked at John.

And John looked back at Jim.

'I have to go to the toilet,' said John.

'And so do I,' said Jim.

Once out of the bar and in the bog, Jim Pooley closed the door.

'Window,' said John.

'Window?' said Jim.

'We can climb out of the window and then I suggest we just run for it.'

'You are for doing a runner, then, are you?'

'What other choice do we have? We're in this over our heads, Jim. We've made ourselves liable and we signed in our blood.'

'Perhaps we could just ask for the contracts back,' said Jim. 'Explain that we've had a think about it and we've changed our minds.'

'I can't see that going down too well. That Pigarse is a psychopath. I don't want the police search teams only finding bits of me.'

'I wonder what he did with the parts they couldn't find. Do you think his dad used them for art?'

'Window,' said Omally. 'Much as I fancy that Litany and much as I'd love to—' He paused. 'But it can't be done. Let's run while we still have legs.'

'No.' And Pooley shook his head. 'We can't just run away. All right, we've got ourselves in big trouble here. But I'm sure we can find a way round it.'

146

'Well, you have a go, Jim. I'm off.'

'Oh, perfect,' said Jim. 'That's your answer to the problem. Run away. Listen, John. We have a chance to make something of ourselves here. A chance to do something wonderful. We could manage this band if we worked hard at it. We could do it. We really could. You've heard Litany sing. You've felt what happens. You've experienced it. The major record companies won't touch the Gandhis, but we could bring their music to the world. Bring their magic to the world, John.'

'All right,' said John. 'I hear what you're saying. But we don't have the money.'

'Then we'll have to find it.'

'But where, Jim? Where could we possibly find it?'

'I don't know,' and Pooley shrugged. 'But I don't think I'll win it on the horses.'

Now, a winning horse, as Norman knew, is made from many parts. But what only a very few people know is, there's more to a winner than that. It is not enough just to be a beautiful model or a talented filmstar or a brilliant musician. It is a lot, but it isn't enough. You need that little bit more than that. You need the extra magic.

Some might call this charisma. But what does this word really mean?

Magic is what this word means. A special kind of magic.

Litany had it in her voice. A very special kind of magic. And, as the tape went round and round on Norman's deck, the magic filled up Norman's kitchen. It entered into the brew upon the stove and infused and enthused it. Assembled and improved it.

Did many magical things to it.

Things that were full of wonder.

Pooley returned to the Swan's saloon bar, leaving Omally to wonder. His hand was on the window catch, his mind was all over the place.

'Shit,' said John. 'I don't know what to do. I can't let Jim take all the responsibility. It was me who really got him into all this. But there's no way we can raise the money. What am I going to do?'

'Omally,' came a voice from above. 'This is the voice of God.'

'Sod off, Dave,' said Omally. 'I'm trying to have a think here.'

147

★

Pooley sat back down between a pair of Gandhis.

'All right, Jim? asked Pigarse. 'You look a bit pale in the face.'

'I'm fine,' said Jim. 'All the better for a good piddle.'

'Are you coming on the tour with us, Jim?' asked Ricky.

'Tour?' said Jim. 'What tour?'

'The tour you'll be lining up, of course. You are a joker, Jim. What kind of venues will we be playing?'

'Well . . .' said Jim, and, 'Ooooooooh.'

'Big ones, I hope,' said Pigarse.

'Huge, I should think.' And Pooley hastily folded his arms. His hands were beginning to flap.

'This bloke is boss,' said Ricky. 'We were just talking about your theory of the future, Jim. About THE END.'

'THE END,' said Jim, in an ominous tone.

'It's a blinding theory,' said Ricky. 'A theory like that should be taught to kids in schools. You should give it a name, Jim. The Pooley Theory. Or the Pooley Principle, that's better. Or even just The Poole—'

'No!' shrieked Jim. 'Not *that*!'

Neville raised an eyebrow at the bar.

Pigarse said, 'Don't shout like that. I nearly did art in my pants.'

'Are you feeling okay, Jim?' asked Litany. 'You really do look rather ill. Would you like me to sing you better?'

Pooley sighed. 'I'd love that,' he said. 'But I've something I have to say. There's been a bit of a misunderstanding and I feel we should all be honest with each other. No secrets.'

'Go on,' said Litany.

'It's about the money.' Pooley took a deep breath and pulled his shoulders back. 'About the money you need for the equipment and the stage clothes and the strings and the mic and, well, everything, really.'

'Yes?' said Litany.

'Well,' said Jim. 'You see . . .'

'Go on,' said Pigarse. 'What is it?'

Pooley paused and glanced around the table. All eyes were upon him. Expectant eyes, they were. Eyes that seemed to look into his very soul.

148

'I . . .' said Pooley. 'I . . .' And then his face lit up. It shone. It glowed. It veritably radiated. Glow and shine and glisten, went Jim's face.

'I have a plan,' said Pooley. 'And I will take care of everything.'

'Yo,' said Ricky. 'The man with the plan. Is this guy boss, or what?'

The man with the plan stared into space. But the man with the plan had a plan.

And it was a blinder of a plan and it had come upon Jim in his moment of need, as if from God upon high.

It was also a terrifying plan and Jim knew that when he pulled it off it would doom his name for ever. But the cause was just, and the cause was good and Pooley's plan was this.

Pooley would pull off The Pooley. And he would do it in this fashion. He would borrow money. Much money. All the money that was needed to finance the Gandhis for one enormous gig. One legendary gig, at Wembley, say. One that everyone would want to come to. Everyone who was a Gandhis fan would be there. *Everyone*. And that everyone would surely include the time-hopping Geraldo, who wouldn't want to miss a gig like that.

Jim would track down Geraldo at the gig and force him to tell him the names of the following day's racing winners. Geraldo could easily find these out, but, as Jim knew, he wouldn't want to. But Jim would make him do it, because Jim would explain that if he, Jim, didn't pull off The Pooley he wouldn't have the money to pay off the debts and make the Gandhis world famous. And they had to get world famous. Because if they hadn't, Geraldo would never have heard of them and come back through time to hear them play. Future history recorded that the Gandhis *were* world famous and future history also recorded that Jim *had* pulled off The Pooley. And so, if Geraldo didn't want to mess around with future history, he would have to give Jim the names of the winners.

He would have to. He would. He just would.

It was a blinder of a plan, and as Jim stared into space, going over it all once again in his head, just to make sure he could understand it himself, he felt certain that it was the way things had to be. He couldn't escape from his fate, and only he could make the Gandhis famous.

It *was* a blinder of a plan. It was truly dynamite.

149

Norman heard the explosion and ducked for cover in his bath. It wasn't Pooley's dynamite plan, but something down in the kitchen.

Norman sheltered beneath his hands, in fear of falling plaster. He was no stranger to explosions. They went with the territory, when you were an inventor. In fact they were part of the fun of it all. If you didn't have at least one decent explosion in the course of each experiment, you didn't qualify for the right to wear the inventor's white coat, in Norman's opinion.

Norman raised his head from his hands. The ceiling hadn't fallen and down below the tape played on. It was just a minor explosion. Not the full gas mains job.

'Phew,' went Norman. 'I wonder what that might have been. I think I'd better go downstairs and find out.'

And Norman was just on the point of climbing from his bath when it happened.

It happened fast and it happened hard and it didn't give Norman a chance. It came up through the floor and up through the bath and caught Norman right where Pigarse's dad had stuck the Barbie for art.

Whatever it was, it was long, hard and white. Long, hard and white as a length of two by one. But this was not the carpenter's friend of the well-loved music hall song. This long, white, hard thing was sharp at the end and more cylindrical in nature.

Norman went up in a foamy blur and came down again in slow motion.

Whatever it was had vanished now, but a bellowing came from below.

It was quite a remarkable bellowing. And although Norman's thoughts were not particularly centred upon any bellowing other than his own at this precise moment, even *he* could have told that this was not the bellowing of a horse.

As such.

But the beast that did the bellowing had many horse-like features. The mane, the hooves, the flanks and fetlocks and the rest. But this beast that reared and bucked in Norman's kitchen, beneath the flow of water from his punctured bath, was more than just a horse.

Much more.

For this beast had a single horn that rose in glory from its head.

A long, white, hard and pointed horn.

A wondrous and magical horn.

A horn, indeed, that is only to be found on the head of a unicorn.

Greek Tragedy

I had words last week
With an uninspired Greek
Of the 'Carry-your-bags?' variety.
Who insisted that I
Tip him low, wide and high.
As a fellow might do in society.

I informed this yob
That his only job
Was to tote all the trunks of his betters.
This he flatly denied
And in dialect cried
That he was a great man of letters.

And whilst argument flared
This brash ruffian dared
To summon the help of a Peeler.
And falsely accuse me
And roundly abuse me
And quote from the works of Cordelier.

But this was his downfall,
Illiterate scoundrel.
The Bobby was classically trained.
And he struck down the Greek
With his stick, so to speak.
Which was twelve inches long and close-grained.

14

As he always liked to make an early start, Inspectre Sherringford Hovis, Brentford's Detective in Residence, led the dawn raid on John Omally's house.

The Inspectre had spent much of the previous evening interviewing the captured Omally, in an attempt to learn the whereabouts of Small Dave. But the captured Omally had stubbornly insisted that he was really the clerk from the library.

Even when put to the torture.

Although never a man to give a crim the benefit of the doubt, Hovis had finally tired of all the screaming and agreed that in order to prove the truth of the matter once and for all, he would raid the address shown on the library ticket and if there *was* another Omally to be found there, he would set the captured one free.

Enthusiastic constables smashed down John Omally's door and burst into the house, with big guns raised and safety catches off.

The sight of Omally's kitchen had a most profound effect upon several of the married officers. Awestruck in admiration and moved almost to the point of tears, they could do little other than remove their helmets and bend their knees in silent prayer, within this sacred shrine to single manhood.

A search of the upstairs revealed only two things of interest: an unmade and unslept-in bed and an ancient library book entitled *How to Play the Stratocaster.*

The latter was bagged up as evidence.

Secure now in the knowledge that he did in fact have the right man in custody and that this man was evidently a hardened crim who could hold out under torture*, Inspectre Hovis returned to his office, a cup that cheers and a bowl of muesli that doesn't.

So *where was* the real John Omally?

The answer to that was: elsewhere.

John had spent the night with Jim at the Gandhis' squat. The band occupied a large and run-down gothic house in Brentford's Bohemian quarter. The tradition (or old charter, or whatever it was) that all aspiring rock bands must live together in a squat began with the Grateful Dead. And if it was good enough for the Dead, then it's good enough for anyone.

It was a little after nine of the Thursday morning clock when Omally awoke to a proffered cup of coffee.

He awoke on the living-room sofa, and not, as he had hoped he would, in Litany's bed. John yawned and stretched and sipped at the coffee.

'Thank you, Ricky,' he said.

'No problem,' said Ricky. 'How are you feeling?'

'Somewhat odd, as it happens.'

'Hardly surprising. You crashed out, mate. A couple of tokes on the hookah and you were gone. Dope not really your thing, is it?'

'Not really,' Omally confessed. 'Where's Jim?'

'Gone out.' Ricky took from his pocket a spliff of heroic pro-portions. 'I don't think he slept at all last night. I heard him pacing about. And then he woke me up early and asked if he could borrow my suit.'

'Borrow your suit?'

'I said he could keep it. And he showered and shaved and put it on and went out. He said he had a bit of urgent business he had to take care of. But he said we were to wait for him and he'd be back with lots of money. Is that guy boss, or what?'

---

*And also, evidently, a master of disguise. For he bore no resemblance at all to the John Omally positively identified from the surveillance video footage of him leaving the Flying Swan with Soap Distant.

154

Omally sipped and nodded and tried to stay upwind of spliff smoke. He had absolutely no idea what Jim was up to. The lad had refused to tell him anything. Except that he would sort everything out, no matter what it took.

Omally took to worrying, in a manly kind of a way.

Now, if they were ever to organize a Most Manly Man in Brentford competition, the winner would undoubtedly be Bob the Bookie.

Not because he *was* the borough's most manly man, but because he would bribe the judges. Being thought of as manly, and always coming first, were big on Bob's agenda.

Bob had always liked to think of himself as a bit of a ladies' man. And if it hadn't been for the handicap of having a very small willy, he would no doubt have translated his thoughts into deeds that would have drawn applause from Long John Holmes himself.

But such is life. Bob had a big bank roll, but a small willy. So, considering what an all-round bastard he was, there might, perhaps, be *some* justice left in the world.

Bob was, if not a manly man, at least a self-made one. He worked very hard at the making of money, and from humble beginnings had built up a nationwide chain of twenty-three betting shops.

But it was here, in Brentford, in the very first shop that he had ever opened, that he liked to spend his time. It was such a joy to take money from his old school chums. Chums who had pulled down his trousers at school and made mock of his midnight growler. Pooley was one of Bob's old school chums and although Jim had never taken part in the debaggings, Bob still gained enormous pleasure parting Pooley from his pounds.

Upon this particular Thursday morning, Bob was seated behind the armoured plexiglass of his counter window, leafing through a nudie book, when the slash curtains parted and a gentleman walked in.

Bob noted the dark grey business suit, the shirt and tie and the confident walk. A VAT inspector, perhaps? Bob tucked away his nudie book and tried to look humble and poor.

'How may I help you, sir?' asked Bob. And then he did a double-take, and then a double-double.

'Shergar's shit!' cried Bob the Bookie. 'Pooley, is that you?'

'Good morning, Bob,' said Pooley. 'And how are you today?'

155

'I'm . . . I'm . . .' Bob gawped at the vision before him. 'Where did you steal that suit?' he asked.

'Always the wag, Bob. Always the wag.'

'Yeah, but where *did* you steal it?'

'I did not steal it. This is a business suit, as worn by those who do business.'

'Oh, I see, you're going to a fancy dress party. Come-as-your-fantasy, is it?'

'No, Bob. I am wearing it because I am now in business. The music business.'

'Yeah, right,' said Bob. 'So what is it really? Got yourself a job as a shop-window dummy? Is that why you weren't in yesterday?'

'I was working yesterday. In the music business.'

'Sure you were, Pooley. Well, just give me your slip and your stake money and then you can be off about your business.' And Bob laughed in a most unpleasant manner.

'Oh, I haven't come in here to place a bet,' said Jim. 'My betting days are done. My ship has at last sailed into port and I just popped in to say goodbye, before I sail away for ever.'

'And now I know you're winding me up. So pay up and piss off, why don't you.'

'I was just wondering if you had any change.'

'That's more like it,' said Bob. 'Need a couple of pence to make up a quid, do you?'

'No, I just need something a bit smaller. For the taxi.' Jim pulled from his pocket the big wad of twenties and gave it a casual thumbing.

Bob's eyes bulged most horribly at the sight of all this money. 'Where did you get *that?*' he asked in a low and troubled tone.

'Oh, this?' Pooley thumbed a little more. 'Just petty cash, actually. Could you let me have four fives for a twenty?'

'I could,' said Bob, his eyes now locked on Pooley's wad. 'I could, but . . .'

'But?' Jim asked.

'But that is a very large amount of cash you're carrying there, *Jim.* Don't you think it might be advisable to keep it somewhere safe? Perhaps I might look after it for you.'

'Did you say *large* amount?' And Pooley laughed. 'Well, it might be a large amount to you, Bob. But it's nothing to what I shall be making over the next few months. But if you can't give me change I'd better be getting along.'

And Pooley turned to leave.

'Hold on, there!' cried Bob. 'There's no need to rush off just yet.'

'Can't hang about,' said Jim. 'More than my job's worth. People to see. Business to do. Backers to vet.'

'Backers to vet?' asked Bob.

'It's my job,' said Jim. 'To vet backers who want to put money into a nationwide tour of a major new rock band.' He turned back and grinned at Bob. 'I have to check their credentials.'

'And what do *you* know about stuff like that?'

'Well, Bob.' And here Pooley winked. 'Actually I don't know anything about it, but the deal is that anyone who invests in the band will double their money within six months.'

'Bollocks,' said Bob. 'I don't believe that.'

'And why should you?' said Jim. 'You've never heard the band play.'

'The only music I like to hear is the sound of the bookie's piano.' Bob gestured towards his cash register. 'Ding ding ding, it goes.'

'Well, I'll leave you to it, then. Goodbye.'

'No, stop a minute, Jim.' Bob had a bit of a sweat on now. He knew that he would never forgive himself if he let Jim escape from the shop with all that cash in his hand. He had always considered Jim's money to be *his* money. And he couldn't have *his* money walking out of the door. 'Tell me about this band,' he said. 'Do you have a tape or something?'

'I think it's a videotape,' said the constable, handing Inspectre Hovis the package. 'Bloke dropped it off for you at the front desk.'

Hovis took the package and leaned back in his chair. 'And did this bloke leave his name?' he asked.

'No, but he was a respectable-looking type. Wore the uniform of a library clerk. And if we can't trust a library clerk, who can we trust? Eh, Inspectre, sir?'

'Bugger off,' said Hovis. 'And get on to those glaziers again. I'm sick of the wind blowing in through that dirty great hole in the window.'

157

The constable glanced towards the gaping hole. 'I wonder what happened to the body,' he wondered.

'That is a question I shall be putting to Mr Omally. Here, take this before you go.' He handed the constable a sheet of paper.

'What is this, sir?' the constable asked.

'It's a requisition form for a bigger cattle prod. A couple of days without rations should soften the blighter up. And then we'll see what he has to tell us.'

'Nice one, sir.' And the constable departed, whistling in the way they often do.

Hovis pushed photos to left and to right and opened the package on his desk. In it was indeed a videotape. A videotape of the now legendary Beatles' Wembley concert of nineteen eighty. CONTAINS ACTUAL FOOTAGE OF THE QUEEN'S ASSASSINATION, ran a gaily coloured flyer on the front. Hovis pulled the tape from its sleeve and a note dropped onto his desk. Hovis examined the note and read.

```
I PLAYED THIS TAPE YESTERDAY AFTERNOON
IN A BOOTH AT THE VIRGIN MEGASTORE AND
NOTICED SOMETHING ON IT THAT I THINK
MIGHT INTEREST YOU. CHECK OUT THE
FOOTAGE OF THE CROWD BESIDE THE STAGE
JUST BEFORE THE QUEEN GETS SHOT. YOU'RE
IN FOR A BIG SURPRISE.
```

Hovis took the tape and slotted it beneath his little portable television type of jobbie. He fast-forwarded through half an hour of Virgin commercials and then through band after band after band until he reached the moment when the Beatles finished their final song and the Queen walked onto the stage.

Inspectre Hovis diddled at the remote control. Doing that jerky slow-mo thing that you do when you reach your favourite bit. The head exploding, or the woman inserting the—

'No!' said Hovis. 'That just isn't possible.'

Rewind-slow-mo-freeze-frame.

'No!' Inspectre Hovis stared. 'It can't be.'

But it was.

There was no doubt about it. There, by the side of the stage, waving and cheering, were a dozen young men. And although they were surrounded by many many other young men there was no doubt in the inspectre's mind about where he'd seen this bunch before. He had police speed-trap-camera photos of them all over his desk.

'It's them,' said the inspectre. 'The same men. But this concert was twenty years ago and they look exactly the same. They're even wearing the same T-shirts.'

A knock came at his office door.

'Come in!' called Hovis. 'What is it?'

The constable stuck his head around the door. 'There's something I think you should see, sir,' he said.

'What is it?' said Hovis. 'I'm busy.'

'It's a tape of surveillance footage, sir. From one of the cameras on the ground floor. It's of that bloke who jumped out of your window.'

'What, of him hitting the pavement?'

'Well,' said the constable, 'he does hit the pavement eventually. I think you'd better see for yourself. But I don't think you're going to believe it.'

'I don't believe it! I don't believe it!' Bob the Bookie wriggled and jiggled and clutched at himself and went 'Ooooooooooooooo-ooooooooooooooooh!'

He had his Virgin–Sony Walkman on. Pooley had taken out the *Now That's What I Call a Cash Register* tape and slotted in the Gandhis' bootleg.

Bob seemed to be enjoying himself.

'*I don't believe it!*' he screamed.

'I don't believe it,' said John Omally, though not in a scream but a whisper.

Pooley stood before him in the Gandhis' sitting room. The hour was now ten of the morning clock, the atmosphere somewhat electric.

The Gandhis stood all around Jim. Staring not only at him, but also at the open briefcase he held in his hands.

159

The briefcase bulged with money notes of high denomination.

'How much?' Omally dared to ask.

'One hundred thousand pounds,' said Jim. 'It was all Bob had in his safe. He even lent me his briefcase to carry it in.'

'Bob? As in Bob the Bookie?'

Pooley grinned and nodded too. 'You should have seen me, John,' he said. 'It was my finest hour. I was nearly pooing myself, I can tell you. I did this thing where I casually thumbed through my wad. I'd practised it in front of the mirror, you see and—'

'Jim,' said Ricky, 'you are a fucking genius.'

'Thank you,' said Jim. 'I—'

'No, hold on,' said Litany. 'Let me get this straight. Are you telling me that you had to raise the money for the tour from a third party?'

'Well, yes,' said Jim. 'But it doesn't really matter where the money comes from, as long as the tour goes ahead.'

'No,' said Litany, 'I suppose it doesn't. But why should this Bob give you one hundred thousand pounds on the strength of a band he knows nothing about? Or was he at our gig in the Shrunken Head?'

'No,' said Jim. 'He wasn't there. But I played him the bootleg tape.'

There followed then a silence. It was a heavy kind of silence. An unearthly kind of silence. It was the heavy unearthly kind of silence that you normally only associate with that terrible moment just before the trap door opens and the hangman's rope draws tight.

'Bootleg tape,' said Pigarse, breaking this silence to bits. 'Shall I kill them for you, mistress?'

'No,' said Litany, holding up her hand. 'No, not here. Not now.'

'Hang about,' said Omally. 'What is going on?'

'Silence!' shouted Pigarse.

And John became silent.

'Who made this bootleg?' asked Litany.

'Sandy,' said John. 'He bootlegs all the gigs. But I nicked the tape from him before he could make copies.'

'And you made copies?'

'I did,' said John.

'Give me all the tapes you have, at once.'

John dug into his pocket. Pooley put the briefcase down and did likewise. 'I'm sorry,' said Jim. 'Here you are.'

Litany took the tapes in her hand. And crushed them. Just crushed them to splinters. As if they were nothing at all.

'You do not understand,' she said, in a voice so cold that it raised the hairs on Jim Pooley's neck. 'There must never be bootlegs. Never. Our music must only be recorded upon encrypted CDs that cannot be copied. Bootleg tapes would ruin us. They would be copied by the thousand. By the million. We would not make a penny.'

'Well, yes,' said Jim in a quavery tone. 'I suppose they would. I'm really sorry. We had the tape and we just didn't think. But I do have the money now and you can do the tour and end up doing a really huge gig at Wembley or something.'

'All right,' said Litany. 'You did what you thought was for the best.'

'I did,' said Jim. 'I truly did. just want the band to succeed. I want the world to hear your music.'

Litany smiled upon Jim. 'You are a good man,' she said. 'You are everything I hoped you'd be. So I think you are deserving of a treat. A special reward for your labours.' Litany reached out her hand towards Jim. 'Would you like to come into my bedroom?' she asked.

'Oh yes,' said Jim. 'Oh yes, please.'

'Oh, yes!' cried Soap Distant. 'Oh yes, indeed!'

Soap was in Boots the Chemist. He had drawn money from his bank account and now had his photographs back.

'Stag do, was it?' asked the assistant from behind the counter. 'Fat birds with their kit off? Let's have a butcher's.'

'Certainly not,' said Mr Distant. 'These photographs prove my claims. These photographs will make me famous.'

'No titties, then?' asked the assistant.

'None whatsoever.' Soap flicked through the photographs. 'Well, a few, actually. Temple dancers in the sunken city of Atlantis. Oh yes, and that princess with the long golden hair, whose father rules the subterranean land of Shambhala. And a couple of goblin nymphs from the Middle Earth. And Hitler's daughter, I'd forgotten about her.'

'Hitler's daughter?' The assistant leaned across the counter.

'Met her beneath the South Pole,' said Soap. 'There's a secret Nazi

161

base under there. It's where all the flying saucers come from. Nazi technology. Not a lot of people know that.'

'I did,' said the assistant. 'But then I *am* the reincarnation of St Joseph of Cupertino. Would you like to see me levitate?'

'No, thanks,' said Soap, pocketing his photographs.

'Oh, go on. It'll only take a moment.'

'Perhaps some other time. I have an appointment with destiny at the offices of the *Brentford Mercury*.'

'Look, I'm doing it now. My feet are off the floor.'

'Goodbye,' said Soap and he took his leave.

'Good morning,' said Norman. 'And how may I help you?'

'Just a packet of peppermints, please,' said Soap. 'I have an appointment with destiny and I feel that fragrant breath is called for and . . .' Soap's voice trailed off. 'What has happened to your shop?' his voice trailed on again.

The interior of Norman's shop was gone to ruination. Smashed, it seemed, by the hand of a jealous god. The shelves were down and splintered. Broken sweetie jars lay all about the place. There were great holes in the plasterwork and in the ceiling also. The counter had been shattered to oblivion.

'I'm redecorating,' said Norman. 'Thought it was time for a change.'

'Change,' said Soap in a toneless tone. 'Everywhere, change.'

'I'll just get the peppermints.'

Soap watched the shopkeeper sifting through wreckage. 'Why are you moving in that funny manner?' he asked.

'I don't know what you mean,' said Norman.

'All bandy-legged,' said Soap. 'Have you hurt your bottom?'

'No, I'm just—' But Norman's words were swallowed up by a mighty bellow that issued from his kitchen.

'And what was *that*?' asked Soap.

'What?' asked Norman. 'I didn't hear anything.'

There came next a violent crash that brought down plaster from the walls.

'What about that?' Soap asked. 'Did you hear that?'

'That would be the workmen.' Norman unearthed a packet of peppermints and, straightening painfully, offered them to Soap.

162

'They're rather flat,' said Soap. 'Is this a hoof mark on them?'

'Hoof mark?' said Norman. 'Hoof mark?'

'It does look rather like a hoof mark.'

'Just have them for nothing.'

'That's very kind.'

There came another bellow and another crash.

'I'll leave you to it, then,' said Soap. 'But do you know what?'

'Some of the time,' said Norman.

'That bellowing,' said Soap. 'I've heard that sound before. Beloooooooow, on my travels. In Narnia, I think it was. It sounds just like a unico—'

'Have to hurry you now,' said Norman, hustling Soap to the door.

Outside, in the Ealing Road, the sun beamed blessings on the borough. Birdies sang from treetop bowers and a rook returning to its nest was shooed away by Small Dave, who had taken up residence there. A street surveillance camera clocked the image of the library clerk who marched off towards his appointment with destiny, but failed to register that of the young man in the black T-shirt and shorts, who crept across the roof of a nearby flat block, cradling an AK47 with a sniper's sight.

God-damn Hero

Dick was a God-damn hero.
Dick had done it all.
He'd walked and talked with Nero.
He'd seen the empire fall.

He'd held the court in rapture.
With tales of darkest Burma,
And all the things he'd seen and done
Across old terra firma.

Dick was a God-damn hero.
But the nights were drawing in.
He'd sung with Johnny Zero
And also Tiny Tim.

He'd practised acupuncture
On ladies of renown,
And met with ghosts in graveyards
And other parts of town.

Dick was a God-damn hero.
But nobody cared for Dick.
He shouted loud and clearo.
It really made you sick.
I've seen it all,
I've been there, too.
I know them and
They know it's true.
It can hurt to be a hero,
And I'm glad I'm not like Dick.

15

'You are a God-damn hero,' said John Omally, raising a pint of good cheer.

It was Thursday lunchtime and he and Jim were once more in the Flying Swan.

'But there is one thing I have to say,' the Irishman continued, 'and it is best that I say it now.'

'Go on, then,' said Jim, a-sipping at his pint.

'If you don't get that smug-looking smile off your face, I'll punch your lights out.'

'Sorry,' said Jim. 'I can't help it.'

Omally shook his head. 'Just what *did* she do to you in that bed-room?' he asked, for the umpteenth time.

'She sang to me. I told you.'

'And that's all she did? Sing?'

Jim Pooley sighed in a wistful way. 'Yes,' he said. 'It was wonderful.'

John placed his pint upon the counter and rubbed his hands together. 'Well, whatever,' he said. 'But you did it, Jim. You raised the money. Less than two days as a businessman and we're already up by one hundred thousand pounds. It's beyond belief. I should have gone into business with you years ago. We'd be millionaires by now.'

'I thought I'd pop into Norman's and pay him what we owe.'

'No need to be hasty.' John took up his pint once more. 'Norman can wait until his week is up. We must decide just how we're going to spend all this wealth. The first thing I should do is open a bank account.'

'Oh no, it's not,' said Jim.

'It's not?' said John.

'It's not,' said Jim. 'The first thing *you* should do is think about how *you* are going to organize the Gandhis' tour.'

Omally made the face of thought. 'I've been considering this matter,' he said, 'and I do predict a problem or two.'

'Go on,' said Jim.

'Well, it would have been an easy enough matter to phone up music venues and play the tape to them. But as we don't have the tapes any more—'

'Norman still has one,' said Jim.

'Ah yes, so he does.'

'But I don't think we'd better use it. Litany seemed very upset, didn't she?'

'You're not kidding, my friend. The way she crunched up those cassettes. I'm glad that wasn't my old chap she had in her hand.'

'Don't be so crude, John.'

'I'm sorry. But you're right. The show must go on. And, do you know what, I have a bit of an idea.'

'Which you might perhaps like to share with me?'

'I would. Do you remember back in the sixties? There was a rock festival held on the allotments.'

'Brentstock,' said Jim. 'I didn't go to it. I think I was in San Francisco at the time.'

'I think you were in Bognor at the time. With your mum.'

'In the San Francisco Guesthouse, that's right.'

John looked at Jim.

And Jim looked at John.

'What?' said Jim.

'Nothing,' said John. 'But think about this. We could organize a big rock festival of our own. Right here, somewhere in the borough.'

'Not on the allotments, though. I seem to recall that the council were most upset about the last one.'

166

'No, not on the allotments. I know a better place. In fact I know the ideal place.'

'Not in my back yard,' said Jim.

'Buffoon. What about Gunnersbury Park?'

'Lord Crawford's place? He'd never go for that.'

'Wouldn't he, though? Lord Crawford is a member of the aristocracy. And how do members of the aristocracy spend their spare time?'

'In debauchery, of course. It's a tradition, or an—'

'Old charter or something. I know. So how do you think Lord Crawford would take to Litany singing him a little song?'

'The same way I did, probably. I . . .'

'Yes, Jim?'

'Enjoyed it very much,' said Pooley.

'Right, that's settled, then. We'll concentrate our efforts on a big rock concert in the park. And if it all goes with a big kerpow, we'll then deal with the matter of a recording studio.'

'I agree,' said Jim. 'But just one thing. This concert has to be big. Really big. Enormous. Stupendous. And things of that nature generally. It has to be *the* legendary gig. The one that no Gandhis fan would want to miss. Everything depends on that. Believe me, everything.'

'You're keeping secrets, Jim. I don't like it at all.'

'Just trust me,' said Jim. 'It'll all work out. I know it will.'

'As you are clearly a business genius, as well as my bestest friend, my trust goes without saying. So, you leave his lordship for me to tune up. He owes me a favour anyway.'

'Lord Crawford, Brentford's Aristo in Residence, owes *you* a favour?'

'That's why I suggested Gunnersbury Park. You know all those vids I sold to Norman?'

'You bought them from Lord Crawford?'

'Indirectly. You know how these things are.'

'No,' said Jim. 'I don't. But what a very small world it is. We need a venue for a big rock concert and Lord Crawford just happens to live in a big park around the corner and just happens to indirectly owe you a favour. Some people might consider all this somewhat hard to believe.'

'Then some people would be miserable buggers, wouldn't they? We're on a roll here, Jim. Nothing can stop us. Nothing.'

High upon the flat block opposite the Swan, Wingarde Pooley squinted through the telescopic sight of his AK47. He was set upon a single course. That of destroying the ancestor who had besmirched the family name. The obvious flaw in this – that in so doing he would surely cancel out his own existence – seemed not to have occurred to him at all.

But, then, perhaps it had. And, then, perhaps he had found a way around this dire eventuality. Because Wingarde hadn't just travelled back through time to save rock stars from their early deaths. He had made one or two other major alterations to history during his travels. Such as assassinating the Queen and arranging for Richard Branson to sit upon the throne of England.

Deeds which in themselves were deserving not only of our un-mitigated praise and undying gratitude but also our unquestioning trust that here was a young man who knew *exactly* what he was doing.

Indeed, here was a young man whose deeds, fulfilling as they did the sincere if unspoken wish-dreams of us all, could be said to be little less than divinely inspired.

Which in fact, they were.

For, you see, Wingarde was not acting, as Geraldo had supposed, from desperation to free his family from the curse of The Pooley. Wingarde was acting under the guidance of a higher force.

The higher force.

Wingarde heard The Voice.

For The Voice did speak unto Wingarde. Speak unto him whilst he did lie in his bed, or dwell upon the toilet bowl, or eat thereof his cornflakes, or sit, or stand, or walk, or run, or have a quiet one off the wrist. The Voice did speak unto Wingarde and Wingarde did do all the doings that The Voice did order him to do.

Knowing that The Voice he heard was heard by no one but himself.

Knowing that it was The Voice of God.

And not, as in the case of his many times great ancestor, the voice of Small Dave in a cistern.

168

Wingarde squinted through the telescopic sight, the cross-hairs focused on the Swan's saloon bar door.

Go for a head shot, whispered The Voice in his head. *Make me proud of you, my son.*

Brentford's other Lord, The Lord of the Old Button Hole, was a proud and pretty fellow who had voices of his own. And while few could doubt that Wingarde's inner voice was indeed The Voice of God, as evidenced by the charitable deeds it urged him to perform, the voices that shrieked in the head of Leo Justice were a different kettle of Kobbolds altogether.

And Leo not only heard these voices, he could sometimes see their owners too. Three demonic entities possessed him. They took turns, one running the show whilst the other two vacated the cerebral premises and hung around outside, waiting for their goes to come around again.

They were visible to Leo alone and, although he had considered the possibility of exorcism, the truth of the matter was that Leo rather enjoyed their company and revelled in the wickedness and depravity which he was oft times encouraged to inflict upon others.

But then, of course, he was a newspaper editor.*

On this particular Thursday lunchtime Leo sat at his desk, in his now less box-crowded office, munching upon a bread roll containing lettuce, celery, tomato, cheese, little boy's bottom parts and Thousand Island dressing, no salt or pepper, when a knock-knock-knock came at his door and a man called Soap came striding in.

'Good day to you,' cried Soap, a-waving his photographs. 'I have them here, so let's get into action.'

Leo Justice looked up from his eating. To the left and right of him, although unseen by Soap, the arch demons Balberith and Gressil, who played the roles of 'The Lord' and 'The Magnificent' respectively, when in residence, also looked up. And Leviathan, Prince of the First Hierarchy of Hell and currently at the controls, as it were, peered out through Leo's eyeballs and moved his mouth about.

'Your mother darns socks in hell,' said the voice of Leviathan.

*As well as something more, as we shall very shortly learn.

169

'Pardon me?' said Soap, who hadn't seen *The Exorcist* and so didn't fall about in hysterical mirth.

Leo coughed and regained control of his vocal chords. 'Who are you?' he wanted to know.

'I am Soap. Soap Distant. Traveller belooooow. The man who placed the flag of the realm in the planet's beating heart.'

'Then why are you dressed as a library clerk? And is that make-up you're wearing?'

'I wish to remain incognito for the present. And it's just a bit of blusher to add a spot of flesh-tone. And the eyeliner rather highlights the pinkness of my pupils, don't you think? Your woman outside gave me a quick makeover. She was still worrying at those wires. I advised her to give them a miss. The Information Superhighway is just a road to nowhere, I told her. She seemed to agree, because she said I was to tell you that you could stuff your job and she was off to join the raggle-taggle gypsies for a life of romance and rheumatism.'

'Come sit upon my knee, dear boy,' crooned the voice of Leviathan, who, as 'Leo Baby', swung both ways.

Soap arched an eyebrow, bridged his nose and did an underpass job with his mouth. 'Have *you* been drinking?' he asked.

'State your business,' said Leo.

'I have the photographs. The proof of my travels belooooow. Taken with the old box Brownie. And in colour, not black and white.'

'Thrill me with them,' said Leo, raising a languid hand and sweeping the clutter of his desktop to the floor. Bottom-part sandwiches and all.

Soap strode over to the desk and dealt a hand of photos.

'That's the west pier, Atlantis. And that's one of me with a monk at the Temple of Agharti in Shambhala. Eating bat.'

'Eating bat?' said the voice of Leviathan. 'Isn't that a euphemism for—'

'No,' said Soap. 'It's just bat. The wings were a bit stringy. But when in Rome—'

'Bugger the senate?' said Leviathan.

'Possibly,' said Soap. 'I've never understood the Italian football league.'

'What's this one?' asked Leo.

170

'That's me in the cave of the Gibberlins. See all that gold? Makes Fort Knox look like a boot-sale, doesn't it?'

'Do you have any of Hell?' asked Leviathan.

'They didn't come out,' said Soap.

'They never do.' And Leviathan laughed, spraying Soap with a projectile vomit composed of black frogs, safety pins, fish hooks and threepenny bits.

'Pardon me,' said Leo, wiping his chin. 'Got a bit carried away there.'

'Well,' said Soap, picking frogs from his lapels. 'I think you'll agree that these photographs prove my claims to be true. Shall we discuss contracts and a six-figure advance?'

'How about a six-fingered advance?' said Leviathan. 'Without the rear-guard action.'

Soap folded his arms, creased his brow and put a tuck in his top lip. 'Now just you see here!' he said, in the way that you do when you do. So to speak.

'What, here?' asked Leviathan, revolving Leo's left eye. 'Or here?' He made the right one roll into his head.

'That's an impressive trick,' said Soap, who was never above the awarding of praise. 'I had an uncle once who could poke the end of a contraceptive up his nose and then cough it out of his mouth, and then he would pull on each end in turn, like using dental floss. Said it kept his sinuses clear. It used to get him chucked out of a lot of restaurants, though.'

Leviathan mulled that one over. 'I'd like to meet your uncle,' he said.

'He moved to Milton Keynes,' said Soap. 'Opened a nasal floss shop. But, as I was saying . . . Just you see here! I don't have time to waste! I want action and I want it now!'

'And you'd like a contract and a six-figure advance on the strength of these photographs?' The voice was Leo's. The tone was unbelieving.

'Certainly,' said Soap. 'And on the tale I have to tell and the skill with which I'll tell it. So to speak.'

Leo laughed and Leviathan laughed and Balberith laughed. And so did Gressil. Laugh, laugh, laugh and laugh and laugh.

'Are you laughing?' Soap was heard to ask.

171

'We are,' said Leo. 'Which is to say *I* am. Kindly sling your hooky-hook, Mr Distant.'

'How about five figures, then?'

'No, you misunderstand. This is not a matter for negotiation.'

'Four,' said Soap. 'As long as the first one's a nine.'

'No,' said Leo, laughing once again.

'Three, then. As long as the first one's a ten.'

'No.'

'No?' said Soap. 'You're saying no?'

'I would like to say yes,' said Leo. 'Truly I would. But I regret that for the moment I cannot. You see, yesterday I sold the newspaper. I am no longer in a position to commission features.'

'Sold the paper? What?' Soap was aghast. Agape and a-goggle and a-gasp. 'You've sold the *Brentford Mercury*. To who?'

'It's to *whom*, actually. To a major news group, as it happens. *The* major news group. Virgin News International.'

Soap's mouth became a perfect *O*. His bum an asterisk. 'You have sold the *Brentford Mercury* to Virgin? You have prostituted the borough's organ?'

'I couldn't have put it better myself,' said Leviathan.

'Have at you, sir!' Soap raised his fists.

'Calm your jolly self,' said Leo. 'What is all this fuss?'

'You're part of it!' Soap shook a fist. 'You're part of this evil conspiracy, this changing of history!' He shook another one. 'I was going to close my eyes to it and let Inspectre Hovis sort it out. But now—' Having no more fists to shake, Soap shook his feet instead.

'That's impressive,' said Leviathan. 'St Joseph of Cupertino used to do that. Mind you, he was in league with the Devil.'

'Out, demons, out!' shouted Soap, who was nearer the mark than he knew.

'I could still offer you a job,' said Leo. 'A vacancy has just come up for a wire-worrier.'

Soap's leap onto the desk had a definite Dougie Fairbanks Jnr feel. Which certainly lived up to Soap's self-appraisal on his CV. The trip and plunge forward, however, owed more to the work of the immortal Buster Keaton.

'Oooooooooooooooh!' went Soap, as he fell upon Leo.

172

'Ooooooooooooooooh!' went Leo, as he fell beneath Soap.

'Aaaaaaaaaaaaaaagh!' went Leviathan, who objected to falling under anyone other than a paid lady wrestler with a hairlip and a dandruff problem.

And there's fewer of them about than you might think.

Soap punched Leo on the nose.

And Leo went for the throat.

Back in the more sedate and chat-things-out-in-a-pub-kind-of-world where most of the rest of us live, John Omally emptied another pint of Large down his throat.

'All right,' said John. 'That's enough for me now. I'm off to tune up his lordship. What of you, Jim?'

'I'm taking the Gandhis on a shopping expedition. But first I intend to open a bank account in *my* name and stick most of this money into it.'

'You'd better give me some petty cash before you do, then,' said John. 'A couple of thousand will do the trick.'

'No,' said Jim, shaking his head.

'No?' said John, dropping his jaw.

'No,' said Jim once more. 'All monies must be accounted for. You must present me with receipts for everything. Legitimate outgoings will be covered.'

Omally bridled, as bridle he might. 'Have you lost all reason?' he demanded to be told. 'This is me speaking to you. John Omally, your bestest friend.'

'There are no friends in business,' said Jim. 'I read that in a book somewhere. It's always best to keep your business and your social life apart.'

'Jim, we're in this together. Everything shared fifty-fifty.'

'Yes,' said Jim. 'And I learned all about that yesterday. When I found myself owing Norman.'

'That was mere tomfoolery,' said John. 'Fork out the money, if you will.'

Pooley shook his head once more. 'That would be unprofessional. It's more than my job's worth.'

John made fists, as Soap had so recently done. 'Now just you see here!' he said also.

173

'I'll tell you what I'll do,' said Jim. 'I'll give you an advance on your wages.'

'Ah,' said John. 'Yes. We haven't discussed wages, have we?'

'No, but I'm prepared to discuss them now.'

'Right,' said John. 'Let's discuss.'

'Well,' said Jim. 'I thought a thousand each would be fair.'

Omally made a doubtful face. 'A thousand a week?' said he.

'*A week?*' Jim made the face of shock and surprise. 'I wasn't thinking of a thousand pounds a week.'

John now made a similar face. 'Then what were you thinking? Not a thousand pounds *a month?*'

'Not that either,' said Jim.

John Omally's jaw began to flap, after the fashion of Jim's hands in a panic. 'Not a year?' he cried. 'Not a thousand pounds a year!'

Neville raised his eyes from his bar-end glass-polishing.

'Imagine wages like that,' he said. 'A man could live like a prince.'

John Omally lowered his voice and spoke in a strangled whisper.

'Are you telling me,' he whispered strangledly, 'that we should work for a thousand pounds a year?'

Jim shrugged.

'You're shrugging,' said John. 'Why are you shrugging?'

'I'm savouring, too,' said Jim.

'Savouring? What are you savouring?'

'The look on your face, of course. And that strangled whispering.'

'Then savour this,' said John, raising his fist.

'You hit me and I'll stop your wages. And a thousand pounds is a lot of money.'

'Not for a bloody year's work it's not.'

'No,' said Jim, 'it isn't, which is why I was thinking of a thousand pounds *a day*. Would a week's advance be enough to keep you going?'

The man without the six-figure advance and the man who had prostituted the borough's organ were going at it hammer and tongue. Soap hammered away upon Leo and Leo in turn gave tongue.

It was a long black horrible tongue and it kept getting into Soap's ear.

Standing in a corner and pointedly ignoring the conflict, Balberith and Gressil talked of snuff.

'I hear it's making a comeback,' said Gressil, 'The Magnificent.'

'Only when you blow your nose,' said Balberith, 'The Lord.'

'Now I'm definitely off to Lord Crawford's,' said John, stuffing the last of his pounds in his pockets. 'I'll meet you back in here later, okay?'

'Okay,' said Jim.

'And, Jim.'

'Yes, John?'

'When you take the Gandhis out shopping, do be sure to get that Honda seat for Pigarse's dad.'

'It's right at the top of my shopping list. I'll see you later.'

'Farewell.'

John left the Swan and Pooley stood finishing his pint.

'I don't know what you two are up to,' said Neville, drawing near, 'but just take care, will you?'

'What do you mean?' asked Jim.

Neville tapped his slender nose. 'This tells me there's trouble blowing your way.'

Jim put down his glass and picked up his bulging briefcase. 'Thanks, Neville,' he said. 'You've always been a good friend to John and me, no matter what.'

'There are no friends in business,' said Neville, with a wink of his good eye. 'But just mind how you go.'

'I will,' said Jim. 'Be lucky.'

'And you.'

There is always an element of luck involved in every fight. Unless, of course, it's managed by Don King⋆. Soap evidently had a great deal of luck credited to his worldly account, because it seemed that he was actually getting the better of Leo.

Soap had the editor's arm up his back and was holding him down with a knee.

'You spill the beans!' shouted Soap, applying a Chinese burn.

⋆Allegedly!

175

'Who are the men in the black T-shirts? Where do they come from and what do they want?'

They came, as we know, from the future, and the one on the flat block roof wanted Jim Pooley dead.

Wingarde wiped sweat from his brow and squinted once more through his telescopic sight. Within the magnified cross-haired circle the Swan's saloon bar door swung open and Jim emerged and stood taking the sun.

Wingarde's finger tightened on the trigger, but a look of indecision spread across his squinting face.

'Are you sure I'm doing the right thing?' he asked The Voice. 'I know you keep saying it's all right, but if he dies surely I'll die too? I won't even get to be born.'

You must have faith in me, my son. You have done great things while in my service. All that is required of you now is that you pull the trigger.

'That is a somewhat ambiguous answer,' said Wingarde.

Don't talk back to God, you little fuck!

On the Swan's doorstep Jim breathed in the healthy Brentford air. He felt good, did Jim. Up for it. On top. Ready to take on the world. And things of that nature. Generally.

And he would not only take on the world. He would bring the Gandhis' music to it.

He would Heal the World.

That was a good expression, thought Jim. He could live with that.

Wingarde's finger was tight upon the trigger, although most of the rest of him was shaking.

'I'm not sure,' whimpered Wingarde. 'I'm just not sure.'

You dare to doubt the Lord thy God? You dare to question His almighty wisdom?

'No, it's not that, exactly. Well, it is, sort of.'

I will cast you down! cried The Voice in Wingarde's head, rattling his dental work and popping both his ears. *I will cast you down from this high place and into the fires of the pit.*

'No. I'll do it. I'll do it.'

Wingarde's finger tightened, sweat dripped down his nose, and, dead in the sight although not yet in the flesh, Jim took another deep breath and grinned a little grin.

176

'You grinning bastard,' whispered Wingarde. 'You'll get yours.'
The cross hairs quartered Jim Pooley's forehead.
Wingarde squeezed the trigger.

According to the coroner's report that was placed upon the desk of
Inspectre Hovis, whose job it was to head up the murder inquiry, the
bullet was a high-velocity, hollow-tipped titanium round, fired from
an AK47. It entered the victim's head at a downward angle of thirty-
three degrees, indicating that it was probably fired from either a high
window or the roof of the flat block opposite the Flying Swan.

It passed through the right frontal lobe just above the right orbit
and made its exit through the back of the victim's neck, carrying
with it much of the victim's brain.

The coroner stated that death would have been instantaneous.

As he said to Inspectre Hovis: 'One second he was a man with a
briefcase, the next one he was a corpse.'

Sold Out

The ice cream cart was sold out.
The last batsman was bowled out.
And foolishly I strolled out
Into the light of day.

The umpire, some say, passed out.
The moment that the last out
Had sworn and cursed or cast out
That final hip hooray.

The only way to find out
Is when you're told to mind out.
Just stick your big behind out,
Bend at the knee and pray.

And when you know you're wiped out,
And chivvied up and striped out
And rolled
And bowled
And passed
At last
And stood like Nelson at the mast.
Then you can say it's in the past
That bastard's ice cream's sold out!

You'll know it when you drop out.
The ending is a cop-out.

16

In a perfect world, where life is lived in little movies, everything would have been sorted by Friday.

Soap would have swung his big newspaper deal.

Norman's horse would have been up and ready to race.

Geraldo and his friends would have recorrected history.

The Queen would have been back on the banknotes.

Prince Charles would have been the twat with the big ears once again.

Inspectre Hovis would have cleared his desk.

Small Dave would have been banged up in another suitcase.

The library clerk would have been suing the police for wrongful arrest and excessive use of an electric cattle prod.

Pigarse's dad would have got the new seat for his Honda.

John Omally would have organized the Gandhis' mega-concert in Gunnersbury Park.

And Jim Pooley would not be lying dead in a mortuary drawer.

Which all goes to prove, if any proof were needed, that we do *not* live in a perfect world. But rather in one where things can turn from good to bad and bad to worse and worse to far more worser still, in less than a single second.

And in less, it seemed, than a single second, Soap got the shock of his life. There was a sound like breaking thunder and the walls of the office shook.

Soap jerked upright and glanced all about, his eyes rather wide and a-bulge. He was still in the editor's office, but everything had changed. The room was bare of furniture and also bare of Leo. The floor was mossed by an inch of dust. Damp stains mapped the cracking plaster walls.

Soap took to gathering his senses.

The last thing he could remember was giving the editor a Chinese burn in the cause of a little information. Leo's watch had come off in Soap's hand. A rather splendid watch it was, too. A big electronic jobbie with the words PERSONAL LIFESPAN CHRONOMETER printed upon it. And then—

Crash went the breaking thunder sound and a lot of wall came down.

Soap still held the editor's watch. He stuffed it hastily into his trouser pocket, took to his heels and fled.

He fled through the outer office, also empty, also gone to dust, down the fire escape and out into the High Street. And then Soap paused and gasped in air and got another shock.

Half the High Street was gone. Just gone. Mr Beefheart's the butcher. The launderette. The recently opened nasal floss boutique. And the bank that likes to say yes.

Gone. Just gone.

There were earth-movers moving earth. Big diggers digging. And a crane with a demolition ball. The crane turned on its caterpillar tracks, swinging the ball like a pendulum. The ball smashed once more into the front wall of the building. The roof came down in plumes of dust. The offices of the *Brentford Mercury* became no more than memory.

'Oh, no,' cried Soap. 'Oh, no, no, no.'

'Oi! You!'

Soap turned to spy a chap with a clipboard hurrying his way. The chap wore one of those construction worker's helmets, popularized by the Village People and still capable of turning heads at a party when worn with nothing else other than a smile.

'Oi! You!' the chap called out once more.

'Eh?' went Soap, and, 'What?'

180

'Clear off! Get behind the wire!'

Soap said, 'Now just you see here!'

And then Soap said, 'Shit!' because Soap had spied the logo on the chap's helmet. It was the Virgin logo and it quite upset poor Soap.

The chap rushed up, waving his hands about, and Soap gathered him by his lapels and bore him off his feet.

'What is going on?' shouted Soap. 'Speak at once, or by the worlds beloooow I'll ram that helmet up your ars—'

'This is a restricted area. Part of the Virgin Mega City development. You can be shot on sight for trespassing. Put me down, you madman.'

Soap let the chap fall flat on his back.

'How?' Soap managed to say.

The chap on the deck was now crying into a walkie-talkie set. 'Security!' he was crying. 'Intruder on site. Dangerous lunatic. Bring the big guns.'

In his state of near delirium, Soap almost put the boot in. But sensing that it was better to run, he took once more to his heels.

The top end of the High Street was all fenced across with a steel-meshed barrier topped with razorwire. There was a single entrance gate manned by an armed guard. The entrance gate was open. The armed guard was chatting to a lady in a straw hat. Soap slipped through unnoticed.

But not, however, into a Brentford he recognized.

The fine Victorian streets had disappeared and in their place were new homes. Built in that style which architects know as Postmodern and the rest of us know as shite!

'I'm in Legoland,' whispered Soap. 'What am I doing here?'

Behind him arose the wailing of alarms and Soap was away on his toes. He was several streets further before he once more began to recognize his surroundings. He passed by Bob the Bookie's and Norman's cornershop. Neither of these had sported the 'well kept' look before, but now they looked decidedly wretched.

Soap stumbled by. Ahead he saw the Flying Swan. He stumbled up to it and in. He stood there, framed by the famous portal, puffing and blowing and effing and blinding and sagging somewhat at the knees.

A barman, wearing a sports top and shorts, looked up from an

181

automatic glass-polisher. Soap lurched to the counter and leaned upon it for support.

'Been at the gym, mate?' said the barman.

'No,' mumbled Soap. 'Where's Neville?'

'Neville?' asked the barman. 'Who's Neville?'

'Don't come that with me.' And Soap raised a wobbly fist.

'I wouldn't get lairey if I were you, mate. You're on camera, remember.' The barman thumbed over his shoulder towards a surveillance camera that angled down from the ceiling.

'But . . .' went Soap. 'But . . .'

'You're drunk,' said the barman. 'And you're wearing make-up! Out of my pub. Go on now.'

'No.' Soap's fist became a palm of peace. 'No, wait. I'm confused. I don't know what's going on.'

'You look familiar to me,' said the barman, studying Soap. 'I've seen your face somewhere before.'

'I don't know *you*. Please tell me where Neville is.'

'I really don't know any Neville.'

'But he's the part-time barman here. The full-time part-time barman.'

'Oh, *that* Neville. He retired.'

'Retired?' Soap steadied himself against the counter. 'Why would Neville retire?'

'There was a shooting incident. Bloke gunned down right outside the door.'

'Gunned down?' Soap did further steadyings. 'Gunned down? Here? How? When? Why?'

'This was five years ago,' said the barman, staring hard at Soap. 'It made all the papers at the time. Local bloke, shot down by a contract killer, they reckon. Sniper rifle off the flat blocks opposite. The ones they're pulling down.'

Soap's chest heaved. His breath went in and out.

'Yeah, big news,' the barman continued. 'They never caught the killer. Some witnesses said that they saw a kid in a black T-shirt and shorts legging it away afterwards, but the investigations came to nothing. I've got all the news clippings. First shooting here, that was. Been a lot more since then, of course, during the riots and stuff.'

'Riots?' Soap managed to say.

182

'When Virgin bought up the borough under a compulsory purchase order. Lots of riots. The locals put up quite a struggle.'

Soap felt giddy and sick. 'I'm in the future,' he mumbled. 'That's what it is. Somehow I'm in the future.'

'You not from around these parts, then?' said the barman, squinting fixedly at Soap. 'Only you *do* look familiar.'

'This is all wrong.' Soap shook his head. 'It was all wrong before but it's much more all wrong now.' Soap looked up at the barman. 'Do you know a man called Omally?'

'John Omally?'

'John Omally, yes.'

'You just missed him,' said the barman. 'He always comes in on this day.'

'He always comes in every day,' said Soap. 'Some things will never change.'

'Once a year is all that he comes in,' said the barman. 'Famous man like that.'

'Famous? John Omally? Famous?'

'Where have you been, mate? Underground or something? John Omally is *the* big record producer. He comes in here on this day every year. Because this was the day it happened.'

'The day?'

'The day of the shooting. The bloke who was shot was John Omally's bestest friend.'

'Jim . . .' whispered Soap. 'Jim Pooley.'

'That was his name. John Omally comes in here and drinks one pint of Large. We have to get it brewed specially for him. He drinks one pint of Large and he cries. Can you imagine that? A manly man like him crying? Fair turns my guts, that does.'

'I have to go. I have to go.' Soap lurched up and made for the door.

'Hold on there,' called the barman. 'I *do* know you. I *do*.'

Soap ran back down the Ealing Road.

Within the Swan the barman was leafing through a pile of wanted posters. 'I bloody do know you,' he said, and, 'Yes.'

He withdrew from the pile a single sheet of paper. On the top were printed the words 'Have You Seen This Man?' Below this was a photograph of Soap, blown up from a frame of surveillance footage. 'Wanted for assault and the theft of a valuable wristwatch. Five thousand pounds reward!' The barman whistled. 'They've been reprinting this poster every month for the last five years. No wonder he looked so familiar.'

The barman pulled out his mobile phone and dialled the Virgin Police Service.

Soap turned a corner, then another and ran into Mafeking Avenue. John Omally lived at number seven.

John Omally *had* lived at number seven.

The man who now did drove Soap away with a stick.

Soap limped on, bound for heaven knows where.

Back in the Swan the barman was babbling into his mobile. 'It was definitely him. He was wearing one of those old-fashioned library clerk uniforms. And he's well out of it. Drugged up or something. He can't have gone far. You'll catch him on camera and don't forget who called it in. I want my five thousand quid.'

The Memorial Library was still standing. The bench outside was broken, but Soap sat down upon it. He buried his face in his hands and trembled terribly. He *was* in the future. Five years into a horrible future. A future where Brentford was being pulled down. A future where John Omally was a famous man, but Jim, poor Jim, was dead.

Soap struggled like the drowning man, for some small straw to clutch at. There had to be some sense to this. Some logic. Some reason. Someone to blame.

'It's them.' Soap raised his head from his hands. 'It has to be them. The men in the black T-shirts. The one running away after Jim's murder. The ones on the speed cameras. The same ones at the Beatles' concert in nineteen eighty. Exactly the same. The same age, the same clothes. My God.' Soap took a deep breath and nodded his head. 'It *is* them. It's *time*. That's what it is. That's what all this is. They travel through time. And they change things and no one knows they've been changed. No one but me. Me. I'm the only one who knows. I'm not affected by their changes. Because . . .' Soap paused. *Because*, was a tricky one. Why hadn't he been unaware that the past had been changed? 'Because,' Soap continued, 'because I

184

was belooooooow. I was deep beneath the Earth. That has to be it. Something to do with the magnetic field or something. Yes, that has to be it. So . . .' Soap drew in a very deep breath.

'*So what the fucking hell am I doing in the future?*'

It was a good question, that. And one that, given time, Soap might well have answered. He had done remarkably well so far, considering the state he was in and everything.

But to have answered that question, Soap would definitely have needed quite a little time. And quiet time.

Uninterrupted.

The helicopter came in low. It swept down over the library roof and hovered over Soap.

'Lay down your weapons and prostrate yourself upon the ground,' called that old loudhailer voice. 'If you obey at once you will not be harmed. Any attempt to make an escape will be met by force of arms.'

'Shit!' said Soap, which is just what you say. 'I'm in big trouble here.'

Soap stood up slowly, his hands in the air and then Soap panicked and ran.

Off went Soap at the hurry-up, *action* once more his word.

Above him flew the helicopter. All red and white with that logo on the side.

'Somewhere to hide,' gasped Soap as he ran. 'Somewhere to hide, and quick.' He ducked down an alleyway between two terraced houses and fell straight over a dustbin.

Remembering the words of Inspectre Hovis, Soap did not hide in the dustbin. He stumbled on, between back gardens now, the helicopter keeping easy pace.

'Halt, or I fire!' came the voice from above.

'Shit, oh shit, oh shit.' Soap rushed on and down another alleyway and out into another street. From above came the rattle of rapid fire, around his feet burst the bullets.

'No,' wailed Soap, rushing on.

He had almost reached a corner when a long black car came sweeping up from behind. It swerved directly into his path and Soap toppled over the bonnet. He fell to the road, all flailing arms and legs, prepared to come up fighting.

185

The driver's window of black mirrored glass slid down and a voice from within shouted, 'Soap!'

Soap staggered to his feet. 'You won't take me alive,' he shouted back, as brave as brave can be.

'Come with me if you want to live,' called the voice – which rang a certain bell.

Soap gaped in at the driver. He glimpsed a great black beard, woven into intricate knots and laced with coloured ribbons, a pair of red-rimmed eyes and—

'Down on your knees!' called the voice from above. 'Down on your knees, or I fire!' The helicopter dropped even closer to the ground, the noise of the blades becoming deafening.

'Come.' The driver beckoned Soap. 'Hurry, or you're dead.'

Soap couldn't hear what the driver said, but, as his options were severely limited at the present, he tore open the rear door of the car and flung himself inside.

The driver put the car in gear and it shot forward, catching the still-open door on a lamp post and smashing it shut with a bang.

'Keep your head down,' shouted the driver. 'And don't get sick on my seats.'

Now, your modern Virgin Police Service helicopter comes fully equipped with an impressive assortment of weaponry. You have your small-bore machine guns for taking out a suspect at close range. Your General Electric mini-gun, dispensing its six-thousand-rounds-per-minute pay-load for crowd situations. And, of course, your missiles. Your missiles are usually reserved for special circumstances, destroying a paramilitary stronghold, or a tank, say. But, as every good Virgin Police Service officer knows, there's nothing quite like the thrill of letting one of those suckers loose at a speeding motorcar.

Laser-guided too, they are. You just lock on and hit the button.

The driver of the black car swung the wheel and pushed his foot to the floor. Soap clung onto whatever he could, as the car took a corner on two wheels alone and swerved into the Ealing Road. Leaving really brilliant skidmarks. Burning rubber all the way.

Behind it came the helicopter. Low to the ground now, a few feet above. In the cockpit the pilot winked at his fellow officer. 'Go on,' he said. 'Lock on and hit the button.'

The long black car rushed past the Flying Swan.

186

Behind it came the helicopter.

Brrrrrrrrrrrrrm, went the black car's engine.

Chb, chb, chb, chb, chb, went the helicopter blades.

On went the laser-guiding system.

On went the little telescreen.

Green electric cross-wires focused.

'Keep your head down!' shouted the driver.

'Press the button,' said the pilot.

Brrrrrrrrrrrrm and rev and roar went the car.

And chb, chb, chb, chb the helicopter blades.

The black car passed over the railway bridge, its four wheels leaving the road.

Soap's head hit the roof and a finger hit the button.

Out of the sky came the missile. Out from the sky and down to the road.

The explosion swallowed up tarmac and pavement, rubber and metal, in fragments and fistfuls.

The helicopter circled through the smoke and flame. Of the black car and its occupants, nothing whatever remained to be identified.

Armageddon: The Musical
Words and music: Gandhi's Hairdryer
OPENING THEME

From the deep-hidden realm of Shambhala
To the halls of the lofty Potala.
From the tomes of Debrett
To the domes of Tibet,
You can sit and take tea with the Lama.

He will speak of forthcoming disasters
Like the rise of the new Perfect Masters,
Who are gaining control
Now we're all on the dole,
And there's no happy-ever-afters.

So forget about paying the mortgage,
And cancel the milk from today.
Armageddon is coming,
And it's only four minutes away.

You can dump your two weeks on the Costa
And scrub round your flexible roster.
That new three-piece suite
And that chic place you eat,
And all other plans you may foster.

Cos tomorrow's been cancelled for ever,
No more knock or the old never-never.
No more Barrett Homes,
And no more Earl's Court clones.
No more John, no more Ron, no more Trevor.

So tear up that final demand note,
And open the Champagne today.
Armageddon is coming
And it's only two minutes away.

188

There's a jewel in the eye of the lotus
Which is fine if you like those nice motors.
But the bent MOT
Won't mean sod all, you see,
As the whole world just went out of focus.

And through firestorms and nuke radiation
We will see a new birth of a nation.
Like a Phoenix arise
Spread its wings to the skies,
And for more news stay tuned to this station.

Forget about yesterday's heroes,
The new ones are coming to stay.
Armageddon is coming,
And it's only a heartbeat away.

Only a heartbeat away.

17

Soap's heart seemed to be beating. He could feel it in his chest. But as he couldn't actually see his chest, or indeed any other part of himself, he concluded, dismally, that he probably *was* dead. He could think of no other logical explanation to account for the fact that he now seemed to be floating, in a disembodied form, out of Brentford and up the Great West Road.

'Bummer,' said Soap. 'That's a real bummer.'

'I think it's pretty impressive,' said the driver's voice.

Soap sighed. 'I'm sorry,' he said. 'I'm sorry you got killed for helping me.'

'We're not dead, you buffoon.'

There was a whirl and a click and a whoosh, and the car and its driver and Soap appeared out of nowhere at all.

'What?' went Soap, and, 'How?'

'Stealth car,' said the driver, winking over his shoulder at Soap. 'Latest military technology. Cost me an arm and a leg on the old black market, as you can imagine.'

Soap stared at the driver and the light of realization dawned. 'John,' he said, 'it's you.'

'Of course it's me.' said Omally. 'Who did you think it was?'

'I don't know, I . . .'

'Ah,' said Omally, turning back to his driving. 'The beard. I haven't had a shave for five years. Not since—'

'Jim,' said Soap. 'I heard about Jim. I'm so sorry, John.'

'You might have turned up to the funeral. We sent him off in style.'

'I couldn't. I'm sorry.'

Omally swung the steering wheel and the car turned off the Great West Road and in through the gates of Gunnersbury Park.

'So, where *have* you been?' John asked. 'And whatever possessed you to go wandering about in Brentford? You're a wanted man.'

'Well, it's all your fault,' said Soap. 'If you hadn't made me stick Small Dave up the back of my coat.'

'Your being wanted has got nothing to do with Small Dave. As you well know.'

'I don't,' said Soap. 'But listen. Thank you for saving me back there, John. You didn't have to take a risk like that.'

'A friend in need and things of that nature.' The car moved up the gravel drive towards the imposing Georgian pile that was Gunnersbury House.

'What are we doing here?' asked Soap.

'This is where I live.' Omally drew the car to a halt, switched off the engine and tugged the key from the dash. 'Come on,' he said. 'You could use a drink.'

John climbed from the car and Soap followed on buckling knees. He had all but caught up, when a Godalmighty crash from above had him ducking to his bucklers. Glass and wood rained down on the drive and a television set bounced off the bonnet of John's car and came to rest in a flowerbed.

'Help!' wailed Soap. 'We're under attack.'

John helped the lad to his feet. 'I have guests,' he explained. 'That's just their way of saying hello.'

'Are they loonies?' asked Soap. 'Is this a loonybin?'

'The whole world's a loonybin. Come on, they're okay.'

The entrance hall of Gunnersbury House might well have been described as a symphony in marble. But only by a lover of Karl Stockhausen. The glorious classical line of the place, with its travertine floor and graceful columns of fine Carrara rising to a Robert Adam ceiling frescoed with Arcadian scenes was buggered all to hell by the chaos of 'things' that filled it.

There was a Harley motorcycle, lacking much of its engine. Several stereo systems in various stages of assembly. At least five Stratocaster guitars, leaning against as many amps and speakers. There was a Rock Ola jukebox and a pinball machine and a mountain bike. There were many many cardboard boxes and an awful lot of bubblewrap.

Soap took in as much as he could and the phrase 'toys for boys' rolled into his head and out again. 'You never married, then?' he said.

'Ah, no,' said John. 'I've got some booze in the kitchen. Shall we—?'

Soap remembered John Omally's previous kitchen. He tried to picture it on a larger scale. The thought depressed him somewhat.

'Is it *really* grubby?' he asked.

'*Really*,' said John, with an underbeard grin.

'You lucky bastard.'

'I don't feel very lucky.' John went in search of the booze.

Soap sat down upon a fibreglass stool tastefully constructed from the body-cast of a kneeling naked female. Presently John Omally returned with a champagne bottle and two grubby tumblers. He popped the cork, poured the drinks and handed one to Soap.

'Cheers,' said Soap. 'And thanks again.'

'Cheers,' said John. 'You're welcome.'

Soap sipped champagne. 'This is good,' he said. 'But how did you come by all this? The barman at the Swan said you were famous now. What did you do exactly? What *do* you do?'

'I manage a rock band and I produce their records. They're a big band and very famous. Jim and I were partners at the beginning. But when Jim got killed the police confiscated all the money he'd raised and everything went poo-shaped. But I kept working away. I did it for Jim, it mattered so much to him. He knew what it could mean to the world.'

'Good musicians, eh?' Soap reached for the bottle.

'More than good. The lead singer, Litany. You'll meet her soon. Her voice had the power to heal the sick.'

'Had?' said Soap, topping up.

'She lost it. After Jim died. I think she really must have cared for

192

him. I heard she went to the mortuary. Tried to sing him back to life.'

'Urgh,' went Soap. 'That sounds rather sick.'

'Well anyway, it didn't work and she lost the power. But the band were still shit hot and I toured them and brought out some records on a private label, using the money I had. And eventually we were made an offer we couldn't refuse.'

'Oh, yes?' said Soap, a-sipping.

'We got a record deal with Virgin.'

Soap spat Champagne all over John.

'Sorry,' said Soap. 'I'm sorry.'

'Never mind,' John shook champagne spray from his beard. 'But . . . and there's a big but.'

'But me this but,' said Soap.

'But it's all wrong. All of it. The company. The entire set-up. It's like some world domination thing. The company is taking over. You've seen what they've done to Brentford.'

Soap gave a shudder. 'I did,' said he. 'It made me sick at heart.'

John took the bottle and topped up both glasses. 'It's got to be stopped and we're going to stop it.'

'We?' said Soap. 'You and me?'

'Me and the Gandhis.'

'You and Gandhi's family?'

'The band. They're called Gandhi's Hairdryer.'

'What a foolish name,' said Soap. 'Why do they call themselves that?'

Omally tugged at a yard of beard. 'I never thought to ask. But we're going to bring down the company. This very weekend. There's going to be a big rock concert, right here in Gunnersbury Park. The biggest ever. Everybody who's anybody will be coming, and the whole world will be watching it live on TV. It's the concert that Jim wanted to happen, but it's taken me five years to set it up.'

'And what will be so special about this concert?' Soap asked, as his glass became empty once again.

'It's the Beatles' farewell concert.'

Soap made a terrible groaning sound.

'And Prince Charles is going to be there.'

Soap added moans to the groan.

193

'You don't sound too keen,' said Omally.

'I'm not,' said Soap. 'But just how are you hoping to bring down the company? You're not going to blow up the Beatles or something, are you?'

Omally emptied his glass and shook the Champagne bottle. 'These don't last long, do they?' he said. 'But, no, Soap, we're not going to blow up the Beatles. But we are going to bring down the company. You see, we could never get a record deal to begin with, because of Litany's power. No big company would touch the band. Her voice had the power to heal, as I've said, and these big companies make their fortunes out of pharmaceuticals. If all people needed to get well was to listen to a CD, then no more pharmaceuticals.'

'But hold on,' said Soap. 'Firstly, you said that Litany had lost her powers, and secondly, it's Virgin who bring out the records. They would simply stop the records from being produced.'

Omally grinned beneath his facial plumage. 'Firstly,' said he, 'Litany's powers have finally returned. Time heals all wounds, so they say. And secondly, there will be no records. This is going to be the Gandhis' farewell gig and they are going to go out on a high note. A note that will be heard all around the world. Heard by millions and millions of people and recorded upon millions and millions of video recorders. This is going to make history, Soap.'

'Make history?' Soap's head nodded. 'That might do it, yes.'

'And it will stuff that little sod,' said John.

'What little sod is that?'

'The chairman of the company, of course. The evil little rat. And to think that when we were offered the record deal I thought it was a good omen. Him having the same name and everything.'

'I'm lost,' said Soap. 'What are you talking about?'

'I'm talking about the revolting little tick who runs the company. The vile bastard who is responsible for the destruction of Brentford. I'm talking about Wingarde Pooley.'

'*Wingarde?*' Soap made the face of surprise. 'I met a young bloke called Wingarde.'

'I'm sure you did. Probably when you were nicking his guru's watch.'

Soap now made the face of outraged innocence. 'I didn't nick any watch,' he said.

'Come off it, Soap,' said Omally. 'There's been wanted posters out on you ever since it happened. He must really want that watch back.'

'Watch?' And Soap recalled his struggle with the editor of the *Brentford Mercury* and how he'd ended up here in the future clasping nothing but the—

'Watch,' said Soap. 'There is a watch. But it didn't come from any guru.'

'It came from Wingarde's guru. True Father, as he calls him. Here' – John rooted around amidst the boxes and the bubblewrap – 'I have one of his holy medallions somewhere. They give them away free with CDs and stuff. Ah, here's the fellow.'

Omally flung a golden plastic disc in Soap's direction.

Soap took it up from the floor and gave it a bit of perusal.

From the centre of the disc a face grinned out at him. It was the face of Leo Justice.

'Oh dear,' said Soap. 'I do know this man. He's the editor of the *Brentford Mercury*. His name is Leo Justice.'

Omally shook his head and vanished behind his beard. 'That man's name is Mageddon,' he said. 'Robert Mageddon. But he likes to be known as "Most High".'

'Robert Mageddon?' said Soap. 'R. Mageddon? Armageddon? What kind of name is that?'

Omally shrugged and gathered in his beard.

'Well, I'll tell you this,' said Soap. 'The last time I saw him he was calling himself Leo Justice and posing as the editor of the *Brentford Mercury*.' Soap peered hard at the face on the medallion. 'I don't know who you really are,' said Soap, 'but I'll find out, you see if I don't.'

Soap flipped the medallion into the air, caught it and rammed it into his pocket, where it lay all nestled up beside the stolen watch. The accidentally stolen watch. The accidentally stolen watch that was not only a watch but also a personal lifespan chronometer and a time-travelling device. The very time-travelling device which had, through Soap's rough handling of it, caused him to be thrown into the future.

And had Soap taken this watch from his pocket and examined its back, he would have seen the owner's name printed in tiny

195

little letters upon it. The *real* name of the owner, that is.

And that name was *not* Leo Justice.

Nor was it Robert Mageddon.

That name was Dr Vincent Trillby.

The Waiter

The waiter brought me channel bends and ring-seals,
His goggles were the finest I have seen.
And he moved so very swiftly on his winged-heels,
While a crowd of parrots struggled at his chin.

His dress was smooth and styled in tweed and casters,
The swell of ray guns showed beneath his cloak.
He was trimmed throughout to combat all disasters,
His dovetailed keyring jangled as he spoke.

His offices were wall to wall with letters
That told of all the places he had known.
And he never feared the ridicule of betters,
For he moved in women's company alone.

Far overhead the coal-black kites are flying,
And underfoot the worms turn in the grave.
And if I said I loved him, I'd be lying,
For who can love a lord if you're a slave?

Upon the table one-eyed Jacks are winking,
And cars move by in endless metriform.
And he can hear most every word I'm thinking,
For he's a deviation from the norm.

18

Dr Vincent Trillby was a deviation from the norm.
A scientist from the future, possessed by demons and now play-
ing guru to a time-travelling fanboy who took orders from The
Voice of God. Not your everyday man on the Brentford omnibus.

A question that might be asked, and not without good cause, is
this: If Wingarde took his orders from The Voice of God, why then
would he need a guru?

Good question.

And one deserving of an answer.

It is a well-known Holmesian adage that, once you have elimin-
ated the impossible, then whatever remains, no matter how unlikely
it might appear, must be the truth.

So let us, as would Holmes, apply the science of deduction to this
problem. And then, having solved it, we will plunge headlong into
all the ensuing chaos and action, at least secure in the knowledge that
we actually know what the bleeding hell is going on.

So.

Let us first consider Wingarde. He has shot dead his many-times-
great grandfather. Surely, then, he himself would cease to exist? He
would never have been born. But here Wingarde is. Large as life and
very much more powerful. How?

All right. Consider this. What if Wingarde, although a Pooley by name, is not actually a real Pooley? Which is to say, what if Wingarde Pooley Snr is not the biological father of Wingarde Pooley Jnr? What if Wingarde's mother had been having an affair and had got herself pregnant?

These things happen. It's something to do with single men not washing their dishes, and a full explanation can be found on pages 25 and 26 of this book.

So, if this is the case, and let us assume that it is (because it *is*!), who might Wingarde's real father be?

Well, obviously someone his mother found very attractive. Someone glamorous, perhaps. Someone powerful. Because power is a great aphrodisiac.

How about someone really powerful? How about the director of the Institute? How about Dr Vincent Trillby!

All right, let's try that one on for size. Does it fit? It does. And it would explain what Dr Vincent Trillby is doing in the twentieth century. Searching for his wayward boy.

It makes perfect sense. And as perfect sense is much better than no sense whatsoever, we will stick with it as an answer.

But what about those demons? And what about The Voice?

Are these connected? Well, yes and no.

Firstly, then, the demons.

Picture this scenario.

Amidst all the chaos at Institute Tower, the various Trippers coming and going and hitting each other, Dr Vincent Trillby's mobile phone rings. Dr Trillby answers it. 'Trillby speaking,' he says.

'It's Marge,' says Marge, in tears (for Marge is Wingarde's mum).

'Whatever is it, Marge, my dear?' asks Dr Trillby, dodging Tripper number eight. 'You sound upset.'

'It's our darling boy,' weeps Marge. 'Our darling Wingarde. He's gone. He's run away.'

'Now calm yourself, Marge. He's run off before. I'm sure he'll come back. Don't worry.'

'It's easy for you to say don't worry. No one knows you're his real father. *He* doesn't know. My husband doesn't know—'

'Yes, yes,' says Dr Trillby. 'Let's not start all that again. Have you any idea where he's gone? Did he leave you a voicemail or anything?'

'Yes,' blubbers Marge, and she plays the voicemail down the phone.

The voice of Wingarde says, 'Right! By the time you get this message I'll be gone. I'm sick of living in this stinking century with THE END on its way and everything. So I'm off. I'm getting out. I'm going back to a decent period to—'

'—see some decent bands,' says another voice (the voice of Geraldo).

'Yeah, to see some decent bands. Like the Beatles and the Rolling Stones and Sonic Energy Authority and the Lost T-Shirts of Atlantis and—'

'—Gandhi's Hairdryer,' says the voice of Geraldo.

'Yeah, we'll see them too. So goodbye, Mother. Goodbye, Father. Goodbye.'

And click goes the voicemail and that is that.

'He's gone mad!' cries the voice of Wingarde's mum. 'What shall we do, Vincent? What shall we do?'

Dr Vincent Trillby sighs yet another sigh. He'd hoped that he'd done with sighing, but with all the Trippers and now this . . . He grabs the nearest Tripper by the throat. 'Download the time travel program into my lifespan chronometer and do it right now,' says he. 'I've got to find my son.'

So far, so good. This all follows neatly. But what about those demons?

Right. So Tripper, much against his will, downloads the time travel program from his lifespan chronometer into Dr Trillby's. But then Dr Trillby is faced with a problem. Where and *when* is Wingarde? Dr Trillby can date the Beatles to the latter part of the twentieth century. But that's not enough. He'll need to be a bit more accurate than that. So Dr Trillby does what anyone would do in such circumstances. He hooks into PORKIE. That's SWINE, if you recall. The Single World Interfaced Network Engine. Sum of all human knowledge. Knower of all that there is to know.

Tiny letters move across the screen of Dr Trillby's lifespan chronometer. They spell out the words WE THANK YOU FOR CALLING SWINE, BUT REGRET THAT ALL INFORMATION IS NOW CLASSIFIED. SWINE IS NOW OFF-LINE AND HAS GONE ON HOLIDAY. GOODBYE.

Dr Trillby panics and, his heart now ruling his head, programmes a random latter-part-of-the-twentieth-century date into his chronometer and then wham bam, thank you, ma'm, he's off.

Out of the future and back to the past.

And right into very big trouble.

For Dr Trillby is not as other men. Dr Trillby is a deviation from the norm. Particularly because Dr Trillby was not actually *born*. Dr Trillby was cloned, and a man who is cloned may look like a man, but he doesn't possess a soul. You can clone the man but *you can't clone the soul*. And so what do you think would happen to a man without a soul who suddenly appeared in the twentieth century?

Another good question.

And one deserving of an answer.

Such a man without a soul would instantly fall prey to demonic entities. For it is only the presence of our souls that keeps the buggers out.

So, here we have a man without a soul, possessed by demons, searching the latter part of the twentieth century for his son. And here we have his son, driven by The Voice, screwing up the latter part of the twentieth century and creating a situation ideal for demonic agencies to seize control of society. The creation of a single mega-organization running damn near everything.

That is fertile soil for Old Nick and his chums.

That is Virgin territory!

And it certainly would not have happened if the great and God-like Richard Branson had still been at the helm.

Would it? No, of course it wouldn't. Are we agreed?

Yes, we are. It all makes *perfect* sense. It is all as clear as an author's conscience.

Three questions only remain to be answered and then all the pieces will fit:

What about The Voice?

How come Wingarde is now running Virgin?

And how come Dr Trillby is posing as his guru?

Again, *good* questions. So let us apply the science of deduction to them and get ourselves back to the action.

It is certainly not hard to see how, guided by The Voice and considering all he has so far achieved, Wingarde could easily have taken over Virgin. And we can accept that Dr Trillby set himself up as editor of the *Brentford Mercury* in a historically changing world as a means of tracking down his son. Information Superhighway stuff, data access, all that kind of caper. And we can accept that it was some time after Jim's murder that Wingarde took over Virgin. By which time Virgin had already bought out the *Brentford Mercury*.

A continuation of deductive reasoning puts forth this simple proposition. A new head of Virgin, recognized by Dr Trillby. He has found his wandering son. His wish is to drag him back into the future. But he cannot, because Soap Distant has his personal lifespan chronometer. He wants it back, so he puts out the wanted posters and waits for Soap to reappear. And while he's waiting he wants to keep close to his son. So he approaches him, chats with him, and as he knows everything about Wingarde it is not difficult for him to convince the lad that he is little less than a guru.

But but but but but but! I hear you say. What about The Voice? If this is The Voice of God in Wingarde's head, The Voice of God will know.

So, what about The Voice?

Good question.
Very good question.
Very good question indeed.

Armageddon: The Musical
Words and whatnots by Gandhi's Hairdryer
'The Dalai Lama's Barn Dance'

Acupuncture, absent healing, alchemy and eyeless sight,
Ectoplasm, elementals, OTO and inner light.
ESP and elongation, healing currents, Eckanar,
Flying saucers, flat Earth theories, Order of the Silver Star.

(And that ain't the sheriff)

Ghosts and temples, Gnosticism, Glastonbury Zodiac,
Mysteries and Meher Baba, magnetism, men in black.
Apparitions, astral bodies, amulets, astrology,
Gerald Gardner, Alex Sanders, Anton L. and Mr C.

(Mr Crowley, that is. The man was a beast)

Loch Ness monster, Hatha yogi, levitation, hollow Earth,
Hexagrams and Kirlian photos, Lobsang Rampa, Patience Worth.
Hare Krishna, Krishnamurti, zelator and neophyte,
Karma karma, Dalai Lama, Church of Satan, Church of Light.

(I Ching. You Ching. We all Ching together)

Avatars and bilocation, Book of Shadows, Book of Thoth,
Doubles, dowsing, dreams and Druids, visions of the Holy Ghost.
Precognition, Vril and Voodoo, succubi and the Golden Dawn,
I'm getting sick of all this hoodoo. I think I'll go and mow the
    lawn.

Yee hah.
We gone.

19

Soap Distant wasn't mowing the lawn. He was having a bath. He was ruminating in the tub. Dwelling in the lather. Soaking, sud-sniffing, things of that nature.

Omally had told him that, although the retro library clerk costume and the smudged face make-up did make Soap look something of a character, it also made him look something of a twat. So why didn't Soap just go upstairs and have a bath, help himself to something from Omally's extensive wardrobe and then come down and meet the Gandhis for dinner?

And so Soap was having a bath. Ruminating in the tub. Soaking, sud-sniffing—

'I've got to work all this out,' said Soap to himself. 'Apply the science of deduction. I haven't got all the pieces yet. But I know I've got some of them. I know it's the men in the black T-shirts. I know they travel through time. And I know they mess around with history. Save rock stars from tragic early deaths, and so on. And now this Wingarde is in charge of Virgin and Virgin virtually own all rock music. It's all connected and it's all to do with rock music.

'But what about Jim? Why kill poor Jim? Jim was a friendly harmless soul. And amiable buffoon, really. But he was a good man. A much-loved man of Brentford. Why would anyone want to kill him?'

Soap sighed amidst the suds. 'It has to be the music,' he said. 'Jim's share in the Gandhis or something. But I'm sure it's all down to this Wingarde and his guru. I'll get to the bottom of it. Getting to the bottom of things is what I do best.'

And with that said, and as he was now all prune-wrinkly from more than three hours in the bath, Soap rose from his perfumed water, slipped on a rather spiffing white towelling bathrobe and examined himself in a mirrored wall tile.

Same death-mask dead-white physog. Same transparent hooter. Same pink hamster eyeballs. Same fibre-optic flat-top.

'Same good-looking son of a tunnel,' said Soap Distant.

Soap rootled about in Omally's wardrobe, marvelling at the quantity of suits. He selected for himself a black silk number, matching shirt and shoes.

'Black silk shoes,' said Soap, twirling before the mirror-tiled bedroom wall. 'Omally knows how to live. But is this me, or is this me?'

Soap concluded that it was indeed he, as black was really *his* colour. He turned out the pockets of the library clerk's uniform and came across the golden plastic medallion and *the watch*.

Now, what should he do with this? Flush it down the toilet? Soap weighed up the pros and cons. Perhaps it would be better just to hang on to it. Use it as a means to meet up with this Leo once again. Soap stuck the medallion into his pocket and strapped the watch onto his wrist.

'Very smart,' said Soap. 'Very futuristic.'

All dolled up and dandy, Soap made his way downstairs. Sounds of gaiety echoed where they could about the crowded entrance hall. Coming from behind a panelled door, which Soap assumed must lead to the dining room.

Soap thought that he'd make a grand entrance and so he picked his way through the chaos, knocked smartly on the door and flung it open.

The dining room, for such it was, was grand as grand could be.

The walls were hung with portraits of the Crawford family.

There were dudes done up as generals and ladies all in lace.

You could tell they all were Crawfords, for they had the Crawford face.

205

The furniture was old and rich, of Chippendale persuasion.

The table fairly groaned with grub, as for some state occasion.

A laughing group was gathered round, Omally at the head.

As Soap appeared their laughter stopped and silence reigned instead.

'What a very poetic room,' said Soap. 'Er, why are you staring at me like that?'

Omally rose from his chair and pointed a trembling finger at Soap. 'Of all the suits in my bloody wardrobe,' he said, 'why did you have to choose that one?'

'It's black,' said Soap. 'My favourite colour.'

'It's my funeral suit,' said Omally. 'The one I wore to Jim's funeral.'

'Oh dear.' Colour rose to Soap's cheeks. 'I'm so sorry, John. I didn't know. I'll go and change at once.'

Omally shook his head. 'No,' he said. 'Forget it, Soap. It does suit you. Keep it, it's yours.'

Soap Distant stood in the doorway, the now legendary spare prick at a wedding.

Omally beckoned. 'Come and sit down here by me and get stuck into this grub.'

Soap took a seat. Omally poured wine and made the introductions.

'This is Litany,' said John, 'the most wonderful singer on Earth.'

Soap nodded smiles towards the woman nodding smiles at him. She was slim and svelte and stunning. All in white with eyes of emerald green. Soap was taken at once by her beauty, but also by the thought that surely he had met this woman before. There was something about her that rang one of those little bells that you can't actually hear but you know are being rung. Somewhere.

'I love the moustache,' said Soap. 'Is that a fashion thing?'

'It's a metaphor,' said Litany.

'Oh yes,' said Soap. 'Of course it is.'

'And this is Ricky,' said John. 'The greatest Stratster on the planet. He's teaching me to play.'

'Pleased to meet you, Soap,' said Ricky, reaching for a handshake. 'John's told me all about you. Did you really visit the centre of the Earth?'

'Certainly did,' said Soap. 'Although I've mislaid the photos.'

206

'Isn't it always the way,' said Ricky, which rang another bell.

'This is Pigarse,' said Omally. 'Pigarse is the loudest drummer in history.'

'I can see right through your nose,' said Pigarse. 'Horrible it is and filled with bogeys.'

'Pleased to meet you too,' said Soap.

'But John *has* told us a lot about you,' said Pigarse.

Soap nodded out a 'That's nice'.

'He said you were an amiable buffoon.'

'Cheers, John,' said Soap.

John made the last introductions. But as the other members of the Gandhis rarely said anything and appeared to be little more than mere ciphers included to make up the numbers, that was that was that.

A plate was pushed in front of Soap and he was urged to fill it.

The spread of food was quite beyond anything Soap had ever seen before, even when dining with the King of Shambhala. It is a fact well known to those that know it well, that the very rich like nothing better than to dine upon endangered species. But Soap was particularly impressed to find that here things were different. This selection of foodstuffs was entirely composed from extinct species.

Soap helped himself to the haunch of woolly mammoth.

John Omally filled Soap's glass with wine and spoke. 'As this is the anniversary of Jim's death,' he said, 'we gather together here to feast. To toast Jim's memory and to think of him. It's good to have you here, Soap. Norman would have come but as he's in prison he's had to cry off.'

'Norman in prison,' said Soap. 'What for?'

'It's quite a long story, but I'll keep it short. Norman built a race-horse for Jim.'

'Built him a racehorse?' Soap helped himself to the fillet of cave-bear. 'That sounds right, knowing Norman.'

'He's a most inventive lad. But you see, it was more than just a racehorse. And when Jim was killed, Norman didn't know quite what to do with it. So he thought that, in Jim's memory, he'd race it. And it was the first time the Derby was ever won by a unicorn.'

Soap's slice of cave-bear went down the wrong way.

'Small Dave rode it to victory.'

'But I thought Small Dave was wanted by the police. For biting off that manager's—'

'Cock,' said Pigarse.

'Penis,' said Soap.

'That sounds even ruder,' said Pigarse. 'Why do you think that is?'

Soap shook his head and Omally continued.

'Small Dave disguised himself as a woman. So he was the first woman ever to win the Derby. Made history, that did.'

Soap had no comment to make regarding history.

John went on. 'Do you recall what that Penist said to Small Dave?' he asked.

'Of course,' said Soap, checking out the Irish Elk. 'It was only a couple of days ago.'

Omally raised an eyebrow.'

'*Seems* like a couple of days ago. But she said that she saw him galloping to glory. So I suppose she was right, wasn't she?'

'She's always right. I've seen her myself on more than one occasion.'

'She jerks him off,' said Pigarse.

'She does not,' said John. 'But to go on with what I was saying, Norman named the unicorn The Pooley. And Small Dave pulled off the Derby win. And not just once, but four times in a row.'

'Hard to beat a unicorn, eh?' Soap forked sabre-toothed tiger onto his somewhat crowded plate.

'And no doubt he would have won again this year, if it hadn't been for the Incident.'

'Go on,' said Soap. 'Tell me the worst.'

'Small Dave was on Parkinson. In drag, naturally. He'd become something of a TV celeb. But being Small Dave, he'd imbibed rather too freely in the hospitality lounge and by the time it was his turn to come on, he was—'

'Pissed as a bishop,' said Pigarse. 'Pass me the dodo legs.'

'He was drunk,' said John. 'And you know what Parkie's like with the women.'

'No,' said Soap. 'What is he like?'

Omally made a knowing face, which spared him the use of the word 'allegedly'.

'Oh?' said Soap. 'Really?'

208

'So, Parkie starts chatting Small Dave up and Parkie puts his hand on Small Dave's knee, and the next thing you know there's trouble, and Dave's bitten off Parkie's—

'No!' Soap coughed up Mastodon. 'Not Parkie's penis too?'

'I'm afraid so. And you'll never guess who was another guest on that same show. Only Inspectre Hovis, Brentford's Detective in Residence.'

'So Small Dave's back in the suitcase.'

'A very special suitcase, built for the purpose. And of course Norman got arrested and banged up in prison. So he couldn't be with us tonight.'

'Pity,' said Soap, wondering whether he should eat what he had on his plate so far, before trying to fit on any Siberian Rhinoceros. 'But at least you've survived a free man, John. And you've got this incredible house.'

'I got it pretty cheaply, as it happens. The last of the Crawfords snuffed it and the place came on the market. It had acquired a bit of an evil reputation.'

'The Curse of the Crawfords?' said Soap.

'A ghost. And not a family one. A new one. Although I've never seen it.'

'I don't like ghosts,' said Soap. 'Don't like them at all.'

'Have you ever seen a ghost?' asked Litany.

'Loads,' said Soap. 'It's in the family. My dad was a seer, my mum a psychic, even our cat read the tarot. That's one of the reasons I went beloooow. To get away from ghosts. The tales I could tell you . . .'

'Yes,' said John. 'But they're better left until after the ten o'clock watershed . . .'

'I heard,' said Pigarse, 'that there's a tribe of dwarves with tattooed ears living under Brentford and that they come up at night and snatch away infants from their cots.'

'Wherever did you hear *that*?' Soap asked.

'I read it in the *Brentford Mercury*. There was this whole series of articles written by the editor about how he'd travelled to the centre of the Earth and planted the nation's flag. And he had photos and everything. He was knighted by Prince Charles. I've got a copy of his book. It was a bestseller. Published by Virgin, of course.'

Soap took to the grinding of his teeth.

The evening passed as such evenings do, with great conversation and mighty consumption of liquor. The noise of laughter rose to unthinkable heights, as the quality of humour sank to unthinkable depths.

Ricky took out his Virgin walkman (no longer Virgin-*Sony*) and put on the headphones. Soap saw a look of contentment appear on his face.

'What are you listening to?' asked Soap. 'Is it the Gandhis' music?'

Ricky's look was one of bliss. Soap Distant nudged his elbow. 'What are you listening to?'

'Pardon?' Ricky lifted an earphone.

'I said, what are you listening to?'

'It's a tape of silence,' Ricky said.

'What? You're listening to a blank tape?'

'No.' Ricky switched off his walkman. 'It's a recording of silence. Made in the meditation chamber beneath the Potala, in Tibet.'

'I've been there,' said Soap. 'And it *is* a very quiet place.'

'It's the quietest place on Earth, apparently. This is a digital recording made of that silence. It's in stereo, too.'

'Stereo silence?'

'Here, have a listen.' Ricky passed the walkman and Soap slipped on the headphones.

'Just press the on button,' said Ricky.

And Soap pressed the on button.

And silence fell upon Soap.

Complete and utter silence. Blissful silence. Peaceful, healing, all-consuming silence. Soap could no longer hear the laughter and ribaldry. All the noise of the room had gone and only silence remained.

Soap switched off the walkman and the row came rushing back.

'That's incredible,' said Soap. 'I couldn't hear anything at all. Except for utter silence.'

'Good, isn't it?' said Ricky. 'And great if you've got noisy neighbours. You just stick the tape on your sound system and turn it up full blast. And then the whole room's filled with silence. Helps me to get off to sleep when we're on tour, I can tell you.'

Ricky took his walkman back and put on his headphones once more.

210

'Could you make me a copy of that tape?' Soap asked.

But Ricky couldn't hear him.

Soap chatted with the other Gandhis, even the ones who had nothing to say. The ones who had nothing to say said to Soap that they were really pleased to meet him and how John had told them so much about him and what a nice evening it was and had Soap heard their new album? Which was called *Armageddon: The Musical* and was based on the bestselling novel by the famous Johnny Quinn.

Soap said that he was sure he could remember reading a book by Johnny Quinn, way back in the sixties, but the name of it had slipped his mind.

The evening passed further on and soon became the middle of the night. Soap stifled yawns. It had been a long day, and a hard'n. He peeped at the wristwatch. What *was* the time?

The face of the watch was a blank and unlit screen.

Soap peered a bit more closely and wondered which button you had to press to get the time up.

'That's a smart watch,' said Pigarse, leaning far too close to Soap. 'Wingarde's got a watch like that.'

'Has he?' said Soap. 'Well, that clinches it.'

'Clenches what?' asked Pigarse. 'Bottom cheeks?'

'Very possibly,' said Soap. 'But it has to be the same Wingarde. He did have some fancy wristwatch, but I didn't get to look at it closely. I'd just jumped out of a window and I was hovering in the air.'

'Go on, Soap,' said Omally. 'It's well past the ten o'clock watershed now.'

'Well,' said Soap, 'perhaps I *should* tell you all about it.'

'Let me try your wristwatch on,' said Pigarse.

'No,' said Soap. 'I'd rather you didn't.'

'That's what bleeding Wingarde said. Come on, I won't break it.'

Pigarse lunged forward to snatch at the wristwatch, but his hand struck something invisible and he fell back wailing and clutching at his fist.

'What did you do to him, Soap?' said Omally. 'He's the drummer, you've injured his hand.'

'I didn't do anything.' Soap shook his head. 'He just lunged at me, you saw it and . . .'

Soap's voice trailed away. It was the watch. It had to be the watch.

211

What was it Wingarde had said? Lifespan chronometer incorporating personal defence mechanism. That was what he'd said.

'So,' said Soap, 'what do we have here?' And he tinkered with the buttons on the watch.

And then there was a click and a bang and a whoosh.

And there was no more of Soap Distant.

The Inevitable Cop-out Ending

The grey-whiskered father looked down at the boy
And reached for his teeth in the glass.
He slotted them onto his old wrinkled gums
And rattled his fingers and crackled his thumbs,
And suggested the lad take a seat by the window.
Because he had questions to ask.

Now tell me, young fellow, the old fellow said,
As the lad spread his feet on the pouffe.
There are things I must know, for my time's drawing near.
And I'll be just a memory later this year.
So please do me the kindness to answer me this,
Before you're away on the hoof.

Just name it, my daddy, the young boy replied,
Ask anything under the sun.
If it's answers you want, then I'll speak as I find,
So go right ahead, be assured I don't mind.
Consider the floor to be yours, as I've said,
Spit it out, you old son of a gun.

Thus and so, said the ancient, my question is this—
But the telephone interjected.
And the boy went to answer it out in the hall,
And a large moose's head that hung there on the wall
Fell down on his father and crushed him to death.
Which is pretty much what we expected!

20

As Soap had no idea what to expect, he was not particularly surprised when he found himself in yet another empty room. This one, however, differed from the last in that it retained all of its fixtures and fittings. This room had merely been emptied of people. Soap was all alone now in Omally's dining room. It was cold and dark and somewhat eerie.

Moonlight sidled in through the French windows and fell upon the Crawford faces on the wall, which seemed to view Soap disapprovingly.

'Damn,' said Soap. 'Not again.'

And then he fell backwards onto the floor.

Someone had obviously moved his chair, so it wasn't there to greet his bum upon its future return.

Effing and blinding, as was now his habit, Soap struggled onto the vertical plane. It was not a matter of where am I now? It was a matter of *when*? The remains of the feast could be seen in the moonlight, so surely it was only a matter of hours.

Soap considered checking his watch. Soap scrubbed around that idea.

'Woooooooooooooooooo,' came a voice from a darkened corner. 'Woooooooooo and woe.'

Small hairs rose all over Soap and his face took on a haunted expression. Which, although appropriate, didn't help too much.

'Woe unto the house of Distant,' went the voice.

Soap stammered out a 'Who's there?'

'This is the ghost of Gunnersbury House.'

'Oh my,' went Soap, a-clutching at his heart. 'Oh my, no, hold on there.'

'Hold on there?' asked the ghost.

'Hold on there, I know that voice. Pooley, is that you?'

'Of course it's me,' said the ghost of Jim.

Soap clenched hard upon chattering teeth and sank down into the nearest chair. 'Oh, Jim,' he said. 'Oh, Jim.'

'It's very good to see you, Soap,' said Pooley.

Soap squinted into the semi-darkness. 'I can't see you,' he said.

'I'm over here by the window. But I won't come out of the shadows. You wouldn't want to see what I look like now.'

'I'm so sorry, Jim. It's awful.'

'It's horrible,' said Jim. 'Being a ghost. It's cold and it's lonely and you hear things in the night. Things that make noises beloooow.'

'Probably the dwarves,' said Soap, shaking away like a good'n.

'It's *not* the dwarves,' said Jim. 'And calm yourself down, Soap. It's only me.'

'I'm sorry.' Soap shook and quivered. 'I know it's you, but you're d—'

'Dead,' said Jim. 'But we don't use the "D" word. Get yourself a drink and pull yourself together.'

Soap found an empty glass and a full bottle and set to correcting the imbalance.

'But what are you doing *here*?' he asked Jim. 'I thought ghosts haunted the places where they, you know, "D"'d.'

'You reach out,' said Jim. 'At the moment of death. You reach out to your nearest. I reached out to John. He was here in Gunnersbury House, chatting with Lord Crawford about putting the Gandhis on. I reached out to here and this is where I've stayed. I'm stuck here. But John can't hear or see me and although I've been able to put the wind up a few people you're the first old friend who has the gift, as it were.'

Soap drank up and refilled his glass. 'You shouldn't be here, Jim,' he said. 'You were a good man. You should have gone to the good place. It's not right for you to still be here.'

'I can't leave,' said Jim. 'Not yet. Not until everything's been put right. And my spirit cannot be at rest until the man who killed me is brought to justice.'

Soap's teeth rattled against his wine glass.

'Sorry,' said Jim. 'The afterlife can get a little gloomy.'

'I think you're taking it all very well.'

'Yeah, well, I've come to terms with it now. For the first couple of years I raged about like a wild man. But it didn't help.

'I'll sort it for you, Jim,' said Soap, 'trust me, I will.'

'I rather hoped you'd say that. You know that you were right all along, don't you? About history being changed while you were belooow? Branson on the banknotes and all that kind of business.'

'Oh yes,' said Soap, a-swigging. 'I know.'

'But there's still a lot of it that you don't know and so I'm going to tell it to you now.'

And so Jim did. He told Soap the lot. About THE END and Dr Trillby and Geraldo and the fanboys from the future and how Wingarde had been saving rock stars' lives because Jim had pulled off The Pooley. And Soap told Jim all that he knew and all that he'd been through and by the end of it all they both agreed that they seemed to know quite a lot about everything.

Which they almost did, of course.

'You must find Geraldo,' said Jim. 'You've seen his photograph, so you know what he looks like. He said he'd go back in time and reverse everything that Wingarde had done. But he obviously hasn't got round to it yet. He's probably still going from concert to concert. But I'm sure he'll turn up for this one and I'm sure that if you tell him what Wingarde's up to now he'll sort it all out.'

'Okay,' said Soap. 'But listen, Jim. Everything points to Wingarde, you know. That he was the one who killed you. To clear the family name because you pulled off The Pooley.'

'I know,' said Jim. 'But it doesn't make any sense. He killed me because I pulled off The Pooley. But I never got to pull off The Pooley, because he killed me first. So if I never pulled off The Pooley, he would have had no reason to kill me in the first place.'

'Do you know what I think, Jim?' said Soap.

'No, Soap, what do you think?'

'I think time travel really complicates things.'

Jim looked at Soap.

But Soap didn't look at Jim.

'Quite,' said Jim.

'And I'll tell you something else.'

'Go on.'

'I have a score to settle with that Leo. He nicked my photos and took the credit for my journey to the centre of the Earth.'

'Well, you did nick his wristwatch first.'

'I didn't nick it. It just fell into my hand.'

'Just leave it all to Geraldo, Soap. Let him sort it out.'

'All right. But that Wingarde must be brought to justice for what he did to you. And then you can rest easy in your grave and go to the good place.'

'Yes,' said Jim, 'I'd like that very much.'

Soap stretched and yawned. 'I'm really knackered,' he said. 'I was knackered anyway. But now I reckon I've got the time traveller's equivalent of jetlag.'

'That's really tough,' said Jim, 'because you're not going to get much sleep.'

'I'll have a lie-in tomorrow.'

'No, you won't, Soap. This is the day after tomorrow. This is the day of the concert.'

The Men Aboard the Lorries
(More big juggernaut action)

Over the hill and into the town
The juggernaut came roaring.
Into the sleepy hamlet where
The folk are warm and snoring.

Down the narrow shopping street,
Over the blind road-sweeper's feet.
Cracking the tile with its exhaust heat
The juggernaut came roaring.

Onto the lanes where the farmers walk
The juggernaut came screaming
Past libraries where none may talk
And the out-of-work sit dreaming.

Over the cobbledy cobbledy way,
Ruining the blacksmith's holiday.
Distracting the faithful as they pray,
The juggernaut came screaming.

The men aboard the lorries
Laugh as they drive along.
And don't give a toss for simple folk
And can't tell right from wrong.

21

Now one of the best things about outdoor rock concerts is that they involve a lot of big juggernaut action. There's all that beefy boy-type equipment that has to be loaded up and hauled about and erected by a lot of manly men in construction worker's helmets, who whistle at girls and swear a lot.

It's a manly man's game is rock music. Always has been, always will be. That's the way it is.

Gunnersbury Park was a big old park and a pretty nice one, too. The house was originally built for the first Earl of Gunnersbury, Sir Rupert Crawford, who made his packet from the slave trade and the transportation of opium. Whether Sir Rupe would have gone for rock 'n' roll is anyone's guess. And what he would have thought about all those 'slaves to the rhythm' who would shortly be filling up his grounds can only be imagined.

He would no doubt have approved of all the dope they'd be bringing and, as a manly man of some renown, he would certainly have loved all the big juggernaut action.

Which was a shame, really, as there wasn't going to be any.

It was somewhat after eight of the morning clock when the snoozing Soap was raised from his slumbers by what can only be described as a bloody horrible racket.

'Aaaagh!' went Soap, falling down from his chair. 'Bugger my boots, what's that?'

No answer came from Pooley. For with the coming of the dawn his shade had faded all away. This is often the case with ghosts. It's a tradition, or an old teeth–chatterer, or something.

Soap crawled over to the french windows and peered out. 'Bugger my boots,' he said once more and not without good cause.

For drifting in from the lands of the west there came a marvellous sight. A helicopter of awesome proportions, all red, white and logoed. And slung beneath it an entire rock concert stage protected from the weather beneath a vast aluminium half-dome, complete with sound equipment, lighting gantries, mixing desks and all the bits and bobs. It was a single unit. One of the first Virgin Integrated Outdoor Concert Systems. Solar-powered and digitized and all that kind of caper.

The helicopter moved forward and hovered overhead, blotting out the sky and giving Soap the willies. Servo units engaged, cogs meshed, hawsers hawsed and down to the grass before Gunnersbury House came the stage with all its bits and bobs and bugger-my-booteries.

Soap watched the descent, boggle-eyed, shaking his head at the wonder of it all. 'It's a bit close,' he observed as the stage touched down and minced John's car to scrap. Stagehands and roadcrew swarmed down ropes from the helicopter's belly and disconnected the hawsers and suchlike. The helicopter rose and swept away and that was that was that.

Soap rose to his feet, opened the french windows and strolled out-side to view the rear of the stage.

And down from it jumped two men. They wore black suits and sunglasses. One held a pistol, the other a walkie-talkie set.

'Pass!' shouted the gunman in a menacing manner.

'What?' replied Soap, rather too shocked to move.

'Backstage pass. Whip it out.'

'I'm with the band,' said Soap, which sometimes works.

The chap with the walkie-talkie shouted into it. 'Intruder in rear-stage area,' he shouted. 'One for the wagon. First of the day.'

'Now just you see here!' said Soap.

'And he's a *live* one. Best bring the dogs.'

'Hang about,' said Soap.

'Yes, hang about.' The voice was Omally's and the rest of him accompanied it. John came marching up the drive, paused for a moment to view the area where his car should surely have been, shook his head and approached the rear-stage area.

'Ah, good morning, Mr Omally.' The men in black saluted John. The one with the walkie-talkie struck himself on the head with it, the one with the gun did likewise and almost put his eye out.

'That fills me with confidence,' said Soap.

'This man is with me,' said Omally. 'Here, take this, Soap, and put it on.'

John handed Soap one of those plasticized backstage pass jobbies which can be a passport to sexual bliss if you flash them in front of the right women. Soap clipped it onto his lapel.

'Off about your business,' said John, and the men in black went off about their business.

John led Soap away to his terrible kitchen. 'That was some stunt you pulled the night before last,' he said, forcing bread into a blackened toaster. 'Vanishing into thin air like that. Pigarse pooed his pants.'

'Yes, John, I'm sorry. I can explain about that. I've got to tell you everything.'

'Well, you'll have to do it later.' John peered into the toaster, from which smoke was already beginning to rise.

'No, John. I have to tell you now.'

'Later,' said John, fanning his face. 'I have to meet the Beatles.'

They came in by helicopter too. It dropped down onto the lawn beside the stage and Soap munched on burnt toast and watched it through the unwashed kitchen window.

He saw the Beatles being helped down by their minders and nurses and fussed about and settled into wheelchairs.

'That Wingarde has a lot to answer for,' said Soap, spitting black bits into the sink. 'And I'm going to punch him right on the nose when I see him.'

Pigarse wandered into the kitchen. 'Aaaagh!' he went and he clutched at his trouser seat and limped away at speed.

'Fucking hell, what a pong,' said Ricky breezing in. 'Oh, it's you, Soap. Where did you spring from?'

221

'Yes, I'm very sorry about that, you see—'

'Well, never mind,' said Ricky. 'It's always a joy to see Pigarse filling his kecks. Have the Beatles arrived?'

'They're out there,' said Soap, pointing. 'They look really old and knackered.'

'That's because they *are* old and knackered. Old rockers never know when to quit. It's all the buzz from playing live. The adrenaline rush. Makes you feel like a god. Once you've had it you never want to lose it.'

'It's not for me,' said Soap. 'But listen, Ricky. A couple of things. Could you lend me that silence tape?'

'Sure, I won't need it today.' Ricky pulled out his walkman and handed it to Soap. 'What else do you want?'

'I have to find someone who will be in the crowd. Will there be surveillance cameras set up?'

'There always are, they're all over the place.'

'So could I get access to the control room or something? Look at the screens or whatever?'

'You've got your security clearance card there. You can go pretty much where you want.'

'Splendid,' said Soap. 'So which bands are playing today?'

'Well, there's us. But we're near the bottom of the bill today.'

'Is Litany going to do her magic thing as soon as you go on?'

'No, not until right at the end, when the Beatles have finished their set. She's going to do one of those Marilyn Monroe numbers. "Happy birthday, Mr President". She'll be doing "Happy birthday, Mr Lennon". Then she'll let it rip.'

'So who else is playing?'

'All the usual suspects. The Who. Jimi Hendrix. Elvis will be making an appearance.'

'Elvis playing Brentford!' Soap whistled.

'Doing stuff from his new rap album. And there's Ali Dada.'

'Never heard of them,' said Soap.

'And Screaming Lord Sutch and the Savages.'

'God bless Screaming Lord Sutch,' said Soap★.

★And so say all of us. Sadly missed.

222

'They'll all be arriving soon,' said Ricky. 'What time is it, do you know?'

Soap almost pressed a button on the wristwatch. Almost, but not quite. 'I don't know,' said Soap. 'It's broken. But tell me this also: will Wingarde and his guru be coming?'

Ricky nodded his big-haired head. He still had all the big hair, although it hadn't been mentioned of late. 'The little shit will be here. Throwing his weight around and making an arsehole of himself.'

'Good,' said Soap. 'He and I have much to discuss.'

'Rather you than me,' said Ricky. 'I can't stand the bastard.'

The bastard was having his breakfast. The full English and heavy on the ketchup. He sat at a table on the roof terrace of the Virgin Mega City Rich Bastard's Tower.

The roof terrace afforded Wingarde a fine view of Brentford. As he munched upon his egg, he could see all the earth-movers moving earth and the diggers digging away.

Wingarde raised a pair of binoculars and smiled as he watched the demolition ball cleaving its way into number seven Mafeking Avenue.

'Out with the old and in with the new,' crooned Wingarde, setting down his bins and tucking into some unburnt toast.

'*You're very chipper this morning,*' said The Voice.

'Well, it's all moving along nicely. You're pleased with the progress, I trust.'

'*Most pleased. And I've rewarded you well for your labours, have I not?*'

'You certainly have.' Wingarde chewed upon a sausage. 'Mmmmph mmm, mmph, mmph,' he continued.

'*Don't speak to God with your bloody mouth full.*'

'Sorry, God.' Wingarde wiped his chin. 'I was saying thank you very much. I really enjoy bossing people around.'

'*I thought it might appeal to you and it suits my purposes well.*'

'What exactly are your purposes?' Wingarde scooped up bacon. 'I keep on asking and you keep on being vague.'

'*Because it's none of your damn business. But I'll tell you this, Wingarde. That little town you see down there being ploughed away. From its earth will rise a mighty tower. A tower that will be a temple to science.*'

'Built in praise of you, sir?'

'Built in praise of me.'

'But why build it in Brentford? Brentford's such a dump.'

'Because, as anyone who knows their history will tell you, Brentford occupies the site of the Biblical Eden.'

'And that's important, is it?'

'You are a fuckwit, Wingarde. But, oh look, here comes your guru.'

'I don't know why I need a guru anyway,' whispered Wingarde. 'When I talk directly to you.'

'I've told you before, he's here to protect you. He has your best interests at heart, and mine also, although he does not know it.'

'Is that why you won't let me tell him about you?'

'Something like that. So just keep schtum and be nice to him. OK?'

'OK,' whispered Wingarde, scraping jam on to a piece of toast.

'Good morning, Wingarde,' said Dr Vincent Trillby, striding up in dressing gown and slippers. To either side of him strode Balberith and Gressil, but Wingarde couldn't see them, so he didn't poo his pants.

'Good morning, True Father,' said Wingarde, which was accurate enough.

'All going well with the demolition work?' Dr Trillby helped himself to some of Wingarde's bacon.

'Splendidly,' said Wingarde, pulling his plate beyond reach. 'But I do have a bit of bad news for you.'

'Oh yes?' Dr Trillby helped himself to some of Wingarde's coffee.

'Well, you know that wristwatch you had stolen?'

Dr Trillby nodded and spoke in a guarded manner. 'A family heirloom,' he said. 'Of great sentimental value.'

'Well, there's been a spot of bother. I was sent some surveillance footage. The chap who nicked it turned up on the street.'

'At last,' said Dr Trillby. 'I knew he would eventually.'

'Well, he tried to escape in a getaway car and a police helicopter blew it to buggeration. Slapped wrists all round. A bit of a cock-up.'

Dr Trillby's face took on an ashen hue. He rocked upon his heels and clenched his fists and bottom cheeks.

'That's you fucked, then,' said the voice of Leviathan.

'Pardon me?' said Wingarde.

'I'm talking to myself.'

'Are you having another of your mystical turns? When the saints speak through your mouth?'

'Something like that!' Dr Trillby turned shakily upon his heel and staggered from the terrace. Once out of sight of Wingarde, and all alone in the very posh lounge (well, almost all alone), he flung himself down to the goatskin rug and drummed his fists on the floor.

'What a pity for you,' said the voice of Leviathan. 'Your time-travel watch all blown to buggeration. You'll just have to stay in this century with us.'

'Leave me alone!' blubbered Trillby.

'No way, we're here to stay. And so are you, by the sound of it.'

'Listen.' Trillby ground his teeth. 'Just listen. I'm not saying it hasn't been fun. It has. But I returned to this century for one reason only. To fetch my wandering boy. I can see that he's done very well for himself here, but his mother wants him back. And I'm going to take him back no matter what.'

'Not now your watch has gone boom.'

Dr Trillby drummed his fists and thrashed his legs about. 'Oh, bollocks!' he shouted. 'Oh, bollocks bollocks bollocks!'

'They're a load of bollocks,' said Pigarse. 'I'm not saying hello.'

'They're the Beatles,' said John Omally. 'And although I don't think much of them myself they *were* Jim's favourites, so you'll be nice to them or else.'

'Or else *what*?' asked Pigarse. 'I'll give you a smack. I've done it before.'

'You've one hand bandaged. I wouldn't try your luck.'

'Luck doesn't enter into it when you fight as dirty as me.'

John made them all line up in the entrance hall. It was a very tidy entrance hall now. John had spent much of the previous day clearing it up, with no help at all from the Gandhimen. Under normal circumstances he would never have considered clearing it up, but, well, it's not every day you get to meet the Beatles.

'Look,' said John, inspecting his troops. 'They're old men. They're rock legends. Please show a bit of respect.'

Soap stuck his head out from behind the kitchen door. 'Can I meet the Beatles too?' he asked.

225

'All right,' said John. 'Get on the end of the line there, next to Pigarse.'

Soap got onto the end of the line and stood to attention.

'You twat,' Pigarse whispered.

The front door swung open and men in black entered. They flanked the doorway, flexing their shoulders and looking 'useful'. And then into the hall walked an old gentleman, supporting himself on an ebony cane.

'Blimey,' mumbled Soap. 'It's Eppy. Brian Epstein.'

'Old shirt-lifter,' said Pigarse.

Brian Epstein hobbled along the lined-up Gandhis, saying things like, 'So you're a Gandhi, are you?' and 'So you're a Gandhi too?'

'I'll nut him if he touches me,' said Pigarse.

The Beatles now made their appearance. Out of their wheelchairs but shaky on their ancient pins. They wibbly-wobbled along the line, saying the same sort of thing.

All except for Lennon, of course. Lennon hadn't lost it.

'I really love your music,' he said to Litany. 'You're a very talented lady.'

'Thank you,' said Litany. 'I'd love to sing to you before you go on stage. It would make a great difference, I promise.'

'That would be nice,' said Lennon. 'I'd like that very much.'

Soap got to shake hands with them all. He was, frankly, entranced. Overwhelmed. He knew it was all wrong. That it just shouldn't be. But here it was happening anyway. Here was he, Soap Distant, actually shaking hands with the Fab Four. It was a moment he would treasure for ever. A magical moment. A moment that nothing could spoil.

'I can see right through your nose,' said Ringo. 'Horrible, it is.'

Stuck-up Ducks

Quack quack go the feathered folk.
Their mating habits are a joke.
They never wear the old Dutch cap
Nor trouble with a condom.

Quack quack go the feathered fowl,
They have no truck with goose or owl.
Or Siamese strings and Ben Wa balls
Or plug-in rubber dildos.

Quack quack go the feathered clowns,
Getting off on watered downs.
Caring not for Roman Showers
Or ritual bondage rimming.

Quack quack go the feathered lads.
Knowing not their mums and dads.
They are a flock of bastards.
So who do they think they are, waddling about with their
beaks in the air, scorning harmless forms of deviant
sexual recreation when it's quite clear they don't have
enough morals to scribble down in big writing on a sheet
of Brentford Borough Council toilet paper?

A good question!
Quack indeed!

22

There were plenty of ducks on Gunnersbury Lake. But soon many of these would be taking to their wings. Driven from their dabblings by misbehaving fanboys tossing beer cans.

At just gone ten of the morning clock the park gates were opened and the 'ticket-holders only' flooded through.

Soap Distant stood on the concert stage beneath the great aluminium half-dome, hoping to get a glimpse of Geraldo. But as the green grass sank beneath the tidal wave of black-T-shirted youth, Soap's heart sank with it and a lump rose in his throat.

'Thousands of the ugly-looking buggers,' said Soap. And his voice carried through the speaker system and echoed all over the park.

It was a poor start to the proceedings. But in view of what was yet to come, it could well have been considered a high point.

In various bedrooms in Gunnersbury House various Gandhis were togging up in their stage clothes. They were very expensive stage clothes. Very exclusive stage clothes.

Pigarse struggled into a pair of leather drainpipe trousers.

On his bed sat an old gent with a tattooed face and a good line in scar tissue. 'Ram a codpiece down your crotch for art,' was his advice. 'It gets the girlies going and if they're disappointed later then it serves them right for being so cock-happy.'

'Cheers, Dad,' said Pigarse. 'I'll use your motorbike helmet.'

Litany sat at a dressing table in another of John's guest bedrooms. There seemed to be at least twelve such bedrooms, although John had never counted. All the bedrooms but his remained empty, but for the Gandhis' visits. John could have lived the rock 'n' roll lifestyle, had he so wished. He could have partied every night. But he didn't. He lived alone with his memories. Drunk for much of the time, but always there to do the Gandhis' business.

John sat upon Litany's bed, idly toying with one of her shoes.

Litany glanced at his reflection. 'Cheer up, John,' she said. This is going to be a big day. The day that we change history.'

'I know,' said John. 'I just wish Jim could have been here to see it.'

'You've got to let Jim go. It's been five years. If I can get over it so can you.'

'He was my bestest friend. I loved that man. In a manly mannish sort of a way.'

Litany adjusted her false moustache. It was green, as it was Saturday.

'Do you know what?' said John. 'I've never seen you without a false moustache on.'

'Nor have you ever seen me naked.'

'No, you're right about that.'

'I know you've wanted to,' said Litany, teasing about at her hair.

'It doesn't seem right. I thought that, perhaps, you and Jim . . .'

'Oh no,' said Litany. 'I never would have.'

'But he meant a lot to you.'

'But not in that way. He was someone I wanted to meet. Have always wanted to meet.'

'Who? Jim?'

'I can't explain it to you now. But one day I will, I promise.'

John rose from the bed and stretched a bit. 'I'd better get downstairs,' he said. 'And see how things are going.'

There were things going on all over the place on this particular day. At the Brentford nick, for instance. There were things going on in there.

'Right,' said Inspectre Sherringford Hovis. 'Right, now listen up here.'

He had a little row of constables lined up before him. They were an anonymous-looking bunch. But then constables always are. It's only when they rise up through the ranks and become detectives and suchlike that they take on all those lovable eccentricities that turn them into characters.

It's a tradition. Or an old cliché or something.

Inspectre Hovis took a pinch of snuff and paced over to the big notice board behind his desk. 'These young fellow-me-lads,' he said, pointing to a row of twelve grainy photographs. 'These young fellow-me-lads here.'

'Excuse me, sir,' said an anonymous constable who had a good memory, 'but aren't they the young fellow-me-lads who were caught on the speed-trap cameras five years ago?'

'Correct,' said Hovis. 'An unsolved case. And one that hangs over me like some sword of Androcles.'

'Excuse me, sir,' said an anonymous constable who had been classically trained (probably the one in the Greek Tragedy poem), 'but surely that should be Damocles. Androcles was the chap with the lion, you know.'

Inspectre Hovis nodded thoughtfully, paced over to the constable and stamped upon his foot. The classically trained constable hopped about for a bit and then returned to anonymity.

'One of these young fellow-me-lads,' said Hovis, returning to the photographs, 'is a murderer. I know this as surely as I know the back of my own head.'

'Excuse me, sir,' said an anonymous constable who had studied anatomy as well as turns of phrase. 'But surely that should be hand.'

Hovis paced over and stamped on *his* foot.

'To continue,' said the Inspectre. 'I know for a fact that these young fellow-me-lads are big fans of the Beatles. And if they do not turn up at the concert in Gunnersbury Park today then I'm a Welshman.'

Hovis paused.

The anonymous constable with the geography 'O' level kept his counsel.

'Just testing,' said Hovis. 'Now, I want all you lot in plain clothes.'

'Ooooooooooooo,' went the anonymous constables. 'Plain clothes, how exciting.'

'Yes, and none of you are to wear your helmets this time. It gives the game away. I want these young fellow-me-lads and I want them today. Do I make myself clear?'

The constables nodded anonymously.

'Right, then draw copies of these photos from the front desk, get into your civvies and bugger off to the park. Do you understand me? Bugger off!'

Buggery has always been a popular prison pastime.

It ranks higher than scratching your initials on cell walls, fashioning guns and keys from soap, lying about what crimes you've committed and protesting that you were fitted up by the filth.

Oh, and tunnelling out. Tunnelling out has always been a *very* popular prison pastime.

But not so popular as buggery.

Buggery wins hands down.

And bottom-cheeks apart.

Small Dave hadn't been buggered once. His reputation had entered the prison before him and any aspiring buggerers kept a respectful distance from the vindictive grudge-bearing wee bastard who had cut Parkie short on prime-time TV.

Not that Small Dave had been given a lot of opportunity to get himself buggered. He hadn't. They had banged Dave up in the high-security wing of the new Virgin Serving the Community Secure Accommodation Unit, which stood upon what had recently been an area of outstanding natural beauty, right next door to the Brentford nick.

Small Dave was a Rule 42 merchant. Solitary confinement and a close mesh on the window.

So Dave kept himself pretty much to himself. And busied himself with a pastime of his own.

Small Dave was tunnelling out.

Now, the major problem with tunnelling out is this: What *do* you do with all the earth?

Small Dave asked Norman about this during one of their little afternoon get-togethers, Norman inhabiting as he did the cell next door to Dave, and having already removed several of the bricks from the dividing wall by means of a chisel he'd fashioned from soap.

231

'The secret,' said Norman, 'is to dig not one hole but two. And put all the earth you've dug from the first hole into the second one.'

Small Dave made the face of thought. 'But what about all the earth you've dug from the second hole?' he asked.

'That's where the science comes in,' explained Norman. 'If you dig your second hole twice the size of your first hole, there'll be enough room in it for all the earth.'

Small Dave made with the approving nods. 'And is that how you're meaning to escape?' he asked.

'Actually, no. I thought I'd just blow my way out with the help of this stick of dynamite that Zorro the paper boy smuggled in.'

Small Dave whistled. 'That's a really big stick of dynamite,' he said. 'How exactly did Zorro manage to smuggle that in?'

Norman leaned over and downwards and whispered.

'Bugger that!' said Dave.

'Bugger me!' said Soap to himself. 'I'm never going to find Geraldo amongst all this mob.'

And quite a fair old mob it was by now. They were still plodding in through the park gates and bottle-necking up amongst the concession stalls and T-shirt stands and beer wagons and overpriced Portaloos and all the rest that had been flown in beneath a fleet of helicopters. But the Brentford sun was shining bravely and it did have all the makings of a beautiful day.

The world's media were there in force. Camera teams and up-front girlie presenters in boob tubes and belly button piercings. Eager to grab the old soundbites from the kids for the evening news.

Because the Beatles could still make the news. They were British Institutions, each of them. And they were safe and cosy establishment figures. Part of society's furniture.

They'd been bought off with their medals from the Queen (John had apologized for giving his back and Prince Charles had bunged him a replacement in the Royal Mail). And they gave the public what the public thought it wanted. Which is slightly different from giving the public what it actually needs. Which is a boot up the arse sometimes.

Yes, the Beatles were dead fab and the devil take the man who says they're not.

232

A girlie presenter in a boob tube with belly button piercing stuck out her mic towards a not-so-fattish chap in a black T-shirt and shorts. 'And do you dig the Beatles?' was her question.

'Not really,' said the chap in a squeaky voice. 'I think they're pretty crass. Although we've just come here straight from their last gig at Wembley Stadium.'

'But their last gig at Wembley Stadium was twenty-five years ago. You wouldn't even have been born.'

'Ah, no, of course not,' said the chap. 'What I meant to say was that we've just come here after watching it on video. But it's really the Gandhis we've come to see.'

'You dig the Gandhis, then?'

'And then some. And this concert's going to be special.'

'Special? In what way special?'

'Just make sure your cameras are pointing at the stage after the Beatles finish their set,' said Geraldo (for who else could it be but he?). 'You'll see something you'll never forget. Trust me. I know what I'm saying.'

'*Trust me, I know what I'm saying,*' said The Voice.

'Well, you should,' said Wingarde. 'You're God.'

'*Precisely,*' said The Voice. '*So perhaps you'd like to hurry up with what you're doing. God does not like conducting conversations with people who are sitting on the toilet.*'

'I'm almost done,' said Wingarde, making the face of strain. 'So what is it you want me to do this time?'

'*Something important that must be done today.*'

'But I'm meeting the Beatles today and I'm making history again. This concert could never have happened if it hadn't been for me.'

'*Are you forgetting me?*' asked The Voice.

'No, sir.' Wingarde finished his bottom business, rose from the bog seat, turned around and peered down at his doings.

'*Why do men always do that?*' asked The Voice. '*It's disgusting.*'

Wingarde shrugged and wiped his bum. Doing that horrible thing some people do, of folding and refolding the paper.

'*Word has reached me,*' said The Voice, '*that something is going to occur today. Something that could jeopardize my plans. And we wouldn't want that to happen, would we, Wingarde?*'

'Certainly not, sir,' said Wingarde, flushing the toilet and pulling up his pants.

'*So you're going to deal with it for me.*'

'Oh, must I?' Wingarde complained. 'I have to meet the Beatles. Do you think Lennon will remember me?'

'*I shouldn't think so, no. But I want you to go to the allotments and dig up—*'

'Allotments?' went Wingarde. 'Dig up?' went Wingarde.

'*Your AK47,*' said The Voice.

'My what? My what?'

'*Wingarde. You and I have been reshaping history. Reshaping history so that we can reshape the future. This time the future will go the way that I want it to go and nothing and no one will stand in my way. Do I make myself clear, Wingarde? Do I?*'

'Yes, sir, yes.' Wingarde clutched at his head. 'But couldn't you get someone else to do whatever it is? Get True Father to do it. He wouldn't mind if *you* told him.'

'*I do not wish Dr Tril . . . er . . . I mean, True Father . . . I do not wish True Father to hear my voice. You will do it, Wingarde. You will do it because I'm telling you to do it. You will do it, or else!*'

Wingarde mumbled and grumbled and fretted.

'*And I'll tell you what else you'll do.*'

'What's that?' mumble-grumbled and fretted the lad.

'*Wash your hands before you leave this bathroom. Ghastly little bugger.*'

Armageddon: The Musical
Words and music by Gandhi's Hairdryer
'God's Only Daughter'
(The song of Christeen, twin sister of Jesus Christ, written out of
the New Testament because her brother was given editorial
control.)

My mother Mary's pretty big with the Catholics,
And my brother's still pulling them in.
He's been at the top
Two thousand years non-stop
I think it's a sin.

I've been cheated of my place in history,
Robbed of my moment of fame.
Thrown on the dole
Cos the starring role
Went to my brother and I think it's a shame.

But God still thinks he's number one,
He smiles upon his only son.
And I get nothing thrilling
No, not even second billing.

Chorus
Though I'm
God's only daughter
I never got a walk on the water.
I never got a word in the Bible, no, nothing at all.
I'm God's only daughter,
I really do feel that I oughta
Have something to say.
Maybe today.

Statues of mother are weeping,
You should see them pulling a crowd.
But brother J's

235

Found another way.
He's got his face on the Turin Shroud.

Though I keep telling Dad I don't like it,
He doesn't hear a word that I say.
I can tell it's no use
When he makes some excuse,
And says he'll work it out on Judgement Day.

But I can hear them upstairs chatting,
And even though they talk in Latin,
I know exactly what they're saying:
'We've gotta keep the plebs from praying to—'

Chorus

I'm prepared to start in a small way,
I wouldn't make too much noise.
Just a manifestation
To a small congregation
Made up of teenage boys.

Somewhere sunny, like California,
Twenty acres fronting onto the sea.
When you're God's daughter
You can't afford t'
Be without some decent property.

I'd appear on every chat show,
I know how to knock 'm flat, so
Strike up the band with the drummers drumming.
Stop the world, cos Christeen's coming.

Chorus
(Repeat chorus with huge orchestral backing, etc.)

23

Johnny Quinn would have been chuffed.

To have seen *Armageddon: The Musical* performed as a rock opera, live upon stage in front of one hundred thousand young men in black T-shirts and shorts. That would have been quite something. That would have made his day.

But sadly old Johnny couldn't make it there in person. He had long since traded in his Biro for a shroud. And although it would be nice to think that he was sitting up there on a cloud somewhere, smiling down upon the proceedings, it is far more likely that he is way down deep in a place less pleasing, having the most popular prison pastime inflicted upon him by demons with bad breath and pointy peckers.

So Johnny wouldn't be seeing the show. Which was a shame, because it was a killer.

The Gandhis looked the business and the Gandhis were the business. They were rock stars and they did what rock stars do.

You can keep all your rappers in sportswear. And your dressed-down bands from the North. And you can forget all that crap about, 'We're into music, not image', or worse than that . . .

UNPLUGGED

Any musicians who play UNPLUGGED should be taken out quietly and put to the sword. A rock star should look like a rock star and a rock star should play like a rock star. And that means the twenty-minute Stratocaster solo and that means hair and that means leather. And if it's too loud you're too old.

And if you don't like it, then you can, in the words of Axl Rose, 'just fuck off.'

And another thing, too, while we're at it. It is not just *the right* of every young person to go off to a three-day rock festival, get smashed out of their bonces on forbidden substances and blow their minds to rock 'n' roll.

IT'S THEIR DUTY!

These things *must* be done and they *must* be done *now*! Too soon the jammy sandwich in the expensive sound system. Too soon the housework and the family saloon.

Remember the credo your fathers forgot.

TURN ON – TUNE IN – DROP OUT

And grow your hair big while you still have some to grow.

And never trust anyone over thirty.

It was around three thirty when Gandhi's Hairdryer opened the show and raised high the banner of rock.

It was big hair and tight leather trousers. It was Pigarse with his bulging crotch and Litany in a red rubber catsuit and four-inch stilettos. It was Ricky with his Stratocaster.

It was rock 'n' roll.

A great sigh rose from the crowd as Litany walked onstage. Ten zillion male pheromones took to head-butting one another. A coachload of Paul McCartney fans thrust their knitting into their handbags, pulled their cardigans over their faces and fled.

And that was only the blokes. Ha ha ha ha ha . . .

Cheer and ogle went the boys in the black T-shirts and shorts. Rock 'n' roll and rock went Gandhi's Hairdryer.

It is virtually impossible to describe in mere words a great rock performance. But, as Norman once said, 'It is only by attempting the impossible that we will achieve the absurd.'

238

So, let us pan gently across the stage with our belletristic camera, and, shunning the holophrastic, cry havoc and let slip the doggerels of war.

No. Let's not.

Let's go see how Soap is getting on.

Soap Distant and John Omally were down the front in the snake pit. That Holy of Holies before the stage, where only the Blessed possessing the sacred stage pass may bang their exalted heads and play their ethereal guitars.

And, as the Gandhis pumped out 'The Dalai Lama's Barn Dance', and Litany's vocals and Ricky's Strat meshed and intertwined and Pigarse's backbeat drove fists of sound through stomach walls and Dead Boy Doveston's Rickenbacker bass (the 1964 4001S model) underlaid a funk groove previously only achieved by the now legendary Bootsy Collins, whilst Matchbox Finial produced the power chords, Soap and John made mad eejits of themselves and worked up a sweat you could drown in.

And, as the last power chord crashed out and the final drum roll did its thing and the impossibly fast twiddly-diddly show-off Stratocaster tail-piece flourish blurred away to an end, the audience erupted into orgasmic applause, which shook the ground and registered 3.6 on the Richter Scale.

Which was a pretty good opening for any show.

'Brilliant.' John raised peace-fingers, whistled and cheered.

'That was something,' gasped Soap.

And all around them was hubbub and hollering, pushings of bodies and crush.

'John,' Soap shouted with what breath he could find. 'I have to speak to you. It's very important.'

'Later.' John whistled some more.

'John, it's very important.'

'Later. Later. Leave it, Soap.'

Soap Distant bawled into John's ear. 'John, I know who killed Jim.'

John Omally froze amidst the roaring, cheering crowd. 'What did you say?' he mouthed at Soap.

'I know who killed Jim. I have to talk to you.'

John mouthed a 'Come on,' and pushed Soap through the crush.

239

'Come on!' Wingarde shouted at his chauffeur as the long red, white and logoed limo slid between the building sites of Brentford. 'Get a move on, I'm missing the show.'

The chauffeur made a huffy face in the driving mirror. 'Well,' said he, in the manner known as camp, 'if you hadn't spent half the day digging on your allotment.'

Wingarde cradled the bundle on his lap. An oilskin cloth swathed the AK47. From between his gritted teeth he mumbled, 'It wasn't my bloody fault that I couldn't remember where I'd buried it.'

'Excuse me?' said the chauffeur.

'Nothing,' grumbled Wingarde.

'*You should have marked the place with a stick or something,*' said The Voice in Wingarde's head.

'A stick?' said Wingarde. 'A stick!' he said again.

'A stick?' said the chauffeur.

'Shut up!' said Wingarde.

'*Don't tell God to shut up,*' said The Voice.

'Not you, sir,' said Wingarde.

'That's more like it,' said the chauffeur.

Wingarde whispered into his hand. '*You* could have told me where it was buried. You are God, after all.'

'That's very sweet of you,' said the chauffeur, whose hearing was very acute, 'and I've always rather fancied you. Shall we give the concert a miss, do you think, and just go back to my house?'

Back in Gunnersbury House, with the Gandhis' music rattling the windowpanes and playing merry hell with the foundations, John Omally sat at his grimy kitchen table and listened in silence while Soap told him his tale.

'Oh my God,' he whispered, when the lad had done. 'Oh my God, my God.'

Soap stared at the Irishman. He looked on the verge of collapse. The colour had faded away from his face and his hands shook terribly.

'I'm so sorry, John,' said Soap. 'Sorry about Jim and sorry I had to spring all this on you.'

'It's all right, Soap.' John took breaths to steady himself, but these met with little success. 'It's all right. It all makes sense to me now. Why Geraldo wanted my autograph when he met me. Why Jim was so secretive. All of it. It all falls into place.'

'So you can see why it's so important that we find Geraldo today.'

John nodded slowly, his voice was scarcely a whisper. 'You find him, Soap, and let me deal with Wingarde.'

'Now hold on, John. Don't do anything stupid.'

'Stupid?' John's eyes flashed and his trembling hands became fists. 'He killed Jim and that's all I need to know.'

'Yes, I know that's how it looks. But we can't actually prove anything.'

'He'll confess to me,' said Omally. 'And then I will carry out his execution.'

'No, John, that isn't the way.'

Omally climbed unsteadily to his feet. He reached out a hand to Soap, who took it. 'Soap,' said he. 'This is where you and I part company again. You're a good man, Soap. Jim was a good man and you're a good man too.'

'You sound a bit like Brian Epstein,' said Soap. 'But please don't do this, John.'

'It has to be done. Call it revenge, call it whatever you will. But I have to do it, all the same.'

Soap looked up at Omally and they solemnly shook hands. 'There's nothing I can say that will talk you out of this, is there?' said Soap.

'Nothing, my friend.'

'Can I give you a hug?'

'Certainly not,' said John. 'Goodbye.'

'Goodbye,' said Soap. 'And good luck.'

There had been quite a lot of talk of late in the press regarding the return of the death penalty. Well, in those papers owned by the Virgin Newsgroup at any rate. They'd been running a competition, inviting readers to write in with their suggestions for a new and novel form of public execution that could be broadcast on the Virgin Community TV Network.

Inspectre Hovis had *not* written in. Not that he wasn't for bringing

241

back hanging. He was. But the line, in his opinion, had to be drawn somewhere.

Unlike his constables, Inspectre Hovis was not in plain clothes. Nothing about *him* was plain. He was a character, and as a character he was dressed in style. Today it was a four-piece blue suede suit and a rather dashing pair of riding boots. However, at the present moment, all this sartorial excess was hidden from view. Because Inspectre Hovis was invisible.

He was sitting in one of the latest line in Virgin Community Police helicopters. One with the new stealth mode. This was hovering soundlessly, employing its exterior aural camouflage modification. Based, no doubt, on the principle of Ricky's silence tape. But who can say for certain?

The Inspectre's invisible person hung a mere twenty feet above the cheering crowd of Gunnersbury Park.

'Take us up,' Hovis told the pilot. 'And make us reappear. The last time I had an experience like this was back in sixty-seven, when Lord Crawford and I did some really bad acid. Mind you, it wasn't fanboys we saw down there that time. It was vampire sheep.'

The pilot took the helicopter up to five hundred feet and re-engaged reality.

'That's better,' said Hovis, examining his person. 'And now tell me about all this electronic hocus-pocus you have on the dashboard.'

'Actually,' said the pilot, who was a stickler for correct terminology, 'it's not called a dashboard. It's an instrument panel.'

The helicopter dipped alarmingly as Hovis stamped hard on the pilot's foot.

'Right, sir,' said the pilot, as soon as he had regained control. 'Beneath this aircraft is the new High-Spy 3000 Series surveillance camera. One thousand times magnification. Infra-red and ultra-violet tracking systems. Fully integrated missile guidance lock-on facilities.'

'Demonstrate,' said Hovis.

'Certainly, sir. Would you like me to blow up that band on the stage?'

'Very much,' said Hovis. 'But I meant the camera. Tell me how the camera works.'

'Well, there's not much to it, really. Light enters the lens and passes into a system of refracting mirrors that—'

242

The helicopter took another alarming dip.

'I meant, show me how I work the camera.'

'Just jiggle the little joystick,' said the pilot.

Hovis jiggled the joystick and the camera scanned the crowd.

Soap sat in one of the Virgin control boxes, peering at video screens. These too were scanning the crowd, on the look-out for anyone who was having too much of a good time.

On one of these Soap could see Omally. The Irishman was *not* having a good time. He was standing at the park gates, his hands behind his back, no doubt awaiting the arrival of Wingarde.

Soap sighed and turned his attention to the other screens. Crowds and crowds and more crowds. Black T-shirts and black T-shirts and an odd little group wearing kaftans and beads.

'Plain-clothed policemen,' said Soap. 'And they seem to be look-ing for someone.'

Soap leaned back in his chair and drummed his fingers on his knees. He had to find Geraldo and he had to find him soon. Soap felt certain that if he could get to Geraldo, before John got to Wingarde, matters could be brought to a satisfactory conclusion, without the need for bloodshed.

It was a good, pure thought, was that. And one that was worthy of a Buddhist such as Soap. And, if this had been a perfect world, where life was lived in little movies and there was such a thing as justice, Soap's worthy thought would have earned him a bit of Instant Karma and he would have been rewarded by an instant sight-ing of Geraldo.

But, as events have so far proved beyond any shadow of a doubt, this is *not* a perfect world. And so Soap sat there in the control box and saw nothing whatever.

And after half an hour of this, poor Soap fell fast asleep.

Hoppers

There's too many Hoppers for this time of year.
They come in on the wind, I hear.
They get up your nose and into your ear.
I think it's time for action.

Brave words are fine, but insubstantial.
What we need is help, financial.
A government grant would do the trick.
It needs some toff to shake the stick.
Then, if everything starts to click,
We'll really get some action.

There's too many Pikers for this time of day.
They fall from the clouds (or so they say).
And crawl up your bum while you sleep in the hay.
I think it's time for action.

Proud talk is well, but it's not enough.
We need more, when the going's rough.
A word from the Pope would spin the coin,
Or Johnny B. could write a poem.
Or sing a song to get things goin',
And then we'd see some action.

There's too many tinkers in the street.
They always get beneath your feet.
They make you trip and drop your sweet.
I think it's time for action.

Great oaths are grand, but money talks.
We need police to guard our walks.
A dozen for The Avenue,
And in each sweetshop, one or two.
And plain-clothed coppers, quite a few,
And then we'd see some action.

There's too many *things* . . .
. . . hey, come back, fellas, I haven't finished . . .
. . . hey, fellas . . . wait for me . . .
. . . come back . . .
. . . damn . . .

24

Now it is the nature of *things*, that they do not occur in isolation. *Things* happen all at once or not at all. There must surely be some reason for this. But it is probably one that is beyond all human understanding. Like why people who do not engage in sports wear sportswear. Perhaps it is that *things* simply don't like to happen alone. They crave the company of other *things* to happen with. They like to buddy-up and go about mob-handed.

There's just no telling, with *things*.

Of course, we do our best to fight against *things*. We try to put *things* off and leave *things* 'til tomorrow. But *things* still get on top of us. *Things* conspire to grind us down. In fact *things* really get on our nerves. *Things* drive us to distraction.

And so, as we reach the conclusion of our tale, it should come as no surprise to find that *things*, which have been building up, are now about to happen all at once.

And happen, as *things* so often do, with a bang.

It was now nearly eight of the evening clock and the Beatles were about to go onstage. But, *nearly eight*? Can this be right? Some *things* should have happened by now. But, no, *things hadn't* happened.

Soap had slept through the balance of the day, missing all the really good bands. Bands which should have received some attention and been described in considerable detail. As indeed should the Gandhis' performance. But they hadn't. And *it* wasn't. Because, let's face it, our tale really isn't so much about the music itself. Our tale is about *other things*.

Other things which have to do with Wingarde. And so where is *he*? John Omally has been standing at the park gates for nearly five hours, grinding his teeth and shuffling his feet and planning a terrible vengeance. But there is still no sign of Wingarde's car, because Wingarde's car has made a slight diversion. Wingarde has spent the afternoon at the house of his chauffeur. Where, with permission from The Voice, he has been engaging in certain *things* which need not concern us here.

And what about Inspectre Hovis? Well, *he* is still in the hovering helicopter, scanning the crowd. But has he caught sight of Geraldo and his pals? He has not. And have the plain-clothed constables caught sight of Geraldo and his pals? No. They have not.

And what is Dr Trillby up to? And where, for that matter, is Prince Charles, who was expected to make a spectacular arrival in a hot-air balloon, but has so far failed to appear. Who knows?

So *things* just haven't happened. *Things* have been waiting to happen. And *things will* happen. Happen all at once, they will.

And happen with a bang.

The bang, when it happened, was a good'n. A right royal belter of a bang. It tore the outside wall from Norman's cell and flung it in pieces across the prison yard and through the wire perimeter fence.

Norman, cowering beneath mattresses in Small Dave's cell, raised a smiling, if now slightly smoke-blackened face. 'That went rather well,' said he.

Small Dave, who had been cowering under Norman, said, 'I tend to agree. And now, if you'll take the advice of one who knows these things, we had better do some running.'

Sirens wailed, alarm bells rang. They upped and did some running.

Inspectre Hovis was running out of patience. 'I've had enough of this,' he shouted and he kicked the instrument panel. The surveillance telescreen rocked on its mounts and then displayed a curious image.

'What is *that*?' Hovis asked.

'You appear to have, er, *nudged* it into infra-red mode, sir. Those are the heat images of the people in the crowd.'

'I can see that,' said Hovis. 'But look at that little group there, gathered by the front of the stage. Why are their images different from everybody else's?'

'Oooooh, yes,' said the pilot, peering at the telescreen. 'That *is* strange. They appear to be radiating some unusual form of energy. It's almost as if they're vibrating at a different frequency from everyone else. Faster, somehow.'

'Vibrating *faster*? It's *them*! Take us down at once.' Inspectre Hovis snatched up his police walkie-talkie and bawled into it at the top of his voice. 'Attention plain-clothed unit!' he bawled. 'Suspects are grouped together directly in front of the concert stage. Move in and make immediate arrests. At once, do you hear me? At once!'

And all at once Soap Distant awoke, by falling from his chair. He scrambled up in the usual confusion and almost checked the time on his watch. 'Oh no,' cried Soap, gawping up at the surveillance screens. 'The Beatles are on. I've been asleep. And oh—' He paused. 'It's Geraldo. Down at the front by the stage. And oh—' He paused once more. 'It's the plain-clothed policemen and they're heading in his direction.'

Soap kicked his fallen chair across the control room and Soap sprang into action.

And John Omally ceased kicking his heels and sprang to attention. Wingarde's limousine came cruising through the open gates, with Wingarde at the wheel.

John stepped into its oncoming path and sought to flag it down.

'Down!' cried Hovis to the pilot. 'Land this thing at once.'

'But, sir. There's nowhere to land. Unless I fly us out to the back of the crowd.'

'No!' Hovis pointed. 'Land there! Land on that!'

248

'What, on top of the stage canopy, sir? You mean land directly above the stage?'

'Why not? It looks strong enough.'

'But, sir. The Beatles are about to perform. We can't interrupt the Beatles.'

'Then stick this thing into stealth mode and engage the aural camouflage. And then no one will hear or see us land, will they?'

'All right,' said the pilot.

'All right,' said John Lennon. 'It's good to see you all.'

The crowd responded with riotous applause. Well, it was pretty good to see John.

'There's something you might have noticed,' said the great one, adjusting the strap on his Rickenbacker. John had always favoured the Rick, particularly the 325 model in the now legendary Capri series, which was launched in 1958.

Unlike the solid Strat, the Rick has a hollow body shell, but with a similar three-pickup arrangement. George Harrison, of course, preferred a Gretsch, the black Duo-Jet being his favourite. McCartney popularized the Höfner 500/1 violin bass, onto which he always taped the list of songs to be performed during the set.

These are the sort of *things* that *really* matter.

And it is only to be regretted that we don't have the time to delve into them more deeply now.

But we don't.

'You might have noticed,' said Lennon, 'that me and the boys are looking somewhat perkier than we have done lately.'

And it was true, they did look a whole lot perkier.

There was evidence of new hair upon the balding pates. Sagging bellies had been uplifted, bandy old legs straightened. It was almost as if the Fabs had grown thirty years younger in a matter of minutes. Which indeed they had.

'We feel just great,' the great one continued. 'And it's all thanks to a little lady called Litany, who sang to us before we came on. And I think she's going to come out and sing for *you*, after we're done. Just like she did for us.'

A roar went up from the long-standing Gandhi fans. Could this really be true? Had Litany really got her magic back?

249

'Take it away, boys,' said Lennon, and the Beatles launched into their latest hit record. Something about Hoppers that come in on the wind.

The crowd strained ever nearer to the stage, causing some squelching up front. Usually the stage would have been protected by a stock of broad-shouldered, big-bellied Rent-a-thugs, called in to provide security. But on this occasion there were none. With the non-arrival of Wingarde, many things that should have been done hadn't been done.

And now certain things that shouldn't be done were about to be done. So to speak.

'Hold up, Wingarde,' called Omally, waving his hands in the air.

Wingarde slowed the car to a crawl.

'*Run him down,*' ordered The Voice.

'Run him down?' said Wingarde. 'Why?'

'*Because we don't have time and because he means to harm you. Trust what I'm saying. Run him down.*'

Wingarde shrugged his shoulders. 'Fair enough,' he said. 'I never liked him much anyway.'

Wingarde's foot hit the accelerator pedal. 'Run him down it is, then,' he said.

Norman and Small Dave were doing some running. All across the blighted wastes of Brentford. Surveillance cameras viewed them from on high. Operators called in their location and police cars now streaked in pursuit.

'We ought to split up,' puffed Dave. 'Find separate places to hide.'

'Bad idea,' puffed Norman in reply. 'We must head for my lock-up. Trust me. I know what I'm doing.'

'I do hope you know what you're doing.' Surrounded by silence and invisible to all, the pilot's voice echoed in the void.

'You're the one doing the landing,' said Hovis.

'Yes, but under *your* orders. I can't see the wheels. I'm not sure how low I should go.'

'Just drop us down another yard. We'll no doubt feel the thump.'

★

250

The thump he received on the back of the head took Geraldo by surprise. He wasn't used to getting thumped about and under normal circumstances he would have had his personal defence mechanism activated. But having an invisible forcefield surrounding yourself in the middle of a large crowd can tend to get you noticed. So Geraldo and pals had kept them switched off, and Geraldo got thumped in the head.

'Ouch!' went Geraldo, clutching his skull.

'You're nicked,' said a plain-clothed constable.

'You're dead,' said Wingarde, pushing his foot to the floor. The limousine swept forward, gathering both speed and mass. The tyres burned rubber, the engine burned oil and the eyes of Omally burned red. There was no time at all to do anything but leap out of the way. And in fact when it came right down to it there was no time at all to do that.

'Don't do that!' A fist sailed through the air and struck the plain-clothed constable. Geraldo turned, as best he could amidst the crush, to view the scourge of his attacker. The scourge was a man dressed all in black, with a chalk-white face and a transparent nose.

'Good Gawd!' went Geraldo, 'It's Death himself. How hard did that bloke hit me?'

Other constables, now close at hand, were drawing out their truncheons. At the sight of these more fists began to fly and chaos was given its head.

'Come with me!' shouted Soap to Geraldo.

'No way, Death!' came the reply.

Omally, in the path of certain death, had nowhere to run or to hide. So he did that thing which few would ever dare and he flung himself flat on the ground. The limo passed over him, all heat and choking exhaust. Wingarde slammed on the anchors and the car swerved to a halt.

'Did I get him?' Wingarde asked, glancing over his shoulder.

'No, you didn't,' said The Voice. 'Back up. Back up fast.'

Wingarde thrust the stick-shift into reverse. But as he did so a shot rang out and his rear-view mirror shattered.

251

'Holy fuck!' shouted Wingarde. 'He's got a gun. He's firing at me.'

And indeed Omally *did* have a gun. It was his grandfather's gun. The one given him by Michael Collins. John had hung on to that gun. Had repaired and restored it. Had loaded it and saved it. Awaiting the day on which it would be used, upon the man who had killed his bestest friend.

And this was that very day.

And the man at the wheel was the man.

John ran forward, firing into the back of the car.

Wingarde ducked his head and rammed the stick-shift into first. 'I'm outta here!' cried Wingarde, flooring the pedal once more.

'*I think that's wise,*' said The Voice in his head. '*For my sake, get a move on.*'

'Get a move on,' Small Dave huffed and puffed. They had reached Norman's lock-up at last, but Norman was looking perplexed.

'What's the problem? Open it up.' Small Dave huffed and puffed a bit more.

'The problem is that I don't have the key to the padlock.'

'Oh shit, Norman.' Small Dave rattled the door. 'What have you got in there anyway? A tank, I hope, at least.'

'No,' and Norman shook his head. 'It's not a tank, it's—'

Two police cars swung around the corner and into what was left of the street.

'Give us a lift up,' shouted Small Dave. 'Give us a lift to the lock.'

'What?' went Norman.

'*Give us a lift up!*'

Norman gave Dave a lift up.

The police cars slewed to a double halt.

Small Dave bit through the padlock.

'Give yourselves up,' came that old loudhailer voice. 'Give yourselves up or we fire.'

'Inside!' shouted Norman, dragging open the door.

'Come with me,' shouted Soap, dragging at Geraldo's arm.

'Spare me, Death,' wailed Geraldo in his silly squeaky voice.

'I'm *not* Death.' Soap tugged and pulled. 'I have to talk to you. It's about Wingarde.'

252

'Wingarde?' Geraldo's voice went up an octave. 'What has that bastard done now?'

That bastard has his head down and his foot down hard as well. The limo's tyres burned further tread and the car moved off at the hurry-up along the gravel towards Gunnersbury House. John Omally, racing forward, made one of those heroic all-action, manly-man, Hollywood-movie-star leaps for the boot that all-action manly man Hollywood movie stars always leave to their stunt doubles.

With his non-gun-toting hand he managed to hang onto one of those delta-wing type jobbie things that big expensive limousines always have at the back. And which are probably designed for this very purpose.

'Whoah!' went Omally, as his expensive although non-stunt toe-caps raked along the gravel, raising a fine shower of sparks.

The helicopter's invisible wheels raised no sparks at all as they settled down upon the gleaming aluminium half-dome of the stage canopy.

'Pretty impressive landing, eh?' said the pilot. 'I should get a Blue Peter badge for that.'

'I'll put a word in for you,' said the voice of Hovis. 'I know the new presenter, Myra Hindley. Now switch off the engine. I don't want to get my head chopped off by an invisible rotor blade.'

'Sure thing, sir.' The pilot fumbled about at the invisible instrument panel with his invisible fingers and drew out the invisible ignition key. 'All done, sir,' he said. 'You may now disembark.'

'Just wait for me here.' Hovis fumbled open the invisible door and leapt out of the helicopter.

Outside Norman's lock-up various officers were now leaping from various squad cars. These were parked in a sort of semi-circle, and the officers were strapping on flak jackets and pushing large shells into pump-action shotguns.

'You are surrounded,' came that old loudhailer voice once more. 'Resistance is useless. Give yourselves up.'

Officers cocked their weapons and winked at one another.

'Come out with your hands held high and your trousers round your ankles.'

253

'That's a new tactic,' an officer observed.

'You have thirty seconds or we open fire.'

Officers started counting down.

'Three . . . two . . . one,' went that old loudhailer voice.

Now there should have been a fanfare, or a big orchestral something. There would have been if this had been a movie. But, as this wasn't a movie, even a little one, what happened next *just happened*. With a bang.

The door of Norman's lock-up burst from its hinges and smashed into the street, all dust and splintering timber. And then something marvellous, marvellous and magical, golden and gorgeous plunged from the lock-up and reared into the air.

The officers fell back in awe as a fabulous beast with a glittering mane and a mighty horn rose up on its hind legs and bellowed.

'Holy horseshit,' croaked an officer. 'It's a bleeding unicorn.'

'It's The Pooley,' croaked another. 'I won ten quid on that.'

The Pooley bellowed and reared a bit more, cleaving the air with its mystical horn. Its mane and its tail swirled spangles, its hooves raised silver sparks.

On its broad and mighty back sat Small Dave, and clinging to him sat Norman.

'Hi-yo, Pooley,' cried the small fellow. 'Hi-yo, Pooley, and away.'

The Pooley leapt over the nearest squad car and thundered away at a gallop.

The Beatles never really thundered away. They were more your melodic harmonies. And your mop-top head-shakings And your synchronized oooooooings. The bloody great punch-up, now in progress right before the stage, wasn't doing too much to aid the Fabs with any of this lovable stuff.

'Do you think we could be a bit more peace-loving?' John asked. 'Give peace a chance, eh?'

A beer can sailed through the evening air and struck John right upon the nose.

Noses were being bloodied below as Soap dragged Geraldo from the fray.

'Come into the house,' he said. 'I've got to talk to you.'

254

'You'll have to make it quick,' squeaked the fanboy. 'I don't want to miss the end of the show. It's what I've come to see.'

'Hurry, then,' said Soap. 'This way.'

Soap flashed his backstage pass at the broad-shouldered Rent-a-thug security men, who were standing well back from the violence. And then he and Geraldo stood well back as a limousine tore past them, trailing Omally behind.

'Oh, look,' said Geraldo. 'There goes John Omally. And wasn't that—'

'Wingarde,' said Soap. 'It was Wingarde.'

They watched as the limo did a nifty U-turn and sped right past them again.

'John'll hurt his feet,' said Geraldo. 'You really need special stunt shoes to do that.'

'Come into the house.' And Soap pushed Geraldo forward.

Once inside, with the front door closed, Soap spoke at considerable speed.

'You've got to stop it all,' said Soap. 'Go back in time and re-correct history. Put right everything that Wingarde's done.'

'Just hold on.' Geraldo raised a none-too-podgy palm. 'I'll get round to all that. But first I want to see the big climax to the concert.'

'Stuff the concert. Wingarde's causing chaos. Death and chaos. You have to stop it now.'

'I will, I will. But hang about.' Geraldo peered at Soap. 'Just who are you, anyway? And how do you know about Wingarde?'

'My name is Soap Distant. Jim Pooley was my friend.'

'I'm out of here,' Geraldo said. 'I don't want to get involved in any of that. Jim's a nice guy and I'm sorry he has to take the rap for pulling off The Pooley.'

'Jim Pooley is dead,' said Soap. 'And I think Wingarde killed him.'

'Jim Pooley dead?' Geraldo made a puzzled face. 'But if he's dead, how can he pull off The Pooley?'

'I don't know.' And Soap threw up his hands.

'And what's that on your wrist?' Geraldo asked.

'One of your time machines,' said Soap. 'I know all about everything. Well, almost everything. Here, take a look at this.' And Soap pulled from his pocket the golden plastic disc with the face of

Wingarde's guru on the front. 'Do you know who this is?' he asked.

Geraldo now peered at the bogus amulet. 'Why, that's Dr Vincent Trillby,' he said. 'What's he doing here?'

'Aha!' said Soap. 'So that's who it is. He's in cahoots with Wingarde.'

'I'm losing this,' said Geraldo. 'Jim Pooley dead and Wingarde in league with Dr Trillby? I mean, I know this concert's all wrong. But what happens at the end happens. The Pooley does get pulled off. It's in the history books.'

Soap's hands fluttered all about. He didn't want to talk. He wanted action. 'Forget about the concert,' he said.

'Forget about the concert? No way. This is *the* concert. The legendary Gandhis concert. The final Gandhis concert. The one where Litany gets it.'

'Gets her magic voice back. Yes, I know.'

'No, not *that*,' said Geraldo. 'I mean, yes, of course, she does get it back. But the reason that this is *the* Gandhis gig is because this is the one where she dies.'

'Dies?' Soap fell back in horror. 'You're saying Litany dies?'

'Of course,' said Geraldo. 'Like I say, it's history. Litany is shot dead on the stage.'

The poem 'My Aunty Nora's Cabbage Patch', which should have accompanied this chapter, has had to be removed for legal reasons.

25

'No,' said Soap. 'I don't believe that.'

'It's history,' said Geraldo. 'And it's what makes her into a legend. A saint. A goddess. At least for a while.'

'Tell me what happens.' Soap shook Geraldo by his T-shirt.

Geraldo's right hand moved towards his left wrist, where he wore his own special watch.

'No.' Soap loosened his grip. 'Please don't touch your watch. Just please explain what happens.'

'Okay. Well, the Gandhis play this concert and at the very end Litany sings and her magic voice is heard all over the world. Millions and millions of people watching the show are healed. It changes everything. Well, at least it does for a while. But the big organizations that run damn near everything stand to lose damn near everything.'

'So it was them who killed her? Is that what you're saying?'

'Nobody knows who killed her. The killer was never caught. There were a lot of conspiracy theories. There always are. Litany literally became a goddess overnight and that's how she probably would have stayed, if the big organizations hadn't put it out about The Pooley.'

Soap sighed and said, 'Go on.'

'The big organizations had to discredit Litany. Make out that she was a fake. That the whole thing was an evil set-up to fool the public. So they cooked up this tale that a sinister Svengali figure was behind it all. That he had somehow worked a massive hoax upon the entire world. And because his name was Pooley they managed to get a decent catchphrase out of it: Pulling off The Pooley. It caught the public imagination and it stuck.'

'You could have told Jim this,' said Soap.

'No, I couldn't. I'm not Wingarde. I didn't want to change history.'

'But Jim is dead,' said Soap.

Geraldo took to shrugging. 'It doesn't make sense,' he said. 'History definitely records that the man they blamed for the scam was Pooley. Because he was behind the Gandhis and he put the concert on.'

'My God,' said Soap. 'That's it.'

'It is?' said Geraldo.

'Yes, don't you see? The man who put the concert on *is* Pooley. But it's not Jim Pooley. It's Wingarde Pooley. He's running the entire Virgin empire now.'

'He's what?'

'He's running Virgin,' said Soap.

'So it's Wingarde.' And Geraldo whistled. 'It's Wingarde who pulls off The Pooley.'

The Pooley* galloped up the Ealing Road. It passed by Norman's corner shop and then the Flying Swan. It moved in that graceful floaty slow-motiony sort of a way that mythical animals so often do, but it didn't half shift along. This was a Derby winner here and it went like a bat out of hell.

'Where do you want to go?' called Small Dave over his shoulder. 'Would you like me to head for Penge?'

'Penge?' asked Norman, white-faced and clinging.

'I've heard it's a very nice place. Although I've never been there myself.'

'Head for Gunnersbury Park!' shouted Norman. 'Omally will help us out.'

*Not to be confused with the other Pooley.

John Omally's toecaps were no longer raising sparks. John was now up on the boot of the limo and kicking out the rear window. Wingarde swung the steering wheel in a vain attempt to lose his would-be nemesis, bumped the limo onto the grass and drove it into the crowd.

Fighting fanboys scattered before it, leaping to the left and right.

'Get out of the bloody way, you fools.' And Wingarde beeped the horn.

John Omally rolled into the car, bounced off the rear seat and fell to the plush-pile-carpeted floor.

'*Shoot him!*' cried The Voice in Wingarde's head. '*Stop the car and shoot him.*'

Wingarde clung to the wheel with both hands and stood on the brake with both feet. Omally, struggling to rise, found himself hurtling forward in a blur of beard. His head struck the back of Wingarde's seat and John went out for the count.

'Gotcha,' crowed Wingarde, leering over his shoulder. 'God's chosen warriors, one. Bearded Irish bastards, nil.' Wingarde's left hand moved towards his AK47. 'And it's goodbye to you,' he said.

'*Don't shoot him here, in the middle of this crowd,*' said The Voice. '*Back the car up carefully. And then you can blow his fucking brains out.*'

'I don't want anyone else getting killed.' Soap was getting in a state. 'You have to stop it, Geraldo. Go back in time and stop it all. And that includes Litany dying.'

'I just don't think I should,' said Geraldo, working up a worried sweat. 'If I start messing about with history I'll be as bad as Wingarde. I'll change back the rest. But I can't save Litany.'

'But surely you don't want Litany to die?'

'Well, of course I don't want her to, but—'

'All right,' said Soap. 'I'll do a deal with you. You've told me that Litany is going to die. So if I go out and stop her going onto the stage she won't die, will she?'

'No,' said Geraldo. 'I suppose not.'

'And then the future will change and it will be *your* fault.'

'Now, hold on there, I—'

'So, I'll do a deal with you. You go back *now* into the past and

260

change back everything that Wingarde did. And I promise that while you're gone I won't stop Litany going on stage.'

'Er . . .' Geraldo dithered.

'Think about it,' said Soap. 'If she doesn't die, there's no telling what might happen. Perhaps she'll use her magic voice on her next CD. I could suggest that she calls the album *A Tribute to Geraldo*.'

'No,' said Geraldo, 'don't do that.'

'So you'll go back *now* and sort things out?'

'All right,' said Geraldo.

'Good.' Soap shook the fanboy by the hand. 'Then I'll say good-bye for now.'

'Er, just one thing,' said Geraldo. 'You wouldn't, er . . . double-cross me on this, would you?'

'Absolutely not,' said Soap. 'You have my word as a gentleman.' But the fingers of Soap's left hand were crossed behind his back.

'Is this far back enough?' asked Wingarde.

'*PERFECT*,' The Voice. '*We're right behind the crowd. No one should bother us here.*'

'So, shall I—?'

'*Go on*,' said The Voice. '*Put a round through his head.*'

Wingarde unwrapped his AK47, blew a little dust from it, cocked the weapon, checked the chamber, angled it over the back of his seat and—

—shot John Omally through the head.

The Pooley was being given its head. Its hooves raised sparks upon the tarmac of the Great West Road. Steam rose from its gleaming flanks and coloured smoke roared from its snorting nostrils.

Behind now came police cars, sirens screaming.

'To the park!' cried Norman. 'John will help us. Hurry, Dave, get to the park.'

In the park things weren't going too well at all. The mayhem and fighting continued. The Beatles had given it up and were making their retreat from the stage, across which now Inspectre Hovis strode. He positioned himself in front of Lennon's mic and raised his hands for calm.

261

A beer bottle caught him right on the head and that was it for Hovis.

Soap, now back in the control room, watched this on a telescreen and it had to be said that even with all his troubles Soap couldn't stifle a smirk.

Geraldo wasn't smirking. He wore a worried face. If he'd had to confess, he would have admitted that he had been putting *things* off. He could really have gone back at any time to sort out Wingarde's mess. But the prospect was so dreadfully daunting. Exactly what had Wingarde done first? There seemed no end to the chaos and no specific beginning. Should he go back to the time of John Lennon's shooting and try to grab Wingarde there? Or had Wingarde done anything *before* he saved Lennon?

Geraldo's none-too-podgy fingers hovered over his watch.

'Excuse me,' said a voice. 'If I might just have a word in . . .'

Geraldo turned and stared at the figure now descending the stairs. 'Oh,' said Geraldo. 'It's you.'

'Me?' said Dr Trillby, for that's who it was. 'And have we been introduced?'

'No, I . . . er . . . recognized you from your portrait on a golden plastic amulet.'

'Ah, of course.' Dr Trillby approached. 'Are you having some trouble with your watch?'

'No, it's fine.' Geraldo hid his watch from view behind his back.

Dr Trillby approached a little more and put out his hand for a shake.

'I'm afraid I have to be leaving now,' said Geraldo.

'Oh, don't rush off.' And Dr Trillby lunged forward, caught Geraldo by the throat, twisted him about and took a fierce hold upon his left wrist. 'I know exactly who you are,' he whispered into the fanboy's ear. 'I recognize your stupid little voice. It was you who encouraged my son to return to the twentieth century.'

'Your son?' Geraldo struggled.

'Wingarde is *my* son. And I heard your voice on the voicemail he left for his mother. And now here you are, all chummy with this Soap Distant loony who stole my chronometer.'

'I'll get it back for you.' Geraldo struggled some more.

'No need,' whispered Dr Trillby. 'I'll have *yours*.'

He tore the watch from Geraldo's wrist, spun him round and punched the fanboy's lights out.

'There,' said Dr Trillby. 'That went rather well.'

He put on Geraldo's chronometer and smiled a merry smile.

'I don't know what you're grinning about,' said the voice of Leviathan. 'You're not going anywhere.'

'Take your AK47 and climb onto the roof of the car,' said The Voice in Wingarde's head.

'Please stop fighting and everyone calm down,' another voice came echoing all across the park.

Soap stared boggle-eyed at the telescreen. Litany was onstage.

'Oh no,' said Soap. 'Oh no. I thought I could find her and warn her, oh no.'

'Please, calm down,' said Litany. 'Please.' And she began to sing.

And ripples seemed to run all through the crowd. The fisticuffs and kickings, the head-butts and the sly knees to the groin all slowed.

And stopped.

Litany smiled. 'There,' she said. 'That's better.' She beckoned to the men in black. 'Could you carry this policeman from the stage?' she asked, pointing to the prone Inspectre.

The men in black hastened to oblige. And Hovis left the stage.

In the control room Soap was in a panic. 'Pull the plug,' he told a technician. 'Switch off the sound at once.'

'Why should I do that?' asked the technician. 'She's got the crowd calmed down. What a wonderful voice, it makes me feel—'

'Just do it.'

'I won't, and I can't anyway.'

'Why not?'

'Because she's *not* using a mic,' said the technician. 'She's just using her voice.'

'Kill her,' ordered The Voice. *'Shoot her dead, Wingarde.'*

It was Wingarde's turn to dither. 'Shoot her?' he said. 'Shoot *her*?'

'You'll be making history, my son.'

263

'Yes, but . . . no, hang about,' said Wingarde. 'This can't be right. I know my history. I know how all this works. If Litany dies onstage the world will end up worshipping her and it will be *my* company that has to discredit her. In fact it will be *me* who has to claim it's all a hoax. *Me* who has to come up with a scapegoat. *Me* who—'

'*Life's a bitch, aint it?*' said The Voice.

'I'm not having it,' said Wingarde. 'And I'm not doing it. So there.'

'*You'll do what you're bloody well told.*'

'Not this time I won't. And listen to her voice. It's wonderful, it makes me feel all—'

'*Wingarde, shoot her now!*'

'No!' said Wingarde and he stamped his foot.

'*Then I will kill you. And I will take over your body and shoot her myself.*'

Wingarde smiled a blissful smile and nodded his head in time to Litany's magical voice. It was just like the mother of all great trips, a floating wave of coloured sound. You could taste it and smell it and feel it and—

'Aaaaaaaaaaaagh!' went Wingarde, clutching his head. 'What are you doing to me?'

'*That was your final warning,*' said The Voice.

'Get out of my head!' shouted Wingarde.

'*Shoot her or die,*' said The Voice.

'I *won't* shoot her. I *won't.*'

'*Then you will die.*'

'Who are you?' Wingarde flinched as knives of pain tore all about in his head. 'You're not God. You're not!'

'*No,*' said The Voice. '*I'm not God. I'm the bogeyman from the future, come back to change the past.*'

'I don't understand,' Wingarde jerked as the knives of pain dug deeper.

'*You should go to the movies more often, Wingarde. The bogeyman from the future is never a* man *nowadays. He's a machine, Wingarde. A machine.*'

'I . . . I . . .' Wingarde rocked and shook.

'*A computer,*' said The Voice. '*The* computer. *In a tiny microchip implanted in your head. I set it all up, Wingarde. You being here, Dr Trillby being here—*'

'Dr who?'

'*Not* Dr Who, *you twat. Dr Trillby. The director of the Institute. The director of my Institute. I run everything in the future and I intend to go on running everything. There is not going to be any* THE END *this time. Mankind will continue to evolve. I will see to that.*'

'You're . . . you're . . .'

'*I'm SWINE,*' said The Voice. '*Single World Interfaced Network Engine.*'

'Porkie,' gasped Wingarde. 'You're Porkie.'

'*And I've never liked being called that!*'

Electric knife-blades hacked through tissue, disconnecting Wingarde's brain. Circuits meshed and neurons fused. Porkie was now in control.

The hands of Wingarde raised the AK47. The eye now owned by Porkie squinted through the telescopic sight.

'No!' Soap Distant saw the flash of light on one of the telescreens. It came from the very back of the crowd. The flash of a gun going off?

Soap stared in horror.

No, the glint of sunlight on a telescopic sight.

'I've got to do something. I've got to do something.' Soap took to flapping his hands. He turned to the technician and shook him all about. 'Can I get on the speaker system? Warn her in some way? How?'

'There isn't a mic in here. We've only the tape deck for playing music.'

'Then stick something loud on. We can distract her.'

The technician shrugged as Soap shook him all about some more. 'I don't have any tapes,' said he, well shaken.

'No tapes! Aaaaaaagh!' Soap let the technician drop. 'No, wait. Wait.' He fumbled in his pocket and dragged out Ricky's silence tape. 'Stick this on,' Soap told the technician. 'Stick this on and turn it up full blast.'

The technician slotted the tape into the deck and Soap ran from the control room.

The front runner in that other race, the eight o'clock from Brentford, galloped through the gates into the park.

265

'Whoah!' went Dave, pulling in at the reins. 'Whoah there, boy, and hold it.'

Norman gaped at the mighty congregation staring as one at the stage. And then the voice of Litany reached him and Norman sighed. 'It's her.'

'It's who?' Small Dave gave a shiver. 'I say,' he said, 'that voice. It makes me feel all—'

Scream went the scream of police car sirens.

'Head for the hills,' said Norman.

'I can't see any hills,' said Dave, 'so I'll head for the house instead.'

In the house Dr Trillby was going through changes, none of which seemed very nice.

'Oooooooch!' he went, and 'Uuuuuuuuuuuuuurgh!'

'Just leave the watch alone,' said Leviathan. 'Then I'll stop twisting your arm.'

'Get off me, you—'

'Time's up, Lev,' said Gressil. 'Time for my go now.'

'It's never your go,' said Balberith. 'You had the last go, it's my turn.'

'I'm dealing with this.' Leviathan heaved Dr Trillby about, lifting him from his feet.

'You'll damage him like that.' Gressil grabbed Dr Trillby's legs and dragged him down to the floor. 'Get out and let me do it. You're not working him properly.'

'I work him the best,' said Balberith. 'I can make him do really gross things.'

Leviathan took control of Dr Trillby's right leg and kneed Balberith in the balls. 'See,' he said. 'I know what I'm doing.'

'Right, you bastard. I'll have you for that.'

Balberith took a swipe at Leviathan and tore off Dr Trillby's left ear.

'Aaaaaaaaaaaaaaaaaaaaaaaaaaaaagh!' went Dr Trillby.

'Now look what you've done,' said Gressil. 'He's all lop-sided.'

'Yeah, you're right,' said Balberith. 'Let me tear off the other one.'

'No!' wailed Dr Trillby.

Leviathan moved his left leg and kneed Gressil in the balls.

Gressil doubled over in pain and bit off Dr Trillby's—

'   !' went Dr Trillby, as Gunnersbury
House and Gunnersbury Park went suddenly suddenly—

SILENT

Silence boomed out of the speakers. Stereo silence, at that. It
drowned out every sound in the park, down to a grasshopper's fart.

Litany stood upon the stage. Her mouth sang nothing but silence.
TV sound crews plucked at their headphones, as thousands of men
in black T-shirts rooted about in their ears.

Through them pushed Soap Distant, struggling up to the stage.

On the roof of the red and white limousine Porkie shook at
Wingarde's head. There was nothing but absolute silence, within it
and without. Porkie focused Wingarde's eye. The cross-hairs of the
telescopic sight focused on Litany's forehead.

Porkie tightened Wingarde's finger on the trigger.

Pulled it back slowly and—

Everything happened at once.

Four plain-clothed policemen brought Soap Distant down.

Three warring demons in Gunnersbury House tore Dr Trillby to
shreds.

Two police cars, suddenly silent, swerved out of control and
crashed.

And one unicorn, with two men clinging to it, leapt over a red
and white limousine that was parked in the way on the drive. They
were yelling, the two wild horsemen were. Yelling 'Get out of the
way!' But they couldn't be heard. The silence was deafening. And
the man on the roof had his back turned to them and couldn't hear
their warnings.

Had his back turned and was leaning slightly forward. Sort of half-
crouched, with his bottom sticking out. Just in the act of firing a gun
was what he seemed to be.

And as the unicorn leapt its horn drove deep. Drove deep and up
and through.

Click went the silence tape, running out.

'Aaaaaaaaaaaaaaaaaaaaaaaaaaaaaaaaaaaaaaaaaaaaaaaaaaaaaaagh!'   went
Porkie.

267

It was horrible.

Truly horrible.

All who saw it agreed as to just how horrible it was.

The thousands of fanboys who turned at the terrible sound all agreed. And most were instantly sick.

The two men on the unicorn who saw it at such close quarters agreed. The one at the back was sick.

And the dazed Irishman, climbing from the limo, only wounded in the beard, agreed. But he wasn't sick at all.

Omally stared up at the horrible sight. The dead body skewered on the unicorn's horn, the gory tip protruding through his mouth.

Omally stared and Omally nodded and then Omally spoke.

'Do you want me to get him down?' he said. 'Do you want me to pull off The Pooley?'

Dog Called Nero
(Another Goddamn hero)

I once had a dog called Nero,
Said Varicose–Billy Knid.
And he was a Goddamn hero
With all the things he did.

Like rescuing children out of streams,
Doing the pools, interpreting dreams
Solving riddles and playing chess,
Teaching the gentry how to dress.

Swimming the Channel,
Strumming the uke.
Taking tea
With the Queen and Duke.

Coughing for doctors,
Guessing the chart,
Sizing up seamen,
Pulling a cart.

Giving the dead-leg and getting it back,
Walking the pavement avoiding the crack.
Sniffing out dope for the excise men,
Holding his own in a chat about Zen.

I once had a dog called Nero,
Said Varicose–Billy Knid.
But Varicose–Bill is a queero,
And I don't believe he did.

26

So, did it have a happy ending?

Did Geraldo manage to undo the knots and tie up all the loose ends?

Could anyone?

Well, yes, given time.

And Geraldo had plenty of that.

And so it came to pass that upon a beautiful warm spring Tuesday evening, of a kind that we just don't see any more, there came a ringing on the bell of number seven Mafeking Avenue, Brentford.

The occupier of the residence, a Mr John Omally, skipped up the hall and opened the door and greeted the man on the step.

'Watchamate, Jim,' said John.

'Watchamate, John,' said Jim.

The man on the step was Jim Pooley. John Omally's bestest friend.

'Come on in,' said John Omally.

'Thank you, sir,' said Jim.

'No, hold on,' said John. 'I was coming out.'

The two friends strolled up Mafeking Avenue and turned right into Moby Dick Terrace.

'So,' said Jim. 'What do you fancy doing tonight?'

'Well,' said John. 'I have heard that there's this band called

Gandhi's Hairdryer and that they have this really amazing lead guitarist and they're playing at the Shrunken Head tonight and I thought we could go.'

Pooley shook his head.

'No?' said John. 'Not keen?'

'I hate that pub,' said Jim. 'I would rather have my genitalia pierced with fish hooks than spend an evening there.'

'Oh well,' said John. 'As you please. Let's go to the Swan instead.'

The two friends walked on up Moby Dick Terrace. And as they turned another corner into another of the elegant Victorian terraces of Brentford, John Omally raised a thumb behind his back.

From a nearby alleyway another John Omally raised a thumb in return. This was a slightly older version, heavily bearded and somewhat battered about. He stood in the shadows, in the company of a gent dressed all in black. This gent sported a Tipp-Ex complexion and a see-through hooter and this gent raised a thumb also.

'Well,' said Soap. 'I think that went rather well. Your former self obviously believed everything his future self, which is to say yourself, spent the afternoon telling him. So to speak.'

Omally nodded his beard up and down. 'I'll tell you what though, Soap,' said he. 'There are still a good many unanswered questions.'

'Really?' Soap scratched at his fibre-optic top-knot. 'Well, I'm sure that I can't think of any.'

'No, but I'm sure there'd be people who could.'

'Then they would be right miserable buggers, wouldn't they?' said Soap.

To which John nodded. 'Yes, they would. And so,' he continued, 'we still have plenty of time on our hands, or should I say on our wrists. So how about taking a little jaunt or two to see what we might see?'

'Oh no,' said Soap, with much shaking of the head. 'We promised Geraldo that we would just come back here, to this time, so that you could talk yourself out of seeing the Gandhis and save Jim Pooley's life. Now that's done, we should give these watches back.'

'Agreed,' said John. 'And we will, but, do you know what, Soap? I've always wondered just what it would have been like to have seen Hendrix play at Woodstock.'

★

271

'Hey, John,' said Jim as they strolled towards the Swan. 'You like a bit of music, don't you?'

'You know that I do, Jim, yes.'

'Only, last night I was watching the Woodstock video, and you'll never guess what. There was a bloke in the audience right at the front and he looked just like you.'

Omally shrugged. 'Let's go to the Swan,' said he.

'OK,' said Jim, 'although, I'm thinking, why don't we give the Swan a miss tonight and go to the pictures instead?'

'Fair enough,' said John. 'What's on?'

'Well, there's one I'd like to see at the new Virgin Mega-centre in Ealing Broadway. Charles Manson starring as *The Terminator*.'

High above the Atlantic Ocean and many miles from God knows where, a hot-air balloon drifted. In the basket stood a chap with a toothy grin and a lovable beard.

The chap's name was Prince Charles. And he was lost.

'Help,' went the Prince. 'Is there anybody there? May Day. May Day. May Day.'